For Crying Out Loud

Cathie Wayland

Theresa Jenner Garrido

L & L Dreamspell
Spring, Texas

Cover and Interior Design by L & L Dreamspell

Copyright © 2010 Cathie Wayland and Theresa Garrido. All rights reserved. No part of this publication may be reproduced, stored in a retrieval system or transmitted in any form or by any means, electronic, mechanical, photocopying, recording or otherwise without the prior written permission of the copyright holder, except for brief quotations used in a review.

This is a work of fiction, and is produced from the author's imagination. People, places and things mentioned in this novel are used in a fictional manner.

ISBN: 978-1-60318-250-8

Library of Congress Control Number: 2010925427

Visit us on the web at www.lldreamspell.com

Published by L & L Dreamspell
Printed in the United States of America

To all our family and friends,

and to all who enjoy life and laughter.

One

I re-readjusted my bright pink, floppy-brimmed, fashionable Southern Belle hat, pushed a few strands of straying hair around, squirmed and tugged at underwear forever sneaking into unnatural crevices, and watched the clock that crept along like Great Aunt Metta with her walker. Lord. The wait seemed interminable. I cracked my neck, fidgeted, and continued perusing each face and form for the long-delayed, much anticipated reunion with my bosom-buddy, whom I hadn't seen in twenty-plus years. Patience was not my forte.

Schooling myself to settle down, I counted to sixty and refused to steal another glance at the clock. Picking up someone's discarded newspaper, I scanned the headlines, noting that Charleston was no different from Greenville or Atlanta. News was news. People were people. Only interesting piece was the blurb about missing three-year-old twins. Thinking about children being abducted was not what I wanted to do so I tossed the paper aside and stole a tiny peek at the clock. The hands hadn't budged a fraction.

Lord. I'd survived the tedious, solo drive down to the Charleston airport. Had overcome timidity and trepidation to allow a scrap of paper with Map Quest's directions to be my guide. Had endured three calls from my ever-anxious husband. Had managed to find a parking space. Couldn't I wait like an adult and not a fretful toddler for my pal of thirty-two years to arrive? Of course I could. Well, maybe I could.

Eyes glazed over with fatigue. Legs crossed and re-crossed. On the verge of pulling out my hair and jumping up and down in frustration, I clenched my hands, sat up straighter, and waited. And waited. An eternity and half a lifetime later, I spotted her, and she, me. Leaping from my seat, nearly tripping over my own purse, I dashed across the room to meet her. A trail of squeals followed behind.

"Ohmigawd." I gurgled, hugging her as best I could, since she towered over me. "Oh, Bernadette, you're here. You're here. Is it really *you?* Oh, I can't believe this. But your hair. Your hair. Where is your Farrah Fawcett hair?"

She threw back her head and guffawed. "Michaela, who in the world even *recognizes* Farrah Fawcett anymore, much less her *hair?*" She patted the fluff on top of her head and rolled her eyes. "My flat and sassy style." Eyes narrowed. "My hair, not my body." Another eye roll. "Can't tell you how long it takes a curling iron to straighten it like this. Natural curly hair be damned."

"Well, it looks great," I chirped. "It's just not how I remembered you, so it threw me."

"Please don't say you were expecting me to look the way I did in 1979."

I laughed. "Heavens no. I just didn't expect this. Ohmigawd. Let me look at you."

Bernie tossed the new do and made a face. "You can study me all you want once we're settled at the condo. All I want now is to grab my bags and get the hell out of here. I feel like a Marine coming home from a deployment." She sighed for effect. "I loathe flying. It took forever to leave Lambert. We circled St. Louis half a dozen times before the pilot decided on the right direction and nosed toward Charleston. I'm beat."

"Yeah, I hear you. The drive down—all by myself, I'm proud to say—then the wait here in the terminal drained all the energy I had. And it's so hot. I can't wait to get to the beach."

We made our way through the concourse area, pausing every few steps to take in every detail of the other, memorize every familiar little mannerism, every little idiosyncrasy that only a best friend would recognize and treasure.

"Oh, my gosh. I *cannot* believe we did it." I chortled for the third time, just staring up at her. A flood of memories cascaded over me and time seemed to stand still.

It'd been twenty-plus years since we shared the corner of the dilapidated teachers' lounge at the small country school where we'd vented and fumed about recalcitrant students and their obtuse parents. Both retired now, this trip had been in the works for some fifteen years. I never thought it'd come to fruition, yet, here we were with enough memories to fill a dozen scrapbooks.

Dear, dear Bernie. I'd never forget the moment we first met. 1975. I'd just made the move from Seattle to Missouri, where my sister and family had settled three years before. I'd been fortunate to find a teaching position in a small, rural parochial school, a reasonable distance from my little apartment-over-a-garage on a farm only a mile from my family.

The first day of the teachers' preparation week, the principal was showing me the building and grounds when we bumped into Bernie in all her blond-hair glory. At almost six feet tall, she towered over my five-foot-three frame, and I remember gazing up at her smiling face and seeing a decided twinkle in her blue-gray eyes. Even though a little taken aback by the twitching of her lips and her teasing smirk, it hadn't taken long before our senses of the ridiculous meshed, and we discovered we were soul mates.

Oh, we had glorious times in that little school. It didn't matter that we were without funds for necessary materials, or that the principal turned out to be a close relative of Attila the Nun. We were the "Hawkeye" and "B.J." of our small world and took great delight in teasing one another, playing practical jokes, and entertaining students and peers with our quips, antics, and mutual love of theater. A day didn't go by that we weren't doubled over in the hallway, convulsed in laughter bordering on hysteria, or belting out a Broadway tune. Yes, those days had definitely gone down in infamy.

But then I got married, moved to South Carolina, and we lost the preciousness of daily encounters, shared laughter, and companionship. We kept in touch, of course, via quirky cards, e-mail, and the occasional phone call, but it wasn't the same. Husbands and growing families took center-stage, and our attentions focused on things other than ourselves. We remained best friends but the camaraderie faded into those mental junk drawers we call memory.

Nevertheless, the moment our eyes met, a surge of heady delight rushed through me. We both broke into blazing smiles and tandem bursts of laughter, powered by the sheer joy of recognition and reconnection. Ahhh…friendship. Could anything be sweeter?

Reverie broken, I said, "You'll love the condo. Two bedrooms and two bathrooms. Perfect."

"How long have your sister and brother-in-law had it?"

"Oh, gosh…two, maybe three years. Everybody in the family uses it."

"I don't doubt it. Remind me to send a card to thank her."

Arm in arm and chattering non-stop, we barged our way through the crowd into the baggage claim area. We'd begin our adventure as soon as we rescued Bernie's suitcases. Anxious to be on our way, I elbowed through the mob gathered about the stainless steel baggage shooter and edged to the front of the line. There I stood, poised to pounce as the carousel conveyor belt whirled luggage around just beyond my reach.

"Whoops," Bernie thrust out one long arm. "That dark blue one's mine." In her excitement, she waved both arms, just missed hitting an elderly gentleman balancing on his cane, and then avoided, by sheer luck, slapping a Burger King cup out of the hand of a surly biker-looking guy. As Bernie's suitcase rolled past us for the third time, we'd all but given up.

A bicep-blessed man stepped in, reached out and snagged the runaway luggage on its fourth tour, hoisted it off the belt and flung it at Bernie with a condescending grin. Dragging the enormous valise across unsuspecting toes and bumping into other weary travelers waiting for the mesmerizing suitcase parade to pass, we managed a hasty retreat from the premises. Twelve minutes together and already we'd garnered way too much attention. What else was new?

Gasping for air from laughing so hard, we struggled down a sloping ramp with the enormous rolling suitcase clipping behind at a healthy pace. When it seemed, even to me, that we'd been walking and tugging and towing our way toward the exit for an epoch, I paused and looked around—this side of frantic. I held my breath, expecting Bernie's annoyance to erupt any second. I didn't have long to wait.

"How far away did you park the damn car, anyway?" Bernie huffed, as we lumbered out of the parking garage and into the sight-slicing brightness of the open parking lot. Already on my case. I knew she suspected I'd forgotten not only the lot and lane, but which car I'd driven. Since I have sort of a reputation— no, a *history*—of getting a little rattled on occasion, this was no surprise. Bernie used to thrive on pointing out my foibles to me every chance she got. This trait hadn't changed.

"I wrote it down." I fumbled in my left pocket. "Just wait… I know it's in here somewhere… Okay. I have it. It's G-18." I announced, chin up, proving that I *did* have the information, and that the situation *was* under control.

Bernie knew better. Nothing tickled her more than getting me a little flustered. It was official. The good-natured war of the words had begun. With a bang.

"We're *past* G and on row J. Is this even the right lot?"

"Yes, it's the right lot. We were talking and I got distracted."

"We're melting here and you got distracted?"

"Oh, please. It's not like you're not used to humidity, coming from St. Louis."

"Different kind of humidity."

"Oh, please."

"I'm dying here."

"Okay, okay. There it is."

Toiling with the bulging suitcase and one carry-on bag, we trudged and perspired our way across acres of molten blacktop to the farthest available parking spot. Keyed-up and nerves on over-drive when I'd arrived, I'd just picked the first spot I'd seen. Only after walking into the airport had I even registered there were closer spaces, not to mention a parking garage that would've been a more reasonable option, considering the oppressive heat.

We dropped the cases while I groped in my cavernous purse for the illusive keys. Exchanging knowing glares across the blistering car roof, we erupted into purling laughter as we gazed at the over-packed back seat and loaded trunk.

"Where in the hell am I going to put this?" Bernie pretended to fume.

"Well, why'd you bring such a humongous suitcase?"

"*Me?* How about *you.*"

"I had to pack for any and all occasions, you know. We might go into Charleston. Then there's the beach and—"

"You should have brought the van then."

Ignoring her, I made a half-hearted attempt to rearrange a few items then sighed. "Just put it on top of that stuff. I'm too hot to care. Let's just get away from the airport."

And so it began…

"Do you really believe we're doing this?" Bernie grinned at me as she tried to maneuver her long legs in the cramped space provided by my Plymouth Neon, even with the seat shoved back as far as it would go.

I returned her smile and inserted the key in the ignition, casting a sidelong glance at this comfortable memory in all her glorious hair and hilarity. My mind raced helter-skelter as a cascade of reminiscences spanning thirty-two years flooded my mind—Bernie's explosive interjections of hysterical laughter punctuating each retrieved recollection.

"Omigosh," I exhaled. "This really is amazing—our being here, that is. I still don't believe we pulled it off. My Joe was *beside* himself with fretting at being abandoned. He's already called three times just making sure I'm all right. He needs looking after, the poor man."

Bernie snorted. "My Jack is positively destitute without *me*. He'll be *lost*, I'm not sorry to say." She leaned back against the headrest and sighed. "I've talked to him at least five times just since leaving St. Louis."

Nodding, I scanned the lot for the exit sign. It shouldn't have been that difficult, but I was too frazzled from the journey, the reunion, and the heat to process. Almost ten minutes had passed, and the continual looping and maneuvering only returned us to our starting point. Renewing efforts to exit the lot, we traveled a serpentine route and found the pay booth. Bernie handed me a ten-dollar bill, and I paid the parking attendant, driving off without Bernie's change.

Who cared? Freedom at last.

Two

Barreling down the lane of moss-draped live oaks at a raging fifty-two miles per hour, I endured my friend's good-natured remarks about my death grip on the wheel of the Neon. My eyes fixed on the road ahead, I refused to be distracted from my mission to deliver us to Edisto Beach and prattled on and on about my beloved Low Country.

"Where is this place, for crying out loud?" Bernie whined. "And enough about ghosts, Gullah folk, and golf courses. Sheesh, sweetie. I love your funny little twitches and head bobs, and involuntary rolling of eyes when you're any way stressed or anxious, but… Enough's enough already."

Bernie never passed up a chance to tease and goad, taking gleeful pride in commenting about my tics, which, of course, caused them to multiply in frequency and duration. "You're being unkind, Bernadette. Now stop," I admonished in my best teacher-voice.

Bernie chuckled. "I know. I'm sorry. Chalk it up to heat and too much perspiration." She leaned forward so I could see her from the corner of my eye. "But, sweetie, you know your innocence and the absolute transparency of your emotions unleashes my witty and acerbic tongue."

"Oh, please."

"You know I can always tell when you're nervous, or excited, or anxious—can designate the appropriate tic to the emotion of the moment. I can read you like a book."

"Yeah, well, it's a good thing I not only tolerate but take delight in your penchant for finding reasons to tease me. You're just lucky I happen to love our constant exchange of remarks and pithy comments designed to spark a laugh—usually at my expense. But you also know I'm always up to the challenge when you torment and taunt me and can give it back."

Bermie laughed outright at this. "Oh, sweetie, you are and will always be my extraordinary friend, and I would do anything for you, anytime, any place. Which is not to say that I don't reserve the right and the privilege of driving you crazy."

After that repartee, we remained silent for several minutes, just enduring the endless drive to my beloved beach town, but the heat was becoming intense. The oppressive humidity had poor Bernie experiencing the palpable sensation of morphing into a giant dandelion. Her hair had always been her nemesis. Bad enough she towered over everyone because of her height, but add seven inches of hair and, well, let's just say it didn't take much to make a spectacle of herself.

"It's not too far, now…just hold your horses," I chided, sensing her growing restlessness. Having her knees embedded in the glove compartment of my compact car may have added to her discomfort. I felt over-heated as well, and my neck was getting stiff from sitting so long.

Just then, a tinny ringing alerted us to someone's cell phone. I glanced at my purse in consternation. The ringing continued, annoying and urgent.

"Answer it. That's my phone." I exclaimed.

This time Bernie was the one admonishing. "Calm down. I'll get it." She rummaged through the cavernous outside pocket of my purse, found the ridiculous piece of molded plastic, and handed it to me. I fumbled with it in one hand.

Bernie stared at me, lips parted, as she listened to one side of the conversation. My "Yes? Oh. Hi, Joe. Yes, we're almost there… What? Well, where are they? Have you looked in all your pants' pockets? Well, Joe, you know they have to be *some*where. Look in every place you can think of. Where did you go last? Just retrace your steps. Okay...okay, well, call me when you find them...I gotta go now. You know I hate driving and talking on the phone at the same time...I do, too. Stay out of trouble, Joe. It'll only be for ten days. Love you. Bye." Had her shaking her head, sighing, and rolling her eyes by the time I clicked off.

I didn't say anything and just handed my tiny phone to her. She chuckled and dropped it into my purse. Clearing her throat, she asked, "Have to say that one-sided conversation was interesting. Sure wish you'd put it on speaker. What the hell was your husband going on and on about? Your facial expressions were priceless."

"Not much. Just that dear Joe has lost his car keys...again."

"Again? Is he in the habit of losing them?"

I released a whoosh of air. "Ooohh, yeah...he loses his keys at least three times a day..."

"Slight exaggeration?"

"Unfortunately, not. Like I said earlier, he really needs looking after."

Don't misunderstand. It's more than gratifying that I found a life partner so in tune with my own offbeat personality, but, really. Are all men such babies?

A century later, we crossed the curving alabaster bridge to Edisto Island. In a matter of minutes, we reached the sleepy little seaside town, crept down Jungle Road at the prescribed 30 miles an hour, then rolled toward my sister and brother-in-law's vacation condo, nestled on the sixteenth green of the trendy Low Country golf course. I slowed to a crawl and turned into the shady parking area. We'd done it. We'd reached our destination.

"We're here," I sighed, relieved, exhilarated, and triumphant that I'd made the trip all by myself, without Joe, and without mishap. For several heartbeats, we sat and stared through the windshield at the low-hanging live oaks, dripping with Spanish moss, and the mass of tropical plants that encircled the condo. The ordeal of unloading and unpacking loomed large, however, and we both felt drained. The challenge of transporting liquor, worthless full-fat snacks, and a case of diet Dr. Pepper—in addition to seventy pounds of comfortable clothing and personal hygiene products—would daunt most women our age. And truth be told, we were both pretty damned daunted already.

"What have you got in here?" Bernie snarled as she hoisted a large canvas bag out of the trunk.

"Nothing. Just two cartons of hard lemonade and a case of bottled water."

"Oh, for Pete's sake, Michaela. They have a store here you know."

"I know, but I was hoping to save us a trip."

Settling in was no easy task. By the time we'd made our third trip to the condo and back, a generous supply of neighbors had gathered at deck rails and barbecue pits to stare at the raucous interlopers stumbling toward their unit like a comedy team run amuck. We each had packed enough for a family of twelve for a month. No denying the serenity of the golf course resort and retreat had been shattered by our arrival.

Speaking of golf. As if on cue, two golf carts lurched onto the horizon. Four portly but nattily dressed gentlemen disembarked, selected the appropriate clubs and continued to pursue their elusive quarries. Sweating and red-faced, these mainlanders pelted the manicured green with the little dimpled golf balls that toyed with the hole, then rolled to rest yards away from the flag.

"Look at that," I nudged Bernie with a pointy elbow in what was once her rib cage. "Free entertainment. I love how they dress. They all want to be Tiger Woods, don't they? Watch this guy's putt," I chuckled then hopped as a Titleist ball bounced across my Croc-clad toes. "Whew. That came too close."

I stooped, scooped up the offending ball, and tossed it back onto the green then caught Bernie's raised eyebrows and winced. "I guess I shouldn't have done that, huh? Oh, well."

Gasping for breath in the dense, humid jungle of moss-laden live oaks, we dragged, bounced, and cajoled the offending necessities up the steep cedar steps to the locked front door. Once again, I groped and mumbled as I searched for the ever-elusive keys.

"Here they are," I muttered, aware of my friend's growing consternation. "Hold this, please." Handing her my tote and a plastic grocery sack, a travel mug, a beach towel and a can of bug spray, I hip-checked the door, and we stepped into blessed air conditioning.

No time to bask in delicious coolness, however. We still had to wrangle and wheedle to establish turf and bicker over every detail from prime refrigerator space to who gets the lighthouse coffee mug. Could we ever have guessed that there'd be so much more to our ten glorious vacation days than sandy sheets, too much shrimp, and an increasing need for pants with elastic waists?

Being female and therefore pros, unpacking was efficient and methodical…Step one: open the closet. Step two: throw in a suitcase. Step three: close closet door. All there was to it. Feeling a tad defiant, however, we skipped step three.

To the casual observer, the urgent need to take this trip might have appeared to be nothing more than a mid-life crisis, or, at the very least, a mid-life dilemma. Whatever the case, we needed this trip more than we'd needed anything in a long time. Years had come and gone, and yet, we found ourselves able to resume our friendship and our lives right where we'd left off those many years ago. Sarcasm, jokes, good-natured sniping were all right on target and interwoven with the commonality of humor.

Bernie, after several fruitless attempts to use her cell phone in the condo, limped outside to search for a signal. Six minutes later, she returned, looking flushed and exasperated. Her "Men." was all I needed to know that her call home had gone through, and she'd been able to talk to her husband. Exhausted, we nodded to one another and headed for our respective rooms for a lie-down. I don't know about Bernie, but I was prostrate and snoring within minutes.

Three

One hour and sixteen minutes later I awoke refreshed and thirsty. After a quick visit to the bathroom and the fridge for a Coke, I planted myself on the couch. On the glass and bamboo table—smartly appointed with a map of the area and the obligatory fish house menu—lay a book Bernie had unloaded from her carry-on: *The Complete Idiots Guide to Middle Age*. Its dog-eared chapters nodded to an untold wealth of pertinent information.

I flipped through several cropped pages until I found a highlighted chapter—*Spastic Colon*. "Whew," I whistled under my breath. A bit too much information, but somehow strangely intriguing, too. I was amazed by Bernie's insistence on marking her territory in this pre-packaged guide to plunging downhill. It'd been quite a few years since she and I had really connected. I could only imagine the medical history she'd had to endure—not to mention the obvious pitfalls of just plain getting older. I focused on this most personal diary of my friend.

Flip…flip… "Hmmm…Goiter. *Goiter?*"

Flip…flip… "'Bingo Arms'…what the hell are 'Bingo Arms'?"

I continued paging and scanning this horrendous collection of matronly maladies, alternating between fascination and horror as I perused the topics of interest to one Bernadette North.

"Dentures…" I whispered. I never would have suspected that Bernie had dentures. She looked so natural.

"Halitosis…" Flip…Flip… "Warts?"

My eyes filled with tears. My poor, poor Bernie. Had so many years passed that my poor, decrepit friend had failed, while I, miles away, had been oblivious? I mean, I hadn't changed. Well, not all that much.

Flip…flip… "Bunions? Gastric Bypass: Pros and Cons? Where There's a Will, There's a Way to Get Even? Amazing." The blinders were down. I had a new perspective now. My dear chum doddered on the edge of senility and old age. Thank God the chapter on Flatulence bore no marking, but Acid Reflux was highlighted in fluorescent yellow. I could relate to that, anyway.

Intrigued, I continued to leaf through the book, marveling at the desperate information chronicled by my faltering cohort. In the back bedroom, I could hear Bernie stirring and groaning. When she sauntered out to the living room, all I could do was stare at her weakening form—a fragile earthen vessel cracking in so many places.

She brightened when she saw the contraband in my hand. I met her raised eyebrows with a lump in my throat and watering eyes. My dearest of dear friends…a poor, pathetic creature, who'd been viable—*alive*—only an hour before.

"Isn't that a hoot?" Bernie bellowed, crashing onto the cushioned chair that matched the couch in fabric and style. "Found that in the little pocket in front of me on the plane. Some old fool left it behind."

More than relieved and quite a bit embarrassed, I mustered a lame grin, and tossed the book aside. "Well. Okay. Ha, ha. Loved it. Loved it." *Damn.*

Bernie's cell phone emitted a funny little ping-squeak at that auspicious moment.

"Is that your phone?" I leaned forward to stare at the funny little flat gray and silver box on the table. "Sure has an odd ring."

"That's not its ring, just noise to let me know I have a text message." She snatched it up and released an exasperated sigh. "Yep. It's Jack again. He's already called seven times today. I called him when we arrived and told him I can't get a signal here. So, just like a kid, he text-messages me…again and again."

"That's so weird. How come you can get an alert to a missed call or a text message but not the call itself? Of course I don't know why I'm even asking since technology and I have never been the best of pals. All I know is my cell phone works just fine, anywhere, anytime," I tried to tone down the smug sound in my voice.

"Yes, well, I discovered mine will work if I stand out on the green." She looked through the large sliding glass door behind her. "Nobody's out there at the moment. Maybe if I hurry I can make my call before some guy yells at me to get out of the way." With a resigned sigh, she slipped on her shoes, pushed through the door, and made her way down the stairs.

I leaned back against the couch cushions, put my feet up on the coffee table, and closed my eyes. At that predestined moment in eternity *my* cell phone rang. With a groan to rival Bernie's sigh, I sat up and reached for the little demon, vibrating on the glass-topped table. One glance and I knew it was from Joe. Dear droll little man. What had he lost now?

Four

Every vacation condo in South Carolina comes complete with essential ingredients: gnats, mosquitoes, sand, heat, humidity, and, if you're lucky, a glorious gallery of characters and personalities who comprise The Neighbors. The tradition of scoping out these special residents always provided both color and comedy for all.

No scripted masterpiece can compete with women-without-mirrors: confident, self-assured, and oblivious to the ravages of rear view cellulite. And let's not forget the portly, post-fit, *studly* men who thrive on striking poses, one hairy hand on hip, while flipping burgers and dodging grease in skimpy Speedos. The image is enough to make one lose her appetite.

We'd trudged out to the car for the last of the supplies and had paused at the foot of our stairs when I did a double take. "Bernie," I hissed, landing another pointy elbow in my friend's ribs. "Look who's coming our way." My gaze riveted on a fifty-something, wild haired, frizz queen sporting crimson lips and audacious boobs trapped in purple spandex. She strode across the pine needle-strewn parking lot, extending a beringed hand, sporting scarlet inches-long fingernails.

"Hey, y'all. Welcome to Fun City. I'm Vicki and that little teddy bear of a man there behind me is Lionel. Lionel, honey," she shrilled across the lot, "come say hey to our neighbors in 215."

Bernie's eyes rolled heavenward. She sent me a meaningful glance, then stepped forward. "Hi," she said, donning her best principal-in-charge smile. "I'm Bernadette, Bernie for short, and this is Michaela, whom her friends call Mike."

Vicki beamed and Lionel offered a sassy wink. I winked back then wished I hadn't.

Needing to lose eye contact with the leering Lionel, I glanced up and spotted a small, pixie-haired child in a bright blue swimsuit peering through the slats of the upstairs railing. She gazed down at us, transfixed. I smiled and waved. Not blinking, she poked a yellow plastic shovel through the cedar slats, aimed, then let it go. The darned thing plunked on my pink floppy hat, bumped to my shoulder, then landed in the pine needles at my feet. She giggled, and the tiny face disappeared behind a colorful Dora the Explorer beach towel, draped over the railing.

"Ahh, the welcoming committee is launching an attack," Bernie commented with a lip curl.

"Cute," was all I said, removing my hat and rubbing my head and shoulder.

"Isn't she just the most precious little darlin'?" Vicki cooed.

"Oh, she is, she is," Bernie nodded. "Cute as she can be."

"I just love her to death," Vicki simpered. "And don't you just love that there little beauty mark on her cute little chin? Just like Elizabeth Taylor's and Marilyn Monroe's. Oh. And Cindy Crawford's got one, too. I'm thinkin' of gettin' one myself."

Not having paid that close of attention to the child's face nor that fond of moles of any kind, I just nodded, while Bernie's shoulders lifted to her ears.

Vicki giggled. "Thank *God* for cosmetics. Right? Well. Sure was nice meetin' you all. We all'll talk again later. Gotta help my man with the dinner. Toodles."

Vicki's red-taloned hand fluttered in a limp wave as she bounced over to join Lionel, hunched over their Weber grill. She leaned over, too, and the resulting display was phenomenal. I glanced up at Bernie and saw the horror I felt mirrored in her eyes. Each of us, desperate to comprehend the amazing elasticity of Vicki's challenged spandex top, which barely contained her size forty-two-triple D bosoms, was almost too startled to move.

The law of physics be damned.

"My girls would never tolerate that kind of confinement," I muttered.

"Girls? What girls?"

"Nellie and Gladys," I said, stabbing a finger at my own size 38 chest.

"You named your breasts?" Bernie's eyes widened.

"Of course. Didn't you?"

The look Bernie gave me was this side of being grossly disrespectful. With tandem shrugs, we turned and headed for our condo, stumbling back up the steps like weary infantry after a grueling march.

By the time we'd reached our porch, mosquitoes had descended upon us in hoards—in quest of an evening meal, no doubt. All I wanted was to get inside, but just as my hand reached for the doorknob, the occupant from the unit next door materialized.

"Yoo-hoo, girls. Don't forget trash pick-up is tomorrow, bright and early," the wispy white-haired, floral caftanned fantasy sang out. "I'm Melba. You know, like the toast. Melba—you can call me Melba though some people call me Mel, but, I prefer Melba, though it doesn't really matter. Trash pick-up tomorrow morning, girls." She paused, frowned, and extended a plump hand. "Have we met? My name is Melba. Like the toast."

"Hello," we chimed in unison. I added, "I'm Mike and this is Bernie."

"Nice to meet you. I'm Melba—"

"Yes, yes," Bernie growled, "like the toast."

"Thanks for the info on trash pick-up, Melba. We'll see you later. Gotta unpack." I waved to Melba-like-the-toast, and ushered Bernie into the condo. Once the door was closed, I wagged a finger at her. "Now, Bernadette, you be nice. That poor woman isn't rowing with both oars, if you know what I mean."

Bernie made a face. "You're telling me? Sheesh."

Heavy footsteps overhead reminded us there was a family

with an adventurous toddler occupying the unit upstairs. Bernie's eyes shot upward.

I snorted, "We've got neighbors coming out our whazoo. That's no doubt the bunch with the adorable little kid who pelted me with the plastic shovel."

"Oh, yes," Bernie nodded, "Most assuredly so. What's more, I think I'm going to like those people. Very perceptive folks. Especially the little munchkin with the beauty mark."

"Oh, please. Not you, too. I was so b—"

From somewhere in the recesses of the small apartment a telephone jingled. Before we could reach the offending noise maker, the answering machine clicked on, retrieving for posterity a perky pre-recorded message alerting us that there was still hope for our bulging bottoms, protruding bellies, and sagging chins at the local pharmacy cum bait and tackle shop. 'Buy *Belly-Free* today to live belly-free tomorrow', the message shrilled.

I made a face. "Who do they think lives here, anyway? A couple of senior citizens?" I gazed into the decorative wall mirror hanging beside the door. "As if we needed that kind of help. I think we look pretty darn good for our ages."

"I wonder if they sell that stuff in gallon buckets," Bernie muttered.

"Oh, pooh." I leaned in closer and shuddered at the noticeable lines fanning both eyes. "You know what really rattles me?"

"No. What?"

"I happened to turn on one of those cable stations and saw an old *Bonanza* rerun."

"And?"

"And it shocked the living daylights out of me when I discovered that Ben Cartwright was more appealing than Little Joe."

Bernie's resulting snort was not at all attractive.

Five

Lionel's barbecue coals smoldered in a soft, gray glow as evening melted onto the horizon. Not a soul in sight. The dinner hour, and Bernie and I prepared an elegant repast of Cheetos, onion dip, potato chips, and Triscuits with cheese. A chunky brownie rounded out the meal. We acknowledged the obvious fact that we couldn't eat this way for ten days. Tomorrow we'd pick up a bag of salad and a few peaches at the local Piggly Wiggly. And maybe some more beer and pretzels.

Lighting a chubby citronella candle, we settled into creaking deck chairs for some downtime before retiring, and crafted our plans for the upcoming days. The subtle scents of growing things teased our noses. Heaven on earth. I let out a long sigh. Bernie opened her mouth to quip but snapped it shut when sweet, fragile Melba from next door wandered onto the deck and appeared delighted yet surprised to see us.

"Well, hello, dears," the older lady cooed. "So happy to see you. My name is Melba. Are you staying here with Elfriede and Simone? They just arrived today."

Oh, Lord, this is going to be a challenge, I thought, not daring to glance Bernie's way.

"Hello, Melba," we said in sync.

"I'm Bernie and this is Mike," Bernie added. "We met you a few hours ago, remember?"

"Of course I do, dears. But where are Elfriede and Simone?"

Melba's eyes slid from us to the porch railing, where a few

seashells lay in a row. Poking at them and rearranging several, the older lady seemed to have forgotten we were there. After an epic-length of time, she lifted her round shoulders, mewed, and shuffled toward her front door, lime green flip-flops popping on callused heels as she made her way back to the cool darkness of her little condo. A gentle turn of her head, a smile in our direction, a wave, a sigh, and she vanished.

"Well." Bernie exhaled. "If that doesn't beat all. Sheesh."

"A tad on the scary side…"

"You're telling me."

We sat in silent contemplation for several minutes, then I couldn't stand it another second. "That's it." I grimaced and twisted and writhed with annoyance.

"Good Lord, what's biting you now?" Bernie leaned away from me.

"My bra. The bra's got to go. And I mean right now." I jumped to my feet, stretched and twisted. "I hate this garment. Don't know why I didn't take it off sooner."

"Jeez Louise, Michaela. You look just like an exercise maven in the throes of warming up for her Pilates routine. Chill."

I just glared at her. "I despise this thing. Who invented the bra, anyway? It's torture. I hate it." I stormed off the porch and into the condo. Two minutes later I returned, relaxed and smiling. Engulfed in an over sized T-shirt, I clutched a sweating bottle of hard lemonade to my recently unshackled bosom. I caught Bernie's bemused and condescending grin from the corner of my eye but chose to ignore the unspoken jibe.

Seasoned friendships are the best. Aged to perfection. You can sense a punch line, explode into painful, gut-wrenching laughter, and comprehend the poignancy of any meaningful moment without so much as a spoken syllable. Only half a day and we were already giving 'Southern Comfort' a whole new scope of delightful innuendo. We had ten glorious, relaxing days ahead of us. Smooth sailing all the way.

"We're heading to the beach tomorrow," I announced to break

the silence. "Did you bring your trunks?"

Bernie, who'd been slapping at mosquitoes, froze. I cocked my head and gave her The Look. "What? Please don't tell me you didn't bring a swimsuit."

A pained expression spread across her face. "Oh, Lord," she groaned.

"What? What's the matter?"

"Sweetie, the prospect of emerging from the privacy of my bedroom, trapped and suspended in lycra and spandex heinously crafted for maximum coverage of dimpled buttocks and gravity-challenged cleavage is depressing and extraordinarily painful."

I did a double take. "You're kidding."

"Uhm hummm," she murmured.

"Uhm hummm, yourself," I countered. "You'd better be teasing me, Mrs. North, because we are going into the water—hideous spandex and lycra or not. Now, let's go inside and watch some TV. Too many mosquitoes out here." I bounced out of my chair. "C'mon, deary...time for the news."

Bernie's face was a mask of reluctance but she ambled into the condo after me and fell into the over-sized easy chair. After placing both feet on the ottoman, she reached for the remote and switched on the TV. Just in time for more on the missing twins I'd read about in the Charleston paper that morning. Flopping onto the couch, I groaned. "I read about those sweet little girls in the paper at the airport. I hate stuff like this."

We listened in sober silence as the announcer described how the identical three-year-old twin girls were snatched from a mall in Columbia while their mother's back was turned and hadn't been seen since last Saturday. An Amber Alert had been sent out, authorities everywhere notified, but as yet no word from any kidnappers had been received. Just plain tragic and I didn't want to think about it. Another thing to add to my already too-long prayer list.

✼

A raucous symphony of sea birds heralded the brilliant

morning sun. Through the palmettos, Lionel and Vicki emerged from 318 in all their radiant glory. Peering at them through the Venetian blinds, we witnessed Lionel treating the world to neon orange Bermuda shorts, bright green pool shoes, a Budweiser beach towel draped over one doughy shoulder, and a tacky baseball cap announcing, 'I'm With Stupid'.

Like a water sprite on hallucinogens, Vicki pranced down the steps behind him on the way to their Lexus. Tight jeans shorts enhanced a muffin-top torso that spilled out from beneath her tie-dyed midriff shirt. Enormous dangling dolphin earrings called to mind native tribes in Zambia, who stretch their earlobes to unnatural proportions for the sake of beauty. Masses of orange hair were swept up in a metallic scrunchee.

"We can't possibly look that bad," I muttered as the Lexus kicked up sand and pine needles in reckless disregard of the posted 13 mph speed limit.

Releasing the blind, I stepped back from the window and exhaled a loud puff of air. I was desperate to leave, already clad in a smart black and white ensemble, complete with matching straw hat and trendy beach bag. No bra. Viscous, cream-like ooze from a liberal application of sunscreen glistened on my exposed body parts. Bernie, on the other hand, was taking her own sweet time getting ready. Finally she slapped a straw hat on her fluff of hair, gathered up her beach bag, and sent me an evil look. I smiled.

"*Why*," Bernie spat the word, "this palpable *exhilaration* at the prospect of swallowing *gallons* of seawater?"

"Are you kidding? Just imagine bobbing up and down in the rhythmic enchantment of waves and tides. The ocean and I are simpatico."

"Humph."

Bernie locked the door as I trundled down the stairs ahead of her. A final glance toward our complex revealed a tiny face at an upstairs window, peeking around the edge of a drawn shade. We looked at each other, then back to the window, but the pixie had vanished. Just then, Jorge the grounds keeper arrived in a whirlwind of sound and fury, billowing leaves and pine cones from his path with his mighty leaf blower.

"Can't wait to get far, far away from that damned nuisance," Bernie grimaced.

No argument there. It'd be a pleasure to leave the noisemaker behind and let Jorge go about his daily routine, grooming the area—humbly, unassuming, ever-observant. "Ohh, yeah," I agreed.

Six

My hands at two and ten on the wheel, I glanced in the rear view mirror, adjusted the seat although it was in the same position it always is when I drive. Then I rectified my creeping swimsuit bottoms, twisted my neck until it popped, re-positioned my floppy-brimmed hat. Satisfied, I reached forward to turn the ignition key, which wasn't there.

"Oh, for crying out loud," I moaned as I flung open the car door, almost decapitating a venturesome squirrel. "I forgot my purse."

Bernie gave me The Look, propped open her door, desperate to coax in a waft of warmish air as she melted into the front seat, and grunted. "Great. I suppose your keys are in the purse?"

"Of course."

"And yet...*silly* me...I went and locked the door." Her sigh teetered on the downside of dramatic.

"Not to worry. I hid a key this morning beneath the shell under the table beside the—"

"*Go.*"

It only took a few minutes before I re-emerged, bag-in-hand, cool and collected. But Bernie was scowling. "What took you so long?" She dripped sweat and sarcasm.

"I didn't want to forget anything else. Here—let's do a last-minute check." I ignored her irritation on purpose. "Let's see... sunscreen..."

"Of course," Bernie exhaled.

"Is it SPF 30 or above?" I asked although Bernie's focus was on something other than me. The sullen look on her face spoke volumes. "Okay, okay," I continued, "beach towel? Flip-flops? Beach book? Swimsuit cover-up?"

"I'm wearing it." Bernie interjected. "Could we just *go*? The beach will dry up before we even get there."

"Oh, what a grouch. I'm just having some fun. Lighten up, will you? Sheesh. Do I sense a wee bit of anxiety and trepidation in my dear sidekick? I realize beach stuff is foreign to you, coming from the Midwest and all, but I, coming from Seattle and raised on Puget Sound, am *one* with the ocean. The salty, crashing waves, the majestic pelicans, and cackling gulls are all part and parcel of my spirit, melded into the untamable power of nature and timeless beauty and—"

"*Enough.*"

"Okay, okay. Jeez, Bernadette, give me a break." I started the engine, backed the car out of its space and maneuvered around a Live oak. Bernie, meanwhile, had removed her straw hat and was clutching it in a death-grip to her bosom. I was wise enough to refrain from uttering even a teensy-weensy comment.

We'd driven a few yards when something tickled my nose and then my ear. "Gnats," I sniped, my attention on the road thwarted by annoying little flying teeth, buzzing around my head. Groping, swiping, and grabbing at the invisible demons, I swatted. "Blasted gnats." I yelped again as one landed squarely on my cheek.

"All right, that's *it*." Bernie shrieked as her final shred of patience slipped through her manicured fingernails.

"Sorry. But they're flying all around my face."

"You're crazy. I don't see a thing."

"Then you're the one who's crazy. They're everywhere."

"Would you go already. Forget the invisible gnats, for crying out loud."

"Fine. Ohh. There. Got one."

"Go."

"Fine." I pressed down on the gas pedal. "Okay, sweetie," I

chirped in my best conciliatory tone, hoping to soothe and placate my riled up friend. "Do you want to go to the sound side or the ocean side?"

"I don't care," grumped Bernie. "Just go *some*where, for god's sake. You pick."

"Well," I began in my best teacher cum tour guide manner, "the sound is delightfully pleasant and lovely…probably just right for someone like you."

Sensing a challenge in my condescending comment, Bernie bristled with disdain. "What do you mean, 'someone like me'?"

Still relishing my role as Queen of the Sea, but sensing I was losing my edge, I hastened to amend, "No, no, dear, don't misunderstand what I said. It's just the *ocean* is, is, well…it's a bit of a *challenge* for landlubbers like yourself."

"And just because I'm from Missouri, I'm not up to it?" sniffed Bernie, perspiration trickling in rivulets from the masses of already disproportionate-sized hair, that seemed to be swelling by the minute.

"Okay, then…" I brightened, swatting again at the bothersome gnats that congregated for karaoke on the bridge of my nose. "We'll go to the ocean side, come hell or high water—no pun intended."

"Fine." Bernie knew she'd snapped so hastened to add, "It's been thirty-something years since I even poked a toe into the ocean so," she coughed, "this should be fun." She leaned toward me. "And I mean that."

"Oh, good," I chortled. "I *love* the ocean. And I know you will, too."

Within minutes, we were rolling into the beach access lot, startled to see so many neon-colored umbrellas peeking over the dunes. Folks got an early start around here. The crashing of breakers onto the rock jetties announced the in-coming tide, and we paused to gaze at the swelling whitecaps pounding the shore. The sounds of summer: laughter—from both gulls and people…shrill cries from children…the coast guard helicopter flying overhead…

the ranger, four-wheeling it from turtle nest to turtle nest across the sea grass dunes...the tinkling of sea shell shards ebbing and flowing in the frothy surf... Summer.

Stepping out of our tent-shaped cover-ups, eyes darting hither and yon for potential critics, we waddled to the water, noodles bent around our middles, ready to embrace the sea.

It didn't take us long to be engulfed in the wondrous ocean, bobbing about like corks, light on our toes, filled with awe at the buoyancy provided by the chemical relationship of saline water to pouchy flesh, wondering how we managed to touch the sand at all.

Minutes melted into timeless euphoria, bouncing and drifting with the flow, leaping into each billowing wave, slapped by an occasional and unexpected crest. Need I say how good life was?

However, how often do the realities of life sneak up and surprise us when we least expect it? This, I believe, is what folks call "Murphy's Law". While I continued to lull about on my float, Bernie bobbed closer to shore then stood straddle-legged in thigh-deep surf, hands on hips, to watch a gaggle of little ones playing in the sand—her back to the monotonous waves. Boogie boards skimmed past as lithe, tanned teens marketed their skills for willowy girls in itsy bikinis who paraded up and down the sand with nothing to hide and everything to show. I relaxed into the moment, content to just watch Bernie experiencing my beach and my ocean. Then the unexpected hit like a lightning bolt.

To my horror, an enormous rogue wave rose up behind Bernie and without ceremony yanked her feet out from under her. Bernie was tossed head-over-kiester once, twice, three times—which was no small task, even for the ocean.

Her black-clad bottom flashed the sky, disappeared then reappeared like some tormented sea creature in the throes of frenzied turmoil. Flopping in mere inches of sand, silt, and shells, there was no doubt Bernie was in extreme distress.

My lightning-like reflexes responded with yelps of surprise and fear, screaming, "Bernie. Bernie. Are you okay? Get up. Get up. Say something—anything."

Bernie rolled over—her suit barely covering the necessities—shells and sand streaming from her mouth, nose, and ears. Disoriented, she sat in three inches of sea and sand with a bemused smile on her face, belying her acute distress. Then, with deliberate and awkward machinations, she got to her feet and, listing from side to side, staggered onto the beach like a party-goer who'd tallied one too many Smirnoffs.

"Oh, my dear…I am *so* sorry," I sympathized, smile wobbling as I made vain attempts to refrain from laughing outright at the image of slow motion somersaults, face in sand, wide hiney winking at the noon day sun.

"Just…get…me…out…of…here," Bernie sputtered, in a game attempt to avoid the pitying yet amused stares of the accumulated by-standers and beach combers. Bernie could be the poster child for 'This Could Happen To You'—a sincere warning to all landlubbers to never, ever underestimate the power of the sea… or the capriciousness of Murphy's Law. Mustering every ounce of dignity remaining in her sandy and shell-bedecked body, Bernie strode with purpose up the beach, snatched up her beach towel, and, refusing to even look back, marched toward the parked car.

"Tomorrow…tomorrow we'll try the sound," I offered, knowing I would pay for this outing for the rest of my life.

Seven

    Still sputtering and spitting out sand and flecks of shells, Bernie squished into the steamy front seat of my Neon, while I offered conciliatory little clucking sounds in hopes of soothing her. "Are you sure you're okay? Oh, honey…I am *so* sorry. You don't hate the water now do you?"
    Bernie blew off my concerns and stared straight ahead, mermaid dreadlocks dripping and clinging to her sand-encrusted scalp.
    The car veered into the condo's parking lot and had barely come to a halt when Bernie forced her way against the door and stumbled up the path to the condo. By her muttering and wincing, I could tell the grit between her thighs chafed as she waddled toward the door like a toddler with a load.
    Dragging our beach bags, I trailed after her, ever mindful of her explosive wrath when challenged. I found the key—an amazing feat in itself—unlocked the door, and ushered her inside. I followed at a respectful distance, trying not to react to the plinking, scratching sounds of beach debris that marked her path down the hallway to the bathroom. "We can sweep up later," I called after her, sensing that my forced cheerfulness probably irked her something fierce as she wanted nothing more than a shower and shampoo.
    Sensing there was no more I could do at the moment, I changed into dry clothes then slumped down onto one of the plastic deck chairs, contemplating the wrath of Neptune and,

what could be even worse, the wrath of Bernie. A flash of color and the cloying scent of heady cologne alerted me to someone's presence. I looked up. The caftan queen.

"Hello, dear. I'm so glad you're back. It gets kind of lonely here when your condo is empty. I'm Melba…like the toast… Where is Constance?"

"Bernie," I corrected. "My friend is Bernie…short for Bernadette."

"Of course she is, dear," Melba patted my hand like I was the one tottering on the brink of dementia.

Swatting at the horde of mosquitoes organizing their family reunion on and around my glistening face, I muttered, "Drat these little buggers," through clenched teeth then grinned up at my neighbor. "Sorry for the visceral display there. I've sprayed but the little demons don't seem to mind, and I've just about had it with their torture."

Melba just shrugged and offered a bemused expression almost impossible to read. "Ohhh…yes…yes…so annoying. One of our Low Country scourges," she tittered. "I just ignore them." Her plump pink hands did a little hula-like wave and then, like a specter, she disappeared back into the dark recesses of her condo, to the company of Maury Povich and Montel Williams, and God knew who else.

Before I could settle back in my deck chair, a creaking floorboard overhead hinted that the elusive family a floor above might be ready to show themselves. Tilting my head back and gazing upwards as though capable of penetrating the floorboards, my neck froze in that ridiculous position. Plagued since my thirties with these muscle spasms, I leaped to my feet, head back, nostrils flaring, grimacing in pain.

"Oh, ow, ow, ow." I yelped, stumbling into the condo, hands outstretched, waving wildly like Patty Duke in *Helen Keller*. "Ow. Oh, jeez…ow." I moaned, seeking comfort and solace from one of my Lidocaine patches and a dose of aspirin. It was times like this I wished I had a massage therapist living right next door.

Therapeutic neck rubs worked miracles. I'm a firm believer that they were what kept me going during my teaching years. I'd long ago tried to talk my Joe into taking classes but he'd refused, proclaiming his expertise as good as any professional's. Well, his backrubs *were* pretty good, but, still, it wasn't the same. I twisted my neck this way and that and the spasm subsided. A minor miracle. I could move again. Thank God.

Turning on my heel to return to the veranda, I froze, detecting the faintest whiff of smoke, wafting on the breeze. Nose tilted toward the wall vent, I sniffed then bristled. "We have rules about smoking around here," I shouted.

"What?" Bernie screeched from her bathroom, floundering beneath cascades of water and shampoo, barely able to hear through sand-encrusted ears.

"Smoking," I hollered.

"Who's choking?" Bernie bellowed from the shower.

"No, I said smoking. Someone's smoking." I tried to explain.

"You're joking?" The blow was louder.

"*Smoking.*"

"Yes, I'm still soaking." Came her sputtering reply, annoying but funny, nevertheless.

"Never *mind.*" I sniffed the air like a bloodhound. Following my nose, I padded about the condo, seeking the source of the disturbing aroma. It would have to remain a mystery, as I didn't see a blessed soul around and neither one of us had the nasty habit. Too much. I felt drained. The muscles, still tight, begged for a nap. It'd been a very stressful morning, and I was on sensory overload.

Like a runaway slide show, terrifying and hilarious images took turns scrolling through my mind at an outlandish pace seldom experienced in this sleepy little beach town, where everyone was committed to beach and surf and golf and made bets on who could move the slowest. They called it, "Edislow" time, and I thoroughly bought into the idea. Especially now. I was beat.

Sitting comatose in the deck chair, my feet resting on the railing, I didn't budge an inch when soft footfalls alerted me to the presence of the little felon from upstairs. Opening one eye, I glanced at the pixie who crouched on the stairs giving me a most thorough but silent examination.

"Hi, there," I greeted the solemn child. "How are you? Having fun at the beach?"

The tousled-head nodded but the little girl didn't say a word or crack a smile. Somewhat bemused by her solemnity, I gazed at her adorable little face with its pointed chin, and focused on the diminutive dark mole—or, rather, *beauty* mark—on the left side of her mouth. I almost laughed aloud, remembering Vicki's gushing over it, and the litany of movie stars that had the good fortune to bear one as well. So funny.

About to say something else to the child, the little kid startled me by bouncing to her feet, turning and scooting back up the stairs to the unit above. So much for our getting acquainted. Cute little girl, though…maybe three or four…still huggable yet old enough not to be a major pest like an inquisitive two-year-old… My thoughts drifted to my grand nieces and nephews. I sure did love those kids of mine.

Still sleepy, I squirmed a bit in the uncomfortable plastic chair, tugged on my shorts and shirt and then settled back to allow a motley assortment of images to tumble around in my mind. Pink flesh rolling and tumbling in the surf, old ladies wearing flowered caftans and cloying cologne, wizened, brown men with mowers and blowers, doughy men and barbecues, pixie faces with beauty marks and—oh, gosh. Too much. Too much. Lycra and spandex and speedos, oh my.

Shaking my head, I sat up straighter in the plastic chair and lowered my legs. I needed a hard lemonade. I struggled to my feet and shuffled into the condo, straight to the fridge. Then with an icy bottle in hand, I flopped onto the floral and rattan sofa that dipped in all the wrong places. That description could just as easily have been used to define my body. One long swallow and I already felt more relaxed. I lay back against the pillow and closed my eyes. A smile flitted across my face—or was it a gnat?

Anyway, this place was again weaving its magic.

What a hoot. I realized that these comical characters bombarding my imagination and challenging my sanity were part and parcel of the uniqueness of this island hideaway. They were the stuff of memories, the smiles and abstract references between old friends. They would be for years to come. Our ten-day retreat had only begun, but already we'd shared gut-wrenching laughter that had brought us both to tears. What would the morrow bring? At this rate, we could write a book.

Eight

Needless to say, Bernie was groggy and sore after her nap. To be frank, I believe she'd been more unconscious than asleep. When she shuffled down the hall, I could tell she felt less than her usual complacent self. Risking her wrath, I raised both eyebrows and asked in a voice dripping with sugar, "Feel a bit droopy after your nap, sweetie?"

She grimaced and the look she pitched my way could've sliced a concrete block in half. "Never," she hissed, "say that word again."

"What word?" *Lord, what had I said?*

"'Droopy'. I loathe that word and all it implies." She tossed her fluffy head. "Sorry. I'm just hungry. So, what else is new? I am *always* hungry. And I'm sore as hell. I had to *slowly* and *painfully* roll off the bed just to get the hell upright. Heard the sound of pennies hitting marble, which turned out to be my knees, then, and I kid you not, literally had to *stagger* into the bathroom, where, only by the grace of God, I *managed* to wash my face and run a comb through my mop. Then, oh, Lord. One look in the mirror, and I knew who the victor of the battle at sea was. And it wasn't me…er, *I*."

I swallowed a grin. "Oh, dear girl, you look all right. I mean… well, you at least look a sight better than you did when you first crawled out of the water." I was enjoying this. "Oh, sweetie, you should've seen yourself. You looked like you'd been run over by a Mac truck or something. You looked—"

"I get it. However, 'Mac truck' is hardly a suitable analogy, seeing I was attacked by something indigenous to the sea. Perhaps barge or frigate or aircraft carrier would be a better term. Anyway. No need to belabor the point. Let's get moving."

"Okay. What do you want to do?"

"Eat. It's after five and I'm hungry. Didn't you say we were going to some wonderful restaurant nearby?"

I sat up. "Oh. Yes, I did. Just down the road a bit, across from the resort's entrance. We can walk it easily."

Bernie grimaced. Walking in sub-Saharan-jungle-like humidity was not her idea of fun. "Mikey, *darling*, you do realize I'm on the downhill side of fifty?"

I wrinkled my freckled, sunburned nose. "Ohh, Bernadette. Don't be so silly. I'm only six months shy of you, and I'm no Wonder Woman. If I can walk it, so can you. It'll be good for us to walk home after a heaping plate of shrimp and hush puppies. And it'll be good to loosen up your sore muscles. You know, get back up on the horse—that sort of thing."

"Fine. Let's get this show on the road."

Taking time only to run a comb through my hair and struggle into a bra, I joined Bernie in the living room. We turned off lights, grabbed our purses and left. Hunger propelled Bernie forward, and she kept up with me just fine. We walked down the winding narrow lane, past two large fresh-water ponds where people congregated to fish on sunny afternoons. Palmettos balanced on reflected images in postcard perfection.

Bernie dawdled, intrigued with the picture-perfect setting. "Darn," she lamented, "I'm kicking myself for not thinking to bring my camera. But who would've thought a short walk to a dockside restaurant would offer such a Kodak Moment?"

"Yeah. I've taken a zillion photos of those two palmettos over there. Awesome, isn't it?"

Bernie nodded and we plodded along.

The restaurant was called—appropriately if not originally—The Dockside. The exterior of the place was weather-beaten, due to countless years of scouring from the elements. It faced a vast marshland of rippling sea grasses, and a canal of sorts, which served as a roadway to open water.

The shabby but comfortable interior boasted a décor, circa 1950's, that no one had bothered to change or improve upon. Hand-lettered signs, amateur attempts in glistening oils of amazing fish and surly sea captains, and the obligatory lighthouse scene covered the faded walls. The most recent addition was the array of glossy decals advertising which credit cards were accepted at this establishment.

We climbed the narrow staircase to the dining room and were told there'd be at least a twenty-minute wait. Bumper crowd tonight. Happy, noisy tourists and a few daring locals filled the place, and it appeared to be doing a record business in the doling out and consumption of fresh shrimp. With a sigh and a protesting growl from our poor, neglected stomachs, we turned around and went back down the stairs to the bar below—a modern beeping device clutched in my hand.

After we ordered our drinks—me, a Tequila Sunrise, and Bernie, a margarita—we made our way out onto an airy screened-in dock area, where patrons could sit and sip their cocktails surrounded by boats and gulls and the subtle scent of diesel fuel. We'd barely tasted our drinks, however, when our little notification buzzer went berserk in a frenzy of blinking lights, which validated Bernie's suspicion that somehow the bartender notified the upstairs hostess as soon as the drinks were purchased. I sure as heck didn't care. I'd carry my drink upstairs. No see no saw.

"Uh, huh," Bernie grunted. "Oh, yeah. They've got their act together quite efficiently."

"Oh, Bernadette…"

Bernie snorted. "I'm serious. They say you have so many minutes to wait so you are forced to buy a drink, and then, when you've paid a ridiculous amount for a plastic cup of booze, your table is ready. Like I said, efficient."

"Oh, Bernie, don't be such a cynic."

Bernie grimaced, but she trouped after me without another word.

Her cross-grained attitude dissolved, however, after she nibbled on one golden brown hush puppy. "Oh, Lord," she exhaled, "this is heavenly. I've never tasted such good hush puppies. These are out-of–this-world good."

I beamed. "I told you. I adore this place and dream of it when I'm off."

"Off? Off what? Your meds?"

"No, for Pete's sake. 'Off' is a term used for those who aren't here…on the island…you know…tourists and the like. If you're 'from off', you're not a local."

Bernie just rolled her eyes. Her mouth was full of hush puppies.

We could barely walk the length of the restaurant when we'd finished eating our way through mounds of superbly fried shrimp, hush puppies, a baked potato with-everything-on-it, and a huge garden salad. That plus at least two quarts of sweet tea, there was no room for dessert. We had to waddle to the register to pay our check. We were more than a little uncomfortable on the walk back to the condo, too. Dodging two cars as we crossed the street and checking out the people riding bikes or fishing helped to take our minds off our distended stomachs.

The final climb up the seven or so steps to our unit was as difficult as the final ascent up Everest. Trudging upward, upward to the cool sanctuary of our condo, we paused long enough to watch the foursome on the green just below our deck. Three men were near the hole, watching each other carefully as they bent over and stared at the slope, held up golf clubs at eye-height to determine a direction or angle or something, and tossed little wisps of grass into the wind.

Just below our deck, a balding, sweaty man in a too-tight polo shirt poked at the foliage in search of his ball. Looking left and right, he dug into his khaki pocket, pulled out another ball, and dropped it at the edge of the landscaping. Confident he'd pulled off his deception, he somehow sensed disapproving eyes boring into the back of his frizzled head and glanced up. Catching our frozen figures in his peripheral vision, he shrugged then turned back to face the green. He knew he'd been busted, so reached down, snatched up the ball, shoved it back into his pocket, and barked to the others that he'd lost the damned ball and would take a penalty on that hole. With one more guilty glance over his shoulder at the two stern teachers staring him down, he hunched his shoulders and scurried toward the golf cart.

Yep. We hadn't lost our touch.

Still chuckling, I fumbled in my purse for my illusive keys. A sudden and most unexpected jolting thud overhead made us both jump.

"Jeez. That was something I didn't need right now," Bernie muttered.

"Yeah. Darn kids and their penchant for slamming doors and jumping off chairs and things. The main reason only young women have children."

"Amen."

Unlocking the door, I pushed my way inside, tossed my purse onto the nearest chair, and ambled over to the fridge. "Want some sweet tea, Bern?"

"Sure. I'm going to the potty then sit out on the deck—"

"—Veranda."

"Veranda. Okay with you?"

"Sounds heavenly. It's a beautiful evening. Spray before you go, though. The mosquitoes are a menace."

"Oh, you and your bugs."

"And light the citronella candle, will you?"

"Of course, sweetie."

Five minutes later we were settled in the plastic deck chairs like a pair of Raggedy Anns with our feet propped up on the railing. Ungainly, and rather awkward, perhaps, but no one could see us that well. No more golfers out on the green. And besides, I didn't care, and it was a cinch Bernie didn't give a horse's patoot.

Leaning back, I let out a dramatic sigh. "Oh, gosh, I do love it here…this is the life…if I had a million dollars I'd buy myself a beach house…how 'bout you, Bern? Feel like a Southern Belle yet?"

Before Bernie could offer a clever rejoinder, our next-door neighbor entered stage left, as if on cue. Melba, in all her floral caftanned glory, flowed out from her perennially dark apartment. Bernie let out a sigh. I tried hard not to roll my eyes or, worse, burst into nervous giggles.

"Hellooo, girls," the plump woman warbled. "I heard you come in… Out for an evening stroll around the grounds?"

"No. Just came back from a wonderful meal at the Dockside," I replied, patting my stomach.

"The Dockside? Ohh, no…not my cup of tea…always too crowded…too crowded…and so noisy…and I'm not that fond of seafood…too fishy…"

"Oh," I shrugged. "Too bad. I adore seafood. I think the Dockside is one of the best restaurants in town."

"Ohh, well…I suppose…always so crowded, though…so I suppose it's good, but I don't get out much…don't tolerate the heat that well…shortness of breath…terrible varicose veins…irritable bowel syndrome…not as young as I used to be…"

"Gosh…that's too bad," I mumbled, not knowing what else to say.

Melba's pale blue eyes swept the veranda then lighted on Bernie. "Dear Simone, how are you enjoying your visit?"

Maintaining her dwindling composure like a saint, Bernie replied, "It's Bernie—short for Bernadette—and I'm having a delightful time, Melba. Thank you."

Our neighbor's limpid blue eyes rolled and her curly head bobbed. "That's nice, so nice, darling. I'm glad someone is enjoying their time here." Her eyes looked skyward. "The Teals, now, oh, my…they aren't. Enjoying their time here, I mean. Poor Brenda is like me—pleasingly plump, that is—can't take the heat…and all those steps…" She gestured toward the staircase leading to the second floor apartments. "But Bobby, the dear, dear boy, is having a simply wonderful time…always smiling…always…and takes that precious, dimpled child with him wherever he goes…a delightful family, really… and little Amanda calls me Aunt Melba…isn't that sweet? Aunt Melba…" Melba sighed, sucked in a deep breath, made that hula gesture with her plump hands again, then turned in a billowing cloud of hot pink and turquoise, and re-entered her unit.

Bernie turned to me and grimaced. "My God. Is she for real? I can't believe that anyone as *clueless* as Melba is living here *alone*. She's confused, she rambles on and on, she can't remember our names…Now I know that sounds a lot like you, but I'm talking about Melba here."

Ignoring the jibe, I wrinkled my nose. "She *is* a character." Pointing overhead, I added in a stage whisper, "What did you think about what she said about Brenda and Bobby?"

Before Bernie had a chance to answer, a door slammed upstairs and footsteps and murmuring voices were heard. I sat up straighter—like a deer sensing danger. Bernie summoned enough energy to lower her elevated legs from the railing. Seconds later two adults and one toddler descended the staircase. None other than the aforementioned Brenda, Bobby, and Little Amanda.

Brenda was indeed plump and had long, stringy brown hair that either had too much mousse in it or was in dire need of a good shampoo. Poor thing was perspiring so heavily that it was probably just too darned hard to keep fresh.

Bobby, on the other hand, was lean to the point of skinny, and had a ponytail longer than my forearm. The muscle shirt he wore allowed a clear view of his multiple tattoos. His dirty flip-flops were almost worn to paper thinness on both heels. Not exactly my pick for the next *American Idol*.

Little Amanda, however, was pixie-cute. Her short, dark brown hair cupped her round face and a dimple showed in each rosy cheek. The tiny mole on the right side of her pointed chin once again snagged my attention. For some inexplicable reason, that tiny mole jumped out at me, and for a nano-second I felt like I was flirting with a senior moment. Chalk it up to too much sweet tea, too much sun, too much food—too much something. I grappled with conflicting thoughts and impressions while Bernie took the reins with poise and self-control—offspring from years of being a principal.

"Hi," Bernie said. "Lovely evening, isn't it?"

Brenda's lips curved upward for a fleeting moment, but her eyes remained focused on her plump feet. Bobby, on the other hand, nodded and returned Bernie's smile. "Yeah, it sure is. We're on our way to get some ice cream." He squeezed little Amanda's hand. "Aren't we, Tadpole?" The pixie gazed up at him and bobbed her head. His smile widened. "Chocolate for Mandy, right?" She nodded even more emphatically. "And strawberry for dada, right?" More vigorous bobbing.

Bernie chuckled and glanced at me. "Mike, here, likes her chocolate, too."

"Or cherry vanilla," I mumbled, having managed to corral my rambling wits enough to join the conversation. "You, uh, have fun now, Amanda. I'd go with you except I'm too full from dinner." Lame but at least sociable.

Bobby's eyes danced. "Did you eat at the Dockside?"

"Oh, yeah," I groaned. "Each of us shoveled down a pound of shrimp."

He nodded. "I know how that is. I always eat too much in that place. It's my favorite restaurant on the island."

"Mine, too. Never can get enough of the Dockside."

"Oh, yeah. What about the fish stew? Isn't that great?"

"Love it. Don't often eat very much as I need to save room for the shrimp and oysters, and what not, but I love the stuff."

By this point Bernie's eyebrows were a furry caterpillar. Common courtesy or not, I guess she'd had enough of our inane prattling about the restaurant. Brenda must have been on Bernie's wavelength because she nudged Bobby and he grimaced. The look he sent her was sharp enough to cut gristle, and suddenly we were interlopers in some internal family struggle.

"Uh, you guys have fun," I said for want of something lighthearted to break the razor-sharp friction emanating from the young couple. "I'm Mike, by the way—short for Michaela—and this is Bernie, uh, Bernadette."

Bobby recovered his mask of congeniality and smiled. "Hi, Mike and Bernie. I'm Bobby and this is Brenda."

"And your darling little girl is Amanda. Melba told us about you." I finished for him. "And Amanda and I met earlier. Curiosity brought her half-way down your stairs."

He ruffled the tot's short bob. "She's my little Tadpole. Aren't you, Amanda?" The tot peered up at him but didn't smile. Bobby's lips formed a smile but his eyes narrowed. With a quick glance at Brenda, he scooped the child up in one sinewy arm and grabbed Brenda's elbow with the other. "See you."

We watched as they disappeared down the remaining flight of stairs, straining to catch the low murmuring coming from Brenda. A couple of loud slams from a car's doors, and silence once more descended upon our little domain.

"Yuck." I muttered. "The thought of ice cream right now makes my stomach turn."

Bernie only grunted, raised her legs, and once more propped them against the railing. Bed sounded good. I was sure I'd sleep tonight and was pretty sure Bernie would, too.

"You know—" Bernie started to say when my cell phone rang. I struggled out of my chair and picked up. "Hi, Joe." I glanced at Bernie and she made a face and mouthed, *Thank God, it isn't mine.* She shifted her legs to a more comfortable position. We'd only just begun our getaway and our husbands had been hounding us. What else is new?

Nine

I awoke to sunlight streaming through my partially closed Venetian blinds. Another day in what I believed was the next best thing this side of Heaven. Punching my pillow and turning to lie on my back, I offered a prayer that my dearest buddy would feel the same. I wished she could see it through my rose-colored glasses, but all she saw was a flat piece of swampland, filled with mosquitoes, gators and snakes, and sea and sand and more sand. The only beach she'd ever been to recently was Myrtle Beach, and, in my humble opinion, that was a nightmare-come-true. Crowded, commercialized to the hilt—awful. Give me the peace and quiet of my little beach town anytime. During the peak season, it was crowded enough.

I rolled out of bed and hustled to my bathroom. Eight minutes later, I puttered about the kitchen, waiting for my pal to show. Just as I expected, the kettle was blowing steam when Bernie finally shuffled in. "G'morning," I greeted her, as she made a beeline for the Dr. Pepper. "Hope you slept well. I sure did. Slept like a log."

Bernie yawned. "Yep. Had a great sleep. So. What's on the agenda for today?"

"Charleston?"

"Charleston?"

"Charleston. See the Market, eat, maybe take a buggy ride around the Battery or Rainbow Row."

"Well…okay…"

"You don't sound too enthused."

"No, I am. Really. Let me have a Pepper then we'll talk." I stepped aside so she could retrieve her drink of choice from the fridge. She popped the lid, poured a tall glass, and sat down at the round glass dinette table. I made a face.

"It's really none of your business, you know," Bernie chided.

"What? What's none of my business?"

"Oh sure, like I'm not supposed to see that you think you're the adult here drinking instant coffee while I'm a soda freak."

"If you're trying to pick a fight, forget it," I sniffed, "because we've got better things to do today."

"Fine. So, let's get dressed and see Charleston. I've only been once and that was for just a few hours, years ago. You know how to get us there?"

That pushed my button. I scowled. "*Yes.* Sheesh. Give me a break, will you? I've been to Charleston a zillion times."

"Were *you* driving?"

"Well…no…but that doesn't matter. It'll be a piece of cake."

"Uh huh…" Now Bernie made a face.

I decided to change the subject. "D'you know what my Joe did?"

"No, but I'm sure you're going to tell me."

"He did laundry."

"Ooookay…"

"Do you know how many times I've told him not to touch the laundry?"

"No, b—"

"If I've told him once, I've told him a million times. He took our sheets off the bed—the dark blue, 500-count set I bought at Belk's that cost an arm and a leg—and added bleach. *Bleach.* Then—get this—he asked whether they'd had white spots on them. White spots. Of course I told him, 'no, they had no white spots on them', and then he sounded really, really contrite and made me feel like the guilty one. *Me.* Oohh. Men. Annoyingly wonderful and wonderfully annoying, at the same time."

Bernie swallowed a mouthful of Dr. Pepper, choked, coughed,

then broke out into a cackle of laughter. I glowered but she slapped the table and chortled. "Oh, Lord. I can just picture your Joe examining the spotted blue sheets—500-count, no less—in complete and total bewilderment. Oh, Lord. I haven't laughed this hard in years."

For some reason, I didn't share my friend's humor. I pursed my lips and turned on the faucet to rinse out my coffee cup. Bernie made a hasty retreat to her room to get dressed.

Exactly one hour and thirty-seven minutes later found us in the Neon and on our way down Highway 174…to Highway 17…to Charleston. Since I exuded confidence, Bernie settled back to enjoy the ride. She fiddled with the air vents until she had the AC aimed right where she wanted it then rested her knees against the glove compartment door. I bet times like these she wished she were five feet two.

We made good time and traffic was co-operating—that is, until we reached the outskirts of Charleston. I could feel my eyes narrowing to a squint and knew the facial tics would soon betray my growing nervousness. I didn't have long to wait.

"What's with the twitching eye?" Bernie asked.

"Nothing…except…"

"Except?"

"Well…here's where it gets tricky. I want Meeting Street…the Visitors' Center…where I'll park…" I gripped the wheel tighter and leaned forward. "There." I hooted. "Visitors' Center. But that's Calhoun. Where's Meeting Street?"

"I don't know. Have they misplaced it?"

"Don't be silly. It's here…somewhere…"

"Just follow the signs."

"I am."

"This lane is a right turn only. Move over."

"Someone's behind me."

"Put your blinker on, for crying out loud."

"It is."

Bernie closed her eyes as we swerved over into the left lane.

"We made it." I chortled. "And there's Meeting Street. I found it. I did it. I did it!"

"I thought you said it was a piece of cake."

I gave her a withering look. "Oh, *please*. It *was* a piece of cake. I got us here, didn't I?"

Bernie smiled even though I knew all manner of epithets were crawling up her throat. "Yes, you did, sweetie. I'm very proud of you."

I beamed.

We got out of the car, making sure we had purses and sunglasses. Of course I had on my perky pseudo-Southern pink hat. I thought I looked cute and didn't know why Bernie wouldn't wear one. With her blond complexion, a hat should've been a given. On the other hand, when you're five foot three you can get away with 'cute'. I guess it's virtually impossible when you're looming this side of six feet.

We'd taken only five steps when a male voice spoke from behind. "Had some trouble switching lanes back there, didn't you?" We both turned—my face a darker shade of pink than my hat. "We were right behind you," he continued. "Some pretty quick maneuvering on your part. Wasn't very well marked, was it?"

I winced then smiled and tried to recover a shred of dignity. "No, it wasn't very well marked. Sorry if I cut in front of you."

The stout gentleman shook his head. "No problem. We got here, didn't we?" He took his equally fleshy wife's arm and sauntered ahead of us.

Bernie looked down at me and grinned. "Don't worry about it. I don't think you cut in front of him…too badly, that is. I didn't hear any screeching of tires or squealing of brakes. Did you?" I shook my head. "And he's probably from up North and will never be down this way again, so don't give him another thought. Let's go. I'm melting. This heat is insane, and it's getting hotter by the minute.

We walked the short distance to the elevator, rode it to the ground floor, disembarked and headed for the Visitors' Center.

Blessed coolness greeted us as soon as we stepped inside. We gave a collective sigh then went straight to the ladies' room. Perspiring heavily, I had to wrestle with my slacks and undies and struggle some more just pulling them up again. At this rate it'd be noon before we got started.

Somewhat refreshed and ready to go, Bernie followed me through the center—ignoring the dizzying array of maps and brochures—through the gift shop and out the door. Blinding sunshine smacked me in the face, and I was thankful for my wide-brimmed, floppy hat. I felt sorry for Bernie's bare head, but at least she had on sunglasses. The glare was already unbearable and we'd only walked a dozen feet.

Two blocks down Meeting Street and the last of Bernie's patience evaporated. "Michaela. Just how far do we have to walk?"

I craned my short neck to squint up at her. "Oh, uh, just a few more blocks, th—"

"A few more blocks? We've already walked two."

"Uh, I know…sorry…Joe and I always park at the Visitors' Center. I-I know it's a rather long walk but—"

"*Rather* long? It's a hundred and ten degrees out, the humidity is somewhere off the charts, I'm almost sixty, over-weight, have bad feet and a bad back, and you're making me *walk* a mile?"

"I'm sorry…I really am…I never thought…I mean…Joe and I are as old and decrepit as you and we do it…'though I must admit we do it spring and fall…never in summer, but…well…it's not too far now…do you want to go back? We can go back, get the car, and see if we can find a closer parking space…" I wanted to sink through the sidewalk.

"Don't be ridiculous. You're being *utterly* ridiculous. Of all the *ridiculous* things to suggest. Of course we're not going back now. But I won't forget this…if I *live* to never forget it, that is."

"I'm sorry," I mumbled. "I've been here a hundred times. Joe does his thing with the USS Yorktown—he's on the board, you know—and we always come down here, and we always park at the Visitors' Center and, er, walk. I guess I just didn't pay attention to any other potential parking lots. I was just so relieved that I was able to drive here without Joe and…"

Bernie's shoulders slumped and she let out a long sigh. "Oh, don't look so crestfallen. Jeez. It's all right…I'll live…I hope. But please tell me we're almost there."

"Oh, we are, we are. See? There, across the street. There's the Market."

The light changed and I led the way across the street, jostling the crowd of tourists like a pro. As soon as we entered the open-aired building, Bernie relaxed. Out of the sun's glare, it was decidedly cooler. The vendors had enough wares to feast your eyes upon, and soon she was no longer dwelling on aching feet and protesting back.

The hand-woven Gullah baskets were wonderful, and I watched as Bernie picked up a few, only to cringe at the prices marked on the little stickers. Beautiful and worth every penny, she still couldn't allow herself the extravagance. Her Jack would've had a coronary if he saw the amount they were asking. I know my Joe sure would have.

Her initial delight soon waned, however, as the stalls continued in a never-ending row that extended the length of several blocks…or so it seemed. After twenty minutes, Bernie'd seen enough.

"Mike," she hissed, pulling on my sleeve. "Mike, I'm getting claustrophobic. Isn't it time we went to lunch?"

I nodded although my attention focused on a display of handmade cloth dolls. The elderly lady who'd made them was leaning toward me, in hopes of snaring another gullible customer. "Aren't these the cutest things you've ever seen?" I flipped over a tiny price tag and grinned. "Very reasonable, too. Think little Amanda would like one?"

Bernie wrinkled her nose. "Oh, indubitably. What toddler wouldn't want a cute, handmade, overpriced, colorfully clothed little rag doll?"

Ignoring her cynicism, I plowed through the display in search of the perfect doll.

Bernie was about to complain further when her cell phone

rang out its whimsical tune. Since she couldn't get reception at the condo, she snatched it from her handbag and answered. "Molly," she mouthed to let me know it was her twenty-four-year-old daughter. A teacher like her old mom, Molly was still recovering from her first year teaching second grade. School was starting in two weeks, and she was in the depths of misery and despair, having just sprained her ankle so badly that she was couch-ridden and told to keep it elevated and iced. There wasn't a thing she could do but sit and watch inane TV shows. She was pulling her hair out and had already called her mom half a dozen times.

While Bernie had her ear to her cell phone, listening, sympathizing and commiserating, I resumed my search through the handmade rag dolls. I picked up one doll after another, examining them like I would fresh vegetables. After seven minutes—I counted them—Molly was mollified enough—no pun intended—to let Bernie go. Dripping perspiration now, she'd lost all patience with the too close, too warm, too historical hysteria. Her gray eyes pleaded with me to leave. Not saying a word, she glared and tossed her ever-expanding shock of hair with ever-expanding impatience.

I grinned, nodded, selected a doll, and paid the tourist-weary vendor. Clutching my treasure, I twisted my neck from side to side and inhaled deeply. "Well, I'm through. Now what? A carriage ride?"

"Lord, no. Now, it's time for lunch." Bernie countered as she shifted from sore foot to sore foot, shorts sticking to sweaty skin, glasses fogged so much she couldn't see.

I knew the thought of trudging blocks and blocks in the intense Charleston heat to the little car was enough to make her want to cry. Only the promise of food could raise her spirits enough to continue her charade of amiability.

Nothing captures our interest and enthusiasm quite as much as eating, so with the carrot dangling before our sweaty noses, we tripped up the brick sidewalk to my favorite barbecue joint. A tad dark…redolent with smoke…but with cushioned benches and oodles of AC. Heaven on earth. We plopped down without ceremony into the massive wooden booth and accepted menus from an eager young man in an apron. I adored *Sticky Fingers* and hoped Bernie would be satisfied with my choice of establishments.

Before we knew it, we'd devoured every shred of our lunch—gnawed the bones, inhaled the seasoned fries—and cleansed sticky fingers with moist towelettes. I tried to be blasé about the six-block trek to the car, but Bernie read right through me and behaved like an inmate on death row.

"Just call the paramedics and get it over with," Bernie moaned as we plodded our way up the streets in historic, downtown Charleston. "Yep, you sure do know how to show a friend a good time." Just a tinge of sarcasm. "I mean, if I had known you were going to park the car in Charlotte and then make us walk to Charleston, I might have objected."

Too hot to counter that snipe, I just pulled the brim lower on my hat and kept walking.

After an endless march to the mirage-like Visitors Center, we almost collapsed when a delicious chilliness swept over us as we staggered inside. We both made a pathetic portrait of womanhood-gone-sour, and were old enough to know better.

Smart and jaunty had been reduced to withered and drooping, and I'm talking about *clothing* here, not female attributes. Smudged mascara and flushed faces told the tale of a bold endeavor brought to its knees by the realities of nature and gravity.

An eternity later, we dropped onto the too-warm car seats, too worn out to say a word. All we could think about was hard lemonade and cool salsa dip awaiting us back at the condo. Sweet, vacant Melba had most assuredly put out an APB advising local authorities that Marlene and Gwen had left early in the early morning for a little jaunt to the big city, but had yet to return.

Such is life.

Ten

One hour and forty-seven minutes later, we arrived on the home scene. Vicki and Lionel were coaxing a meager flame from their smoldering brazier. At least two pounds of richly marbled steak awaited the char. While Lionel blew on the ash-laden embers, Vicki happened to look up, saw us, flung back her shoulders and snapped to attention, almost clocking Lionel with her astonishing boobs, clad today in bright yellow lycra. Gravity is a wondrous and remarkable element of nature, except when it wrecks havoc upon the female figure after fifty-some years of battle. Vicki had indeed put up a valiant fight, but the dear gal had already lost the war with gravity. Yet she seemed oblivious of what the strife had cost her.

"Well, hey, y'all." Vicki shrilled as we lumbered up the walk from the car. "Where y'all been all day?"

Without waiting for our reply, Vicki sashayed across the pine needles, kicking up dust and pine cones as her flip-flopped feet snapped, snapped, snapped in cadence with her bouncing progress in our direction. Away from her watchful eye, Lionel was now free to handle the fire in a manly manner, and quickly—one eye on his wife's back—directed a potent squirt of fire starter on the tiny anemic flame. Within seconds, billowing smoke engulfed the hapless Lionel as he coughed and swore and flailed his arms in a mad effort to suck in some air. Glancing over her shoulder, Vicki hooted.

"Careful, hon," Vicki yelled in his general direction. "Don't forget that Rogaine is highly flammable. Recollect what happened last summer when y'caught your head on fire. Ohooeee. *That* sure was a sight."

Vicki then turned her attention back to us. Too weary and discombobulated to do anything but gape at the pageant of smoke and fire and color and sound, we just stood there with mouths open. We'd just driven all the way to Charleston and back, hiked blocks and blocks—all in blistering, Sub-Saharan heat—but nothing compared to the spectacle in progress in our own backyard.

Furious and more than a tad frustrated, poor Lionel clomped up the wooden stairs to his deck, clueless to the additional horror he imposed on the innocent bystander. Someone *really* needed to have a frank and serious talk with him about where polyester material goes when thwarted in the attempt to conceal well-endowed buttocks.

I managed a surreptitious glance at Bernie then wished I hadn't. The open disdain she had all over her pink cheeks was enough to cause the giggles to well up in me. Putting a hand over my mouth, I jerked my head toward Vicki then raced up the steps to our deck, where I collapsed onto a chair. I heard Bernie mumble something about Charleston, heat, and my need of a bathroom.

"Well, y'all must have had quite a day," Vicki's shrill voice commiserated. "Sure is hot enough to boil taters. I spent my day at the pool…readin'."

When Bernie said, "Oh?" I almost laughed outright. Then she added, "What are you, uh, reading?" She couldn't quite keep the disbelief from her tone.

A shrill giggle, then, "Oh, *you* know…one of them trashy romances where the girl's skin-tight dress is fallin' off her shoulders on the cover, and her hair's floatin' in the wind 'cause there's always a breeze, an' it looks like her boobs is gonna fall out any minute. Say. Did y'hear that an alligator was seen in the lagoon—"

"No—"

"I saw one last year but haven't this year, *yet*—"

"Too b—"

"—And honey, ohmi*gawd*. Have you seen the couple to the west of our place—"

"N—"

"—She has absolutely *no* fashion sense whatsoever. My gawd. I'd *die* before going out in public like that."

Doubled up with suppressed laughter, I left the chair, leaned over the railing and peered around the building to watch Bernie's reaction to the amazing Vicki.

"Awful." Bernie's voice dripped irritability and impatience.

"Oh, I agree. And, dear little Melba." Vicki tossed her frizzy red head. "Do you know I just *happened* to be lookin' out our window, and I *saw* her—Melba, that is—lookin' through the *trash* cans, takin' trash *out* instead of puttin' it *in*. Isn't that the most *disgustin'* thing you've ever heard?"

"Actually, no. Well, it was nice chatting with you, Vicki, but nature is calling." And with that, my friend made her way up the steps and found me doubled over, convulsed with mirth. She glared at me. "Why haven't you opened the door, for crying out loud? I need to use the bathroom and I'm exhausted."

Of course it took me an interminable length of time to find the damn key. I could hear Bernie's breathing getting heavier and heavier until she exploded. "You would think by this time it would cease to be a surprise to you that you need a key to enter this place. I mean, for crying out loud, Mike. What's with this ritualistic search and discovery every time we want to go inside? I mean, again and again and again… Why didn't you keep the key under that blasted seashell?"

"After thinking about it, I decided it was too obvious a place. So there." I stuck out my tongue, opened the door, and made an exaggerated motion for her to enter. She sauntered in, threw her purse onto the table, and marched into her bathroom. I, on the other hand, dashed for my bathroom in order to rip off the bra that I'd endured for more than six excruciating hours. Only then could I relax, allowing my 'girls' the luxury of unrestricted bobbing and swaying. In less than a minute, we both were back in the living room feeling much better.

"I need a drink," Bernie announced.

"You and me both. A Pepper or a hard lemonade?"

"Neither. Give me a Smirnoff, please."

I got our drinks and joined her on the couch. She accepted hers gratefully, took a long swallow then sighed. "Oh, that's good. That's really good." She eyed me, brows in a knot, as I reached for my purse and started rummaging in its cavernous maw. "Jeez Louise, Mike, do you really need that big of a purse? What have you got in there?"

I sniffed. "Nothing but what's essential. Let's see…Kleenex, moist towelettes, Chap Stick, wallet—oh. And two Piggly Wiggly receipts…loose change—how'd that get down there—a comb, my cell ph—"

"Enough. Please. I get it. I get it. Sorry I brought it up. I now fully comprehend your difficulty in retrieving a simple set of keys. You need to downsize, sweetie."

"I've tried. No use. I really need this stuff."

"Then use the blasted seashell."

"Too risky."

"Then wear the damned key around your neck."

"Uh huh…good one." I yawned, put my bare feet up on the coffee table and tugged at my over-sized T-shirt that had bunched up behind me. "Gosh I'm glad to be free from that binder."

Bernie looked at me with a slight shake of her poofy head. "Well, at least, sweetie, your boobs don't land in your lap when you flop down on the sofa. The curse of 'Cooper's Droop', which is how we laughingly referred to boobs at waist-length when we were young and perky."

This time it was my turn to look askance. "*Excuse* me? I don't believe I've ever heard of 'Cooper's Droop'."

"Oh, you have, too. We talked about it all the time…"

"When?"

"Back when we were in our twenties."

"Did not."

"Did, too." She frowned. "Somehow, though, it's just not as funny or weird looking as when we were young. Imagine that…"

Above us a door slammed. I rolled my eyes heavenward. "Well," I shrugged and stretched. "We know they're home. Weird because we usually can't hear anything from the neighboring units. My brother-in-law says the walls are well buffered or something. That young couple sure must be active." I took another swallow of my hard lemonade.

Bernie nodded. Then a smirk danced across her face. "You are something else."

"What's that supposed to mean?"

"Just that you are quite the accomplished social drinker, aren't you?"

I made a face. "Well, yes, as a matter of fact, I am. My doctor told me when I was in my forties I needed to take a glass of wine before bed to alleviate stress. And now I thoroughly enjoy my hard lemonades and an occasional light beer."

"Ohhhoo…2% wine coolers and light beer. And sometimes two in one day. It's amazing…utterly amazing…how decadent and worldly you've become with gloriously liberating age. I can see that you revel at living on the edge."

"I like martinis, too," I returned.

"Oohhooo…I'm impressed."

I refrained from further commenting and picked up my paperback instead.

That's when Bernie's cell phone made the ridiculous message alert squeak.

"Ohh, darn." She scooped it off the table, took one look at it, and grunted. "It's Molly." Her blue-gray eyes were as beseeching as an old bloodhound's. "May I, uh, use your phone to call her since mine only can offer text messages?"

I grinned. "Sure. Give her the house number so she can call you here whenever she wants. Doesn't cost anything for in-coming calls, and you have an extension in your bedroom. Don't know why we didn't think of that alternative earlier."

Bernie's hound dog look evaporated. "Thanks. You're a dear. I'll do just that." She exchanged her phone for mine, punched in her daughter's number, and sat back in her chair. "Hi, hon, it's mom. Got your text. You know my phone isn't working here. From now on, call this number…"

Tuning out Bernie's conversation with her distraught daughter, I reached for my tote and pulled out the cute little handmade cloth doll and held it up to admire the detail. I couldn't wait to see the expression on little Amanda's face when I gave it to her. Bobby and Brenda certainly wouldn't mind the sweet, thoughtful token from the older gals downstairs. Smiling and quite pleased with myself, I leaned back and closed my eyes. Amanda's heart-shaped face came to mind, but something wasn't right. I couldn't put my finger on it; couldn't quite wrap my mind around it. Damn. Why was I having these senior moments? I was way too young for senility. And, no way I'd broach the subject with my dear comrade, as it would just give her more grist for her mill.

I decided this would be a good time to soak in my tub.

Eleven

It was past seven in the evening. After my long soak in the tub and Bernie's even longer chat with Molly, we hadn't budged from the plastic deck chairs, alternating between reading and quipping, and drinking from tall glasses of sweet tea that had replaced the hard lemonades and Smirnoffs. When the mosquitoes began their mass exodus across our front lawn to the promised land of our veranda, well, we decided it was time to go inside. *Jeopardy* was on, anyway, and we both relished the heady euphoria of correctly answered questions.

We watched our television game show and again were impressed by our own quick wit and keen intelligence—and this after having been retired from teaching for eons. We answered question after question—correctly, mind you—before the flustered contestants could even open their mouths, let alone buzz their buzzers. It was a source of constant amazement to us that each of us was so richly endowed with personal traits that went unnoticed among the general public. Our past principals certainly hadn't appreciated us to the full extent. But, alas, great women often go unrecognized in their own time.

We were aroused from our reverie when a howling whir and a billowing cloud of pine needles and lawn debris announced the bi-weekly arrival of Jorge and his meticulous clearing off of sidewalks and decks and lawn furniture of dust and feathers and worse. Going about his work with the diligence of a qualified and competent maintenance engineer, Jorge moved about the units, eyes averted, rarely engaging any of the neighbors with a glance or grin. He was the soul of propriety…courteous and efficient, attentive to the details of his job, yet unobtrusive. He was what every woman looks for in a husband…hard-working and delightfully closed-mouth.

My sigh must have been audible because Bernie stirred. "You tired?" she mumbled through a yawn.

"Not enough to go to bed, if that's what you mean," I replied via my own yawn. "You?"

"Hmmm, just relaxed. Haven't had my snack yet." Bernie yawned again, almost swallowing herself. "What about you?"

"I'll stay up a little while longer. Can't go to bed on an empty stomach, either." I shifted and yanked on my shirt for the umpteenth time.

Attention diverted by the messages scrolling across the bottom of the television screen, we sat up straighter. "Ugh…heat's here to stay," Bernie murmured as area temperatures rolled along the message line. Then came an announcement for a new comedy show, followed by an ad for the Piggly Wiggly—referred to by the locals as 'The Pig'—another Amber Alert for the missing twins, and then back to weather.

"Those missing twins sure have—" I started to say when a sudden pounding on our door startled us both out of three years of life expectancy. I bounded to my feet and headed for my bedroom, calling over my shoulder that I was bra-less and therefore couldn't answer the door. Summoning the fragments of energy she had left, Bernie stumbled to the door and peeked through the peephole.

I watched from the shadows of the hallway as she opened the door. Bobby from upstairs. A wide grin pasted on his fuzzy face. Bernie returned his smile, albeit with raised eyebrows.

"Well, hello," Bernie said.

"Hi. Sorry to disturb you guys, but…" he paused, looking rather embarrassed. I wondered what was up.

"But?" Bernie prodded.

He flushed crimson. "Oh. Sorry. I hate doing this," he grimaced, "but Brenda's right in the middle of making cookies and discovered—the numbskull—that she didn't have any eggs. So…I was wondering whether we could, uh, borrow two eggs? If you had any to spare, that is. Don't want to take your last ones. I'll go to the store tomorrow and replace them, and—"

Bernie held up a hand. "Whoa. I'm sure we can spare you a couple eggs. Wait just a sec." She left him swaying on the deck and retrieved the eggs, which he accepted with a sheepish grin and downcast eyes.

"Thanks. I'm really sorry about this—interrupting you, I mean."

"Like I said, it's no problem. Tell Brenda to give us a sample and we'll call it even-steven. Okay?"

He chuckled. "Sure. She makes great cookies, too. Packed with nuts and chips and stuff." He brandished the eggs over his head. "Thanks, again. See you tomorrow."

As soon as she'd closed and locked the door, I stepped away from my hiding place. "Well, that was weird."

Bernie tossed her head. "Just Bobby…from upstairs…needing to borrow two eggs. Seems Brenda's baking cookies and didn't have any."

"Yeah, I heard. But baking cookies at this hour?"

"For heaven's sake, Mike. You look like I'd said the girl was hawking Avon products on the roof."

"But who'd ever want to bake cookies at this hour?"

Bernie shrugged. "Oh, I don't know. I remember being a young mother, having worked a full day at school, deciding to bake something as late as nine o'clock—just because I was finally alone and could do something in absolute, blessed silence. It's really not that strange, sweetie."

"Hmmm," I frowned, not sold on the idea.

Bernie returned to her chair and put her feet up on the ottoman. "Almost bedtime. I don't think I'll eat anything after all, and I think I'll really sleep good tonight." She sent me a gravid look. "It's been an incredibly emotionally *exhausting* day." My eyes shot darts of disdain so she changed the subject. "Say, Mike... a thought just struck me. I know we're not particularly fashion mavens, couldn't care less what we're wearing most days, but... well, I couldn't help but notice something..."

I fetched a sugar-free cherry Popsicle from the freezer and sat down. "What?"

"Our neighbors," Bernie thrust her chin upwards. "Don't you think they seem a bit *miscast* for this place?"

"Miscast? In what way?"

"Oh, I don't know. It's just...well, bike rentals begin at $10 an hour, and there isn't a menu item at any restaurant less than $9.95—and that's only a hot-dog..."

"Well, yes, I know, but—"

"Beach-front houses go for a few grand for just a week, and I'm sure the second street in isn't that much less. And, these condos are going for a pretty hunk of change, too, sooo..."

"So, what's your point?" I interjected with some annoyance as my cherry Popsicle painted pink stripes down my wrist.

"My point is," Bernie retorted, "that our upstairs daddy is wearing last decade's flip-flops, and they've seen better days. And didn't you notice Brenda was a bit of a slob, by anyone's standards, with those polyester stretch pants and throwback T-shirt from a love-in somewhere back in time when you watched *Mod Squad*?"

I choked, releasing dribbles of pink Popsicle from the corners of my mouth. "*Mod Squad?*"

"Well, *Hawaii Five-O*, then."

"Oh, *please*."

Ignoring me, Bernie continued. "And the little dolly, so cute and all, yes, but I'd swear mom bought her outfits at a garage sale from the 50-cent table." Before I could utter further protest, she held up her hand. "I know, I know...I sound like an uppity snob, don't I? But I'm serious here and not trying to be impertinent."

"Okay...but you *do* sound rather poochie—"

"—*Poochie?* What the hell does *that* mean?"

"It's my word for snobbish, uppity, putting-on-airs, etc. etc."

"Oh, for crying out loud, woman, you're an English major."

"I know. I coined that word and now it's mine. Poochie. Take it or leave it. *I* know what I mean." I shrugged, tossed the Popsicle stick at the trashcan, missed, and lumbered to my feet to dispose of it properly. "Anyway, I sort of agree with you. Was wondering about it myself, actually. There is something funny about little Amanda's chin, too. Can't put my finger on it, but it's there. The whole lot seem like, like…well, like green peas in a sea of garlic mashed potatoes."

Bernie rolled her eyes. "That's probably the stupidest thing I have *ever* heard you say, but—and I admit this grudgingly—I think I understand."

Twelve

The next morning I was itching to go to the beach. Here we were, a few streets away from the ocean, and my dearest of chums would rather watch Turner Classic Movies and eat chips and dip. Well, I enjoy my share of chips and onion dip, too, but come on. It's the beach, for crying out loud. The beach. With its miles and miles of blissfully warm saline water in which one can float and drift to her heart's content.

"Bernadette. Time to get up." I called from the kitchenette. "It's a beautiful day and we should go to the beach—sound side, of course. Before it gets too hot…before it gets too crowded…before what little energy we have dissolves…bef—"

"Enough already," echoed from her bathroom.

Four minutes later, she shuffled into the living room, wearing her wrinkled terrycloth bathrobe and slippers that made muted little taps as she walked. She stuck her upper body into the refrigerator, rummaged through its contents, and then reappeared with a diet Dr. Pepper. She frowned at me. "The beach? *Again?*"

"What do you mean, 'again'? We've only been once." Her eyes sent electric currents my way. "We'll go to the sound. It's calm. No waves. You'll love it. Very relaxing and safe. Families take their toddlers there. Okay?"

"Fine. But I'm warning you, Michaela Mercer Rosales…if I so much as get one teensy weensy drop of water up my nose… well…it won't be pretty…"

I had to grin. "Oh, I know. It wasn't very pretty the last time." Her look could've melted the polar caps, so I swerved to another topic. "How 'bout a bowl of cereal? We've got all these cute little individual boxes of—"

"Just give me the bag of mini bagels and the cream cheese."

I handed her the two items then poured myself a bowl of Frosted Flakes. We ate in communal silence.

Fifty-four minutes later found me leaning over the deck railing, looking out across the sixteenth green, waiting for Bernie to finish meditating in order to achieve the desirable mood for our pilgrimage to the beach. The cerulean sky held puffs of marshmallow clouds that looked good enough to eat. Birds everywhere, accompanied by a hypnotic drone of insects and tree frogs. A simply gorgeous day for the beach. I did love it here, and wanted Bernie to like it, too.

Lost in my reverie, I jumped a foot when a piping voice said, "Cookie."

Startled, I turned around to find the little tot from upstairs standing beside me with a paper plate covered in plastic wrap, through which half a dozen cookies lay in a neat circle. I smiled. "Well. You certainly *do* have a cookie. Looks like you have six of 'em."

The pixie beamed. "Bwenda made them. She likes t'make cookies, and dada likes to eat a lot. Me, too."

Her trebly voice was endearing, and she was as cute as could be in her bright pink bathing suit. I crouched down to get on her level. "Well, they sure look yummy. Did you help make 'em?"

"No. We was in bed. I had one for br'fast." She pushed the plate at me. "They're for you and your mommy."

That nearly knocked me over, and it was all I could do not to convulse with laughter. "Oh, thank you. My *mommy* and I will enjoy them. Tell, uh, Brenda that we said thank you. Will you do that?"

A disembodied voice from above interrupted our pleasant conversation. "Amanda? Amanda, get back here. Now." The voice belonged to Brenda, and by the sound of it, she was peeved.

I looked up but couldn't spot her. "Good morning, Brenda," I called out. "Amanda just brought us the lovely cookies. Thank you. They look wonderful."

The dumpy young woman appeared and leaned over the banister, long hair hanging untidily, reminiscent of the Spanish moss dripping from the tree beside us. "Oh. Hello, Ms., uh, I'm sorry…I forgot your name…"

"I'm Mike. My friend is Bernie."

"Oh, yeah…well, uh, I hope you enjoy the cookies. I, uh, like to bake. C'mon, Amanda. I said get up here."

The child buttoned her beautiful green eyes for a moment then stuck out her lower lip. Two spots of color appeared on her round cheeks and the tiny mole on the left side of her chin wobbled. "I'm coming." she shrilled as she turned to leave, hesitated, waved at me, and then scooted up the stairs like a little monkey. One adorable kid, but damn. That innocuous little mole was becoming my nemesis or magnificent obsession. Why was the stupid thing bothering me so much? Was I turning into my grandmother, who'd suffered from dementia as early as her mid-forties? Good God, what a thought. I really needed to let go of this fixation before I lost my mind. We needed the beach.

Bernie opened the screen door behind me, which made me jump a foot. "What was that all about?"

Glad to rid my head of its dizzying thoughts, I grinned. A surge of mischief welled up inside. "Hey, there," I giggled. "That? That was just little Amanda bringing down this plate of chocolate chip cookies for my mommy and me to enjoy. Brenda sends them with her compliments. The child is as cute as they come." My grin widened.

Bernie never misses a trick. Her eyebrows knotted and her lips pursed. "For your 'mommy' and you? Your *mommy*? Your MOMMY!"

"Shh, lower your voice."

She glowered. "Well. I have never been so insulted in my

life. Your *mommy?* I am only six months older than you are. Six months."

"I know that, sweetie. For crying out loud, the child is just a baby. You're tall, have gray hair…you look like a 'mommy'…you know what they say about children and honesty and speaking their little minds…"

Her eyes were mere slits. "And you are petite, albeit a little round in parts, a little droopy in others, and have your share of gray hair, so—"

I patted her arm. "Just block it from your memory, dear. You, of all people, know that what children say sometimes must be taken with a grain of salt. What a great segue. Speaking of salt, the ocean's waiting for us. I'm already so hot I'm getting addlepated."

Bernie, no doubt hoping to delay our departure, put hands on ample hips and raised her eyebrows. "So…how did Amanda like the little doll you bought her in Charleston?"

She had me there. "Oh, shoot. The doll. I forgot. Let's run upstairs right now and give it to her before we leave. Man. I can't believe I forgot about the doll." I dashed inside, set the plate on the counter, snatched up the sack and pulled out the rag doll by one leg. "Let's go," I said over one shoulder and clambered up the stairs to the unit above us. Bernie tapped on the door. We heard garbled voices from inside but couldn't make out what was said. Then a door slammed, resulting in our tandem startled jerks. After what seemed a lifetime, Brenda opened the door a crack and peered at us as though she'd never seen us before.

"Yeah?" Brenda's face pressed so close between door and jamb that it looked pinched. "D'you want something?"

Fumbling for words, I managed to slap a smile on my face and say, "Uh, sorry to intrude…but…Bernie and I saw the cutest little doll when we were in Charleston and, well, we thought of Amanda and…wanted to give it to her." Lame but the younger woman's in-your-face rudeness had taken the wind from my sails.

Brenda grimaced, glanced over her shoulder then squeezed through the crack in the doorway, shutting the door behind her.

Her thin lips couldn't quite manage a smile. "Yeah? Well, you shouldn't have." By the tone of her voice and the look on her oily face, we believed her. "Uh, well, thanks anyway. I'll give it to her."

I'd garnered some chutzpah. "Oh, gosh, Bernie and I had sort of hoped to give it to her ourselves. Would that be okay?"

"Uh, yeah, I mean, no, I mean she's taking a nap," Brenda responded. "I'll give it to her as soon as she wakes up. Okay?" Before I had a chance to even blink, Brenda snatched the doll from my hand, yanked open the door, and slipped through. The door slammed right in our very startled faces.

"Well." Bernie sputtered. "That was unbelievable. And you went to so much effort to get the kid a present, and then she… and you…in front of me…and Amanda…" Bernie's groping for words betrayed her total unfamiliarity with the very idea of being at a loss for something pithy to say.

"Yeah…"

"Well, I never."

With a collective grunt, we marched back down to our level, retrieved our beach bags and headed for the car. Bernie had the look of someone headed to the dentist for a root canal instead of a delightful romp on a sunny beach. More than ever I was determined to show her a good time. Come hell or high water, my chum would leave Edisto loving the ocean.

The little parking area by the beach access was already crowded, but I managed to squeeze the Neon in between the bicycle stand and a golf cart. We dragged our stuff from the back seat, shuffled through fiery-hot sand, found a fairly secluded spot on which to drop our bags, then squirmed out of our cover-ups, and toddled to the water, which lapped and licked the shore in a benign manner.

"See?" I chortled. "It's not threatening at all. It's as calm as a lake."

Bernie muttered something I couldn't catch and entered the olive green water like Marie Antoinette to the guillotine. After only a few minutes, however, I could see her relax. Who wouldn't?

Bobbing around in bath-warm seawater is soothing and relaxing; a perfect panacea for what ails you. I could feel my own tight muscles unwind. Pure bliss.

"What's that?"

Bernie's question startled me. I stopped floating and stood. "What's what?"

"That thing over there." She pointed out to sea.

Craning my neck and shielding my eyes from the dancing sparkles made from the sun's glare, I stared in the direction she indicated. "What? Oh, that? That's somebody's little buoy-thing for their crab pot."

"No," she sniffed. "Not that, you ninny. *That.*" She waved her hand. "That large brown thing floating over there."

I looked, saw it, registered it and sucked in my surprise. "Oh, wow. It's…it's…wow. It's either the largest horseshoe crab I've ever seen or…or…"

"What *is* the damn thing?"

I moved closer but not too close. "Wow. I think it's a…it's a—wow. Bernie. It's a turtle. It's a sea turtle. A huge one. Look at the barnacles on her back. They're at least an inch in diameter. Oh, wow. I've come here a zillion times, and I've never seen a sea turtle this close up. Isn't she something?"

For once, Bernie hadn't a scathing thing to say. By her enthralled face, I could tell she was as pleased as I was at seeing one of Nature's miracles. We followed the beautiful sea creature as she paddled up the sound toward the point. Enthralled, we left a good two yards between the wild animal and us but kept up with her, none the less. Having waded a good distance up the beach, we said a reluctant good-bye and turned to head back to where we'd left our things.

"Ohh," I sighed, "I can't believe we saw that. I can't wait to tell everyone back home."

"It *was* remarkable," Bernie agreed.

"Now, I wish you could see a dolphin."

"Well, I won't hold my breath, but it would be interesting.

Why not? Surprising things do happen."

"And then, maybe you'll be lucky enough to see the alligator that lives in the pond back at the condo."

Bernie snorted. "Oh, yeah, right. Like I'm buying *that* story."

"It's true," I insisted with a touch of exasperation. Sometimes her cynicism really irked me. "We see alligators in those ponds every summer. The boys see one every time they play golf or go running early in the morning."

"Uh, *huh*…"

"Oh, for crying out loud, Bernadette. Sometimes you make me so mad."

She laughed, then grimaced as a speedboat came perilously close to shore on its way up the coast. "Sheesh. Slow down, buddy!"

I was mad, too. "They think they're so great. They have enough money to *buy* the darned thing but haven't a clue how to *handle* it. I think you should have to take a test in order to operate a boat as big and fast as that."

No sooner had I voiced that vehement declaration than another equally fast boat sped by, also too close to the shore. Bernie groaned. "Oh, for crying out loud. Wake up, you people." She shook a fist at their wake.

After venting our frustration, we relaxed and spent a good half-hour more paddling around in the warm water. Deciding we were waterlogged and hungry, we threw the towel in, so to speak, and left the water. We'd each grabbed her towel and were drying off when we couldn't help noticing the group of people gathered in a clump, staring at the water several yards down the shore.

"Wonder what they're looking at?" Bernie mused as she tossed her frothy hair with one hand.

"Looks like they found something," I muttered, pulling on my cover-up.

Two teenage girls strolled by, chattering in high-pitched voices about blood and guts and gore. My radar jumped ten degrees. "Hey. Excuse me. Girls." They stopped and looked at me. "What happened back there…where all the people are gathered?"

One of the teens made a face. "It's a turtle...a big one...she got ripped in half—"

"—Her fin or foot or something was almost off and there was a lot—"

"—Of blood and guts in the water. It was awful."

I felt light-headed. Bernie groaned. "Oh, no." she exclaimed. "A turtle? A sea turtle? Injured?"

"No," one of the girls shook her head, "dead. They called the rangers. They're coming to get it. Somebody said a boat's propeller got it. It was awful."

We were speechless. The girls shrugged and continued on their way. Bernie looked at me and I stared back. "Our turtle..." My voice croaked. "Oh, Bernie, it was *our* turtle...she'd lived all those years...free...older than dirt...she was so huge...all the barnacles..."

Bernie's mouth was a straight line. She didn't say anything, but I knew she was as upset as I was, maybe even fighting back tears. We picked up our bags and walked to the car without saying another word. Somewhere deep in my heart I had a niggling hope that our turtle wasn't dead but just injured, and that the rangers might be able to save her. It could happen. Anything can happen. Maybe she'd get another chance to lay eggs in the warm sand and swim to her heart's content hither and yon. Of course it could happen. If there was one thing we'd learned from our decades of teaching kids, it was that every life has a meaning and a purpose and a value. Even a lowly sea turtle.

We were backing out of the tiny parking lot when Bernie sat up straighter and pointed toward the beach. "Mike, look."

I squinted into the sun and was surprised and a little startled to see Jorge, our conscientious, efficient little gardener, taking long strides down the beach, away from us, toward the rangers talking to a large group of vacationers. "Jorge? What's *he* doing here? And why's he headed for the rangers?"

He seemed so out of context without his trusty leaf blower

that we just sat and stared for several heartbeats in mute bewilderment. For some inane reason, it was difficult picturing the maintenance crew enjoying a day at the shore or interested in the wildlife. But why not? After all, the beach belonged to everybody. The idea that our gardener was heading for the two men in uniform was ridiculous. He was just curious like everyone else.

Thirteen

Exhausted by the time we reached the condo, all I wanted was a shower and a nap—not necessarily in that order—and by the way Bernie's head hung and shoulders slumped, she did, too. We made it inside without bumping into Vicki and Lionel or Melba-the-toast. Thank God. I didn't think I could be civil if we'd had to pause to chat with any of them, and I had no doubt Bernie'd be downright belligerent. Once inside, we headed to our rooms. We'd think about dinner later. Much later.

Two hours and fifty-three minutes later, to be exact. We both had slept. Then, had awakened feeling like we'd been on an all-day drinking binge. Cool showers revived us enough to make it out to the living room, where we turned on the boob tube to watch the news.

Bernie selected a Smirnoff while I cradled a hard lemonade to my once-again-reprieved bosoms. Bernie flopped down in her favorite chair, raised her legs, snagged the ottoman with one foot and dragged it closer. Lifting her bottle in salute, she took a swallow then grinned. "You know? I really enjoy watching other cities' newscasts—especially the weather and sports. No matter where you travel in these United States, the sportscaster is a clone of every other sportscaster in the nation. Always youngish, chipper, full of laughs, and keenly serious about stats. And always with a name like Zip, or Rock, or Chip. Always. Don't suppose Charleston is any different."

I nodded and took a long draught from my own bottle. A

gentle burp followed but mercifully Bernie didn't catch it. Or, was just too tuckered to bother. Our attention on the TV, we listened, laughed, and learned nothing more than the Cardinals were doing okay, the Braves were smugly self-assured, and the Mets were on a roll. After sports came more of the hard stuff.

An elegantly coifed, albeit ultra-conservative newscaster, donning a mask of compassionate interest lest she acquire the least adverse reaction to her blatant trespassing across raw emotions, was interviewing the parents of the missing twins that had invoked the Amber Alert we'd been seeing and reading about. The mother, young, blond, but sadly drained of all color and personality, was leaning against her inarticulate husband. The picture of two little girls with long, blond hair, dressed in identical pink dresses was poignant enough to give me heartburn. I took a long swallow of my drink and allowed my eyes to leave the TV screen and focus on a flock of pelicans flying in perfect formation over the fifteenth green.

Bernie's grunt drew me from my reverie. "Lord, this whole thing sickens me," she muttered.

"The news?"

"Yes, the news. Much as I appreciate the need to keep up with all that's going on in the world, I've grown increasingly tired of one depressing story tripping on the heels of another. I've seen enough sordid unhappiness in my long career as a middle school teacher, and even more as a principal, where the most tragic of dramas played out every single, damn day, right before my eyes. I simply don't want to hear or see any more. Especially now, on my vacation. So, dearie, let's switch channels and—"

"No, wait." I'd just seen something that snagged my attention and wanted to hear more. Ohmigawd, Bernie. Did you hear that? Gangs and G-men. Right here. No way."

"Good grief, Michaela. Settle down. What in heaven's name are you ranting and raving about? I was talking about teaching and all the sordid, sad and depressing things I've had to—"

"—G-men, Bernadette. Listen."

"*G-men?* Sweetie, nobody uses that absurd term anymore. What are you going on about?" Bernie remained lackadaisical, while I was so excited I nearly dumped my drink in my lap.

"Weren't you listening? They were talking about a 'Bonnie-and-Clyde' copycat burglary team. Imagine that. Bonnie and Clyde. Here."

"What are you *talking* about?" She'd lost her listlessness and was sitting up straighter.

I sighed. "The news, Bernadette. There've been a series of robberies in and around Charleston. Isn't that amazing? Just like Bonnie and Clyde." I glared at her pointedly. "*Surely*, you've heard of Bonnie and Clyde."

This time Bernie sighed. "Yes, Michaela, I've heard of Bonnie and Clyde. Supposed to have committed countless murders and robberies in the 30's. There was a great movie made in 1967, starring Warren Beatty and Faye Dunaway. Did you see it? I saw it twice. In the theater, that is."

I slumped down in my chair and closed my eyes as though in pain. "Fine," I mumbled. "I should've known you'd be a walking encyclopedia regarding movie trivia. How do you do it? You missed your calling. You should've been in the C.I.A."

"Central Intel—"

"—No, Cinema Investigators of America," I quipped.

The droning of a leaf blower drew our attention away from our bickering and the TV. Jorge was at it again. Bernie cocked her head to listen, then turned to me. "Sheesh. How often does he do that? Wasn't he just here?"

"Yeah, he was. Maybe something interrupted him yesterday…"

"Or maybe someone complained that he wasn't doing a good enough job."

"I hope not. Seems to do a good enough job to me."

"I have no complaints."

"Me, neither."

"Except for one. I'm too warm."

"Yeah, it is muggy, isn't it?" I sat up. "Oh, look. They're rehashing the bit about Bonnie and Clyde. Look at the composite drawings. They l—"

"Hush. Now I want to hear."

We listened while the announcer recalled how eye-witnesses described the perpetrators as having blond hair, black hair, red hair; as being tall, short, with and without mustaches, and so on. Bernie grunted. "Obviously they're using disguises or people in Charleston are remarkably near-sighted."

I chuckled. "It's just like a movie."

At that very moment, the condo lights blinked and we were thrust into semi-darkness. The TV snapped off.

"Power failure? What the heck." I moaned, struggling to my feet, as if by standing, I could somehow bring back the electric pulse that cooled us and refrigerated our snacks.

"Great," Bernie exhaled. "100 degrees outside and the power goes out. That's really great."

"Well…I guess it happens," I shrugged and resumed my seat in the corner of the couch, propped up by two over-stuffed pillows. "Nothing we can do about it but wait it out. I'm sure the powers that be will fix it soon."

"Oh, fudge," Bernie grumbled.

"Hmmm, too hot for fudge…"

I saw Bernie roll her eyes even though I pretended not to look her way. "Well, it's not too hot for shrimp and salad. I say we go to dinner," she said, as if the thought of eating was somehow novel and unique rather than a mainstay of each day's endeavors. "Do you have enough energy to go out?"

"Yeah…I guess. I can always summon enough energy to go to the Dockside."

Through the large window of the sliding door, we could see Jorge gazing at his blower with a puzzled expression. Gathering the extra-long cord, he strode across the yard toward the next unit. Curiosity whetted, we leapt to our feet to watch what he did next. To our astonishment, he inserted the plug in the outside electrical outlet, and the blower burst into life. He went on with his duties with only an occasional glance over his shoulder at our darkened complex.

"Did you see that?" Bernie exclaimed.

"I certainly did. So, what is the meaning of that?" I shot out, hands on hips and tapping a foot as though addressing a recalcitrant sixth grader.

Bernie chuckled. "Well, Sister Mary Clancey, let's not get our wimple in a knot. Like you said, they-who-are-in-charge will be duly notified and act upon it as quickly as possible. I say we go eat. By the time we get back, I'm sure we'll have lights."

"Let there be light," I mumbled.

"Exactly."

Engrossed with the delightful prospect of a delectable shrimp dinner at the Dockside, we grabbed our pocket books and ambled out of the condo, down the wooden steps, and into the warm, moist evening air—swatting mosquitoes like pros. I was already engaged in the thirty-eighth chapter in my series of discussions—or, rather, monologues—regarding alligators, Gullah, pirates, and Spanish moss. Bernie murmured occasional yet pithy comments now and then so I was satisfied. I knew she was listening and enjoying my tales, whether she showed it or not.

So committed were we in making seafood history, we paid not the slightest attention to our darkened unit. The fact that it was the only unit lacking illumination bothered us not. We couldn't have cared less, confidant that 'They' would have the problem rectified by the time we got back. I mean, what did *we* know about fuses and wires and cables and such? Sheesh.

We were right. The TV was on and so were the lights when we returned from dinner. We hadn't been inconvenienced in the least.

Fourteen

Morning arrived right on time. How delightful that the sun made its punctual appearance on the horizon every day. And even more delightful, Bernie was beginning to appreciate the magic of my South Carolina. Weeks before we'd even set out on this most amazing of escapes from our mundane, everyday lives, I'd regaled her with cautions and warnings and foreboding innuendoes concerning the dark and melodramatic history of the long-time residents of this Low Country.

Ghost stories hid in every glade, and mysteries hung like moss in the branches of the live oak trees. Strange goings-on and eerie howling emanated from unkempt cemetery plots and churchyards. Countless swamps, easy enough to enter, had too often swallowed the path, so that a confused intruder might wander around for hours or days or maybe even forever, in a fruitless search for a way out.

Yes, the Low Country was all of that. But. The only really truly *accurate* depictions of this wondrously sinister place were entrusted to the memories, however foggy, of the Schenonne Family. And it just so happened that the descendants of this renowned Island family had a little business on the side, where they carried upland tourists—excuse me, those 'from off'—on fantastic treks into the Past, while regaling them with legends and myths and real-live ghost stories. I had painted this family so well that, even though she wouldn't admit it, Bernie was hoping to meet one. She didn't care if it was a fourth cousin, once removed.

Determined to demonstrate once and for all that my love of this place was sane and justifiable, I made reservations for us to take the tour. Perhaps I should rephrase that and put the words in caps or italics, for there needs to be noticeable clarification, careful distinction, and undying respect here. The sleepy beach town boasted at least three 'tours' from which a hapless visitor could choose, but only one could merit our undue attention. *The* Tour. As far as I was concerned, the *only* tour. In a bright turquoise van, no less.

I'd just replaced the phone in its cradle and turned to beam at Bernie. Bernie, on the other hand, just sniffed and drawled, "Okay…and?"

"Today at ten sharp." I refused to let her cynicism pull my spirits down.

"Today? At ten? Sweetie, it's 9:37."

"I know, but we're already dressed, and it only takes a few minutes to get to the place where we're supposed to meet the van. Let's go, kiddo."

"As long as there's no reference to the sanctity of inhaling the exhilarating essence of pluff mud—or whatever you call the stuff—I guess I can go for it," Bernie sighed. "I'm not exactly thrilled at the prospect of riding about in a hideously garish extended van for hours on end with…well, a gaggle of loud, obnoxious tourists." She sent me a pointed look. "Will we have to get out and do much walking around? I'm still recovering from the Charleston debacle."

I shook my head, adjusted my bra straps and muttered how barbaric a contraption—emphasis on *trap*—the bra was and how much I would like to destroy the ones I owned. After a final twitch, tug and readjustment, I felt I could tolerate the confinement for the next few hours, for a good cause. I grabbed my purse. "Okay. Let's go, girl."

Bernie's reluctance was palpable but she followed me to the car. We raced out of the resort complex at a mind-blowing 19 miles per hour.

"It's the posted speed," I snapped, sensing Bernie's condescension at my driving prowess. Hours later…well, about nine minutes that only *seemed* like hours…I nosed the car into the gravel parking lot of Mama Ethyl Mae's Pit Bar-B-Q. The quaint establishment boasted a flashing pink neon sign, depicting a deranged pig sporting a chef's hat and wearing a flowered apron.

"Lord," Bernie muttered, "I have the feeling this is going to be a long day."

"Oh, pooh," I chided as I cast a suspicious eye at the sandy lot, noting that ours and one sleek little Toyota were the only cars on the scene—not counting the turquoise van—with just minutes until take-off.

As if on cue, a large, sunny, smiling gentleman in a Panama hat and wearing a bright floral Hawaiian shirt flung open the rusty screen door of the café. He allowed a middle-aged woman dressed in a smart black and white capris ensemble, cropped gray hair and over-sized glasses, somewhere between forty and sixty, to mince ahead, then ambled in our direction.

While the woman stood aside, a smirk on her dour face, he extended his right hand and flashed a toothy smile, shining with Southern hospitality and genuine warmth. We had no doubt this was our tour guide, the epitome of Old South, Low Country style and good looks. Low-slung, wrinkled Bermuda shorts—the fellow was a veritable world map—flared out from his generous thighs, and hairy, pink-skinned legs, stopped on command at the white crew socks pulled to the calf. Tan deck shoes, worn down at the heels, with frazzled tassels completed the image. His shirt buttons protested as he leaned forward to embrace us, first me then Bernie.

"Hey, y'all. Lookin' for me? I'm Dixon Lee. My mama usually handles these tours, but she come down with a little sumpin', don' know what, nothin' serious, but anyways, here I am, and I'm all yours for the next two and a half hours." Dixon Lee boomed with good will and an ingratiating smile. He turned to Miss Sour Pickles and nodded. "This here is Miss Nicole Suzette Daniels, who will be accompanying us on our little jaunt."

"Good morning," Pickles puckered.

Our guide cocked his head and thrust his round chin our way. "And you are?"

"I'm Mike," I lifted my hand in an affected wave, caught myself and blushed.

"And I'm Bernie," Bernie said, trying hard not to add a sarcastic footnote. I shot her a severe warning glance; one crafted and well-utilized from my teaching days, which insisted she refrain from any snappy comeback that could get us stranded somewhere past the back and beyond of some forgotten bayou. Acerbic is Bernie's middle name.

The gallant Dixon Lee flung open the doublewide van door—perfect for allowing women of stature to position themselves in comfort in the high-backed seats. Bernie and I climbed aboard and settled on the third seat, allowing Miss Sour Puss to commandeer the entire second row seats. Curious locals slowed their cars as they passed, noting the loading process, no doubt amused and entertained by who was paying Dixon Lee some outrageous amount of Yankee spending money for a tour of their own back yards. I could tell it pained Bernie that she was one of the aforementioned fools.

Dixon Lee flipped his hat, bowed, and flashed his toothy grin to all, squinted at the sun, nodded to the spirits and boo-daddies who haunted the region, and hauled himself into the driver's seat. He left the parking lot on two wheels, spraying gravel and dust at the oncoming cement truck barreling down the two-lane road.

White knuckled hands gripping the armrest, I hissed, "This is going to be great…if we live long enough to see anything."

Bernie pursed her lips and pawed through her bulging handbag for Excedrin and Pepcid AC, no doubt anticipating a wild and hot ride, bouncing along backcountry roads. Both items were absent, however, and the tour had officially begun. My pal sat back in resignation. I, on the other, hand, was beyond excited.

"Are you, by any chance, related to the Schenonne family here abouts?" I asked, leaning forward against my restraining seat belt.

"Yes'm, I surely am," the ever-cheerful Dixon Lee replied. "My family can trace its holdings here back to the 1600's. And I'm related to half the county."

I shot Bernie a triumphant look. "Awesome."

"We will, of course, be visiting Cassina Point, the home of Carolina Lafayette Seabrook, who married a Northerner," Miss Pickles enunciated from her spot by the left window of the second row seat.

Dixon Lee's head bobbed up and down. "We surely will, Miss Nicole."

"It's Nicole Suzette."

"I beg pardon. Miss Nicole Suzette."

I glanced at Bernie but kept my mouth closed. Sitting behind Pickles offered us the welcome opportunity of making faces at her pert little head.

"I believe Seabrook House was built in 1798," Nicole Suzette articulated.

"No, ma'am…more likely around 1810."

"I see. And didn't Lafayette visit the plantation in the 1820s? I recall from my extensive reading on the subject that he named the owner's daughter, Carolina Lafayette, after himself."

"Yes, ma'am." Dixon Lee's voice had lost a tad of its enthusiasm. Bernie, on the other hand, was beginning to look like this tour might turn out to be a lot of fun, after all. Prissy-butts like Miss Nicole Suzette offered the world scope for the imagination—to borrow a phrase from *Anne of Green Gables*—and were often highly entertaining. I did, however, feel a bit sorry for poor Dixon Lee.

Dixon Lee narrated the journey at a pleasant Southern pace, pausing occasionally for significance and impact as he pointed out battle sites and scenes of mysterious crimes, recalled legends and myths. He delighted in lowering his voice, dripping with drama, as he described the frightening aspects of ghosts and spirits and haunts known to some locals as 'boo-daddies'. I confess I was mesmerized by each tale, consigning each minute detail to memory, and reveling in the ghastly and ghostly enhancements of life in the swamps.

Bernie, by contrast, loved the color and the charm and the experience of walking among tombstones, and sitting in a private pew at the historic Presbyterian Church built over two hundred years ago. She was far less intrigued by the spirit world than I was. If truth be told, Bernie was more impressed by the cold lemonade and homemade Benet cookies that Dixon Lee produced halfway through our tour, than by any other highlight of the trip. That cautious, sometimes cynical "Show-Me-State" mentality, I guess.

Miss Pickles proved to be an unending source of entertainment. Bernie, fed up with the woman's priggish superiority, decided to re-name her. Whispering, "Miss Motor Mouth" to me as we trailed behind our two companions, she made grotesque faces, which, of course, had me choking down convulsive mirth. The title suited the annoying woman better than Pickles since she couldn't shut up. I decided to give the woman some competition. It'd be a challenge to match her penchant for knowledge, offering one trivial snippet after another.

Soon Dixon Lee, Miss Motor Mouth, and I vied for Historian of the Year, as our gaudy vehicle careened along gravel road and pitted asphalt. The temperature inside the van rose—whether from the glaring sun or the rapidly heating oral fisticuffs, is anyone's guess. All I know is that after several hours of Southern charm and hospitality, not to mention the verbal diatribe—complete with a few choice tales that threatened to surpass *Harry Potter* with sinister sorcery and insidious intrigue—my dear comrade had had enough. When the turquoise van magically reappeared at our starting point, Bernie let out a sigh that should've been heard all the way to Fort Sumter.

Realizing that the meter had ceased ticking on our ghostly ancestral lowland tour, I tumbled from the van and offered profuse compliments to the ever-smiling Dixon Lee, who nodded, smiled, and nodded again. Bernie, on the other hand, took ages to disembark, pushing the door open further with a foot while fanning her flushed face with a folded brochure.

We waited as Miss Nicole Suzette handed over a neat twenty-dollar bill—no tip—shook Dixon Lee's hand and turned on her heel to march to her car. Bernie shrugged, opened her purse and doled out the cost of the tour plus a sweet tip for his good sportsmanship and trouble.

Dixon Lee tugged on the brim of his hat as we strolled past him toward the now-stifling Neon. We waved at Dixon Lee and he waved back. As soon as he'd entered the small café, I heaved a sigh of pure bliss. "I thought the tour was terrific. Didn't you think it was terrific?" I stuck my pointy elbow in my pal's ribs. "Well? Didn't you?"

As I fumbled around for my car keys, Bernie stared off into the blurred green of shrubbery across the road. When I poked her again, she winced. "*What?*"

"I thought he was charming, and so knowledgeable…didn't you? It was a perfect outing except for Miss Poochie. Sheesh. She got on my nerves. I wanted to throttle her so many times…but I think he really enjoyed being with *us*, and I learned some great new stuff and…Bernie. Bernie, are you even listening to me?" I demanded, a trifle cross.

"Huh? Yes, I, uh, agree…uh huh, you're so right, " she mumbled.

"Oh, and thank you for paying for it. You sure gave him a generous tip."

Bernie wrinkled her nose and smirked. "I thought he handled Miss Know-It-All quite well. And Missy Motor Mouth, too, for that matter. I would've strangled her on Botany Bay Road an hour into our trip if it had been up to me."

Her cute little word play hadn't gone over my head, but I refused to give her the satisfaction by reacting to the jab. Instead I said, "Well, that was very sweet of you. I'm sure Dixon Lee appreciated the gesture. It's gotta be hard being polite to tourists, day in and day out, especially if they're anything like Miss Prissy-Butt."

"But there's something I just don't understand…"

"What?" I asked a trifle impatiently since I still hadn't found my keys.

"Well…why don't they ever leave the condo?" Bernie's eyebrows were in a knot.

"*What? Who* are you talking about? And what does that have to do with the tour?" I fired at her. "Are you suffering from heat stroke?"

Bernie ignored me. "I mean, if you're on vacation with a small child in a posh resort—well, an upscale resort, anyway—and there's tons to do and places to go, like interpretive centers, and beaches and swimming pools—not to mention alligators and cranes taller than the child—well…why do you stay holed up in your unit, day and night? Hmmm?" She drew in a long breath.

I just glared at her. "Bernadette, I have *no* idea what you're talking about. Did you take your pills this morning? Is it acid reflux? Your leg cramps again? Constipation? What *is* your problem? And you say *I'm* fruitcake." She'd really lost me.

Bernie sighed. "Ohhh, nothing, I guess. Chalk it up to my over-stimulated imagination…and too much Dramamine. And too much Nicole Suzette. What's for dinner?"

I shook my head in sad disbelief. Depressing how some people faded mentally when they passed a certain age. Still shaking my head, I proceeded to dump the entire contents of my purse on the scorching car hood, located my incorrigible keys, adjusted a bra strap, then ducked into the oven-hot car. I'd come to the conclusion that my best friend was either a complete idiot or was hallucinating from heat stroke…maybe both. God, I dreaded getting old.

Fifteen

The following morning we slept in. In layman's terms, nine o'clock is probably not considered 'sleeping in', but for retired teachers too used to the nauseating ritual of rising before dawn is even *thinking* about dawning—well, trust me…it's sleeping in.

I awoke first, struggled into something decent to wear, and dragged myself into the kitchen, where I put on the kettle. I'd just sunk into the cushions of the couch with a steaming cup of coffee when Bernie scuffled in. Without so much as a greeting, she fetched a can of Dr. Pepper, poured it over ice cubes, then turned bleary-eyed toward me. "G'morning," she said hoarsely.

"Same to you," I said with what I hoped passed for a twinkle in my eyes.

"How'd you sleep?" she asked with one eye shut.

"Good. Didn't move an inch the entire night. How 'bout you?"

"So-so. Too many wicked dreams."

"About boo-daddies and headstones?"

Her withering look squelched that. "No." She flopped down in her chair and put her feet on the ottoman. "I'm still stewing about the fact that our upstairs neighbors don't leave their apartment."

I made a face. "For crying out loud, Bernie. How do you know they don't ever leave? Weren't they going out for ice cream the first time we met them?"

Bernie's face clouded. "Yes…yes, they were. But that's been the extent of their comings and goings as far as I have observed. They're *always* going out for ice cream. And ice cream, to my mind, does not constitute a dream-vacation."

"How do you know they only go out for ice cream? We've been in and out ourselves. Gone to the beach, to Charleston, to half a dozen restaurants, on the tour, and—"

"I know, I know," she interrupted, waving a hand in agitation. "I realize that, but…all the same…something bothers me about them…and I can't put a finger on it."

I set my coffee mug on the table and leaned forward. "Yeah, well, maybe so, but, listen to this. Remember the descriptions of the Bonnie and Clyde wannabe's?"

"Wannabe's. What kind of a word is th—"

"Quiet. Just listen. You remember how they described the couple who've been running a robbery racket all over Charleston and thereabouts…well—and don't interrupt 'til I'm finished—who do they remind you of?"

"Dangling prep—"

"*Bernie.*"

"Sorry."

"Well…who do they remind you of?" I squirmed in my excitement. "Who fits the description of those robbers? Hmmm?"

"I don't know. You tell me."

"Vicki and Lionel."

"*What?*"

"You heard me. Vicki and Lionel are the perfect portrait of a married couple bent on a life of crime."

Bernie narrowed her eyes and just stared at me. Then she whispered, "You…have…got…to…be…kidding."

"No. I'm serious. Don't they fit the bill like a cliché?"

"Vicki? And poor Lionel?" Bernie snorted—rather an unladylike sound to be sure. "Why, Vicki has more brains in her pendulous boobs than in her frizzled head. And Lionel…why, he can't even keep his pants on. I mean…I've seen his plumber's butt more times than I've scratched my mosquito bites. You are *absolutely* out of your ever-loving mind, Mike. You read way too many novels, my dear. *Way* too many. Maybe you should get a part time job or something. You're bored. You haven't enough to do. You miss teaching. There you are. Go be a mentor or something. Be a sub. Get back into the rat race."

I sank back into the sofa cushions and folded my arms across my chest. "Fine. You dwell on the harmless young couple and their precious baby upstairs. I, on the other hand, will concentrate my attention on our neighbors in the next complex. I think Vicki and Lionel positively reek from their numerous illicit endeavors."

"Well, I agree they reek, but the rest of that story is ridiculous. Lord…" Bernie sighed.

※

It was after two in the afternoon when we got the craving for some ice cream. Bernie also wanted to rent a movie—*Dreamgirls*—since I'd never seen it, and she thought it worth viewing… especially by someone who'd taught years of drama to middle school students. I didn't argue. I knew I'd enjoy seeing it. We were too tired to venture out into the late afternoon heat wave for anything more strenuous than dinner, so our evenings were free. And there was never much to watch on TV.

Grabbing our purses we headed out only to come face-to-face with Melba, who was standing on the veranda, starring up at the sky. She jumped a foot when we came outside.

"Oh. Hello, there, Norma…and Mary…how are you? I thought you had left…haven't seen you around…are you still here?" Melba twittered like a bird that'd just flown into a window.

Bernie slapped on her best parent-teacher-conference smile. "Hello, Melba. Yes, we're still here. How have you been? The heat hasn't been too much for you has it?"

Melba's eyes rolled. "Oohh, no…I'm used to it…sometimes I just wander around my little place in the all-together…you know what I mean… nekked as a jaybird…just trying to beat the heat."

"Good…good…" Bernie nodded, probably desperate to block the mental image of Melba, *nekked*, wandering around her apartment.

The dear woman stepped closer to Bernie and craned her

neck to peer up at her. "How are you, Mary? Are you enjoying your stay with us?"

"Uh, yes…yes, I am."

I wanted to giggle and was struggling to keep myself in check. Melba was as vacant as a condemned building. I wasn't sure she was rowing with both oars—not to mix my metaphors.

Bernie stepped back as unobtrusively as she could and grabbed my arm, none too gently. "Mike and I are off to get some ice cream and rent a movie. We've been at it so much that we're both a little exhausted and need some down-time."

Melba's lips wobbled at the corners. "Ohhh…I understand…I understand. I'm just waiting here for my nephew and his wife… they called…said they had something for me to keep while they vacation out west…in Arizona, I think…or was it Reno? No…I think they're going to San Diego…" she batted her eyes. "It doesn't really matter, does it, girls?"

"Uh…no, it doesn't. Nice for you to have some company," Bernie muttered.

"Oh, they come by often…to leave things with me…I have that extra room, you know…and their apartment is so cramped… so tiny…and he needs his office space…the dear boy…my sister's boy…like my own…and Jessica is such a darling girl…so clever… why, she can even—"

"That's great. Well, hate to run away but we have to go. 'Bye, Melba. We'll be seeing you." And with that, Bernie pulled me after her, dragging me down the stairs and tripping me in the process. As soon as we'd rounded the corner and were out of earshot, she hissed, "Jeez Louise. That woman needs help."

"I know, I know," I giggled. "But, gosh, Bern, I feel a little sorry for her, too. *And* us."

"*Us?*"

"Yeah, us. Imagine women our age so hell-bent on getting to the ice cream parlor that we have no patience for a sweet, simple old soul. Some day it'll be our turn. Jeez, I'm already having more senior moments than I care to talk about. I dread the day when people are in a hurry to get away from me and don't have time to give me a little compassion."

Bernie's face lit up. "Oh, sweetie…don't I give you the attention you crave, heaped with oodles of compassion?"

"Well…I guess…" I opened my purse and stuck a hand in.

"And don't I listen to your long-winded, pointless, rambling stories about ghosts and Gullah?"

"Ummm, yes…"

"Then consider yourself blessed to have a best friend like me." She leaned against the car. "Sweetie, need I remind you I have Christmas shopping to do?"

I glared up at her and continued to rummage for my damned car keys.

As luck would have it on a blistering summer afternoon at the beach, the ice cream shop was crowded. We didn't mind too much as it allowed us a decent time to review the many flavor selections offered. Finally, after much thought and careful weighing of pros and cons, I decided on a cherry vanilla scoop with hot fudge, whipped cream and a cherry—oh. And a sprinkling of chopped walnuts. Divine.

Bernie, on the other hand, and with no imagination whatsoever, chose a double scoop of 'Killa Vanilla' in a plain old waffle cone. Be still my beating heart.

We carried our concoctions to a table, relieved that most of the patrons were taking theirs with them. Both of us hated to eat standing up, juggling purses and treats and napkins. I invariably had an accident whenever I did. Sitting down didn't afford me much leeway, either, but at least I had a fighting chance.

Gazing around at the happy patrons crowding the tiny shop, jostling one another for prime position at the counter and discussing among themselves the multitude of flavor possibilities, we couldn't help but smile. Happiness is contagious and we old gals were enjoying more than just our sweet treats. I was picking the stem off my cherry when I happened to catch a familiar face. Bobby from upstairs, minus his two gals, was standing just outside the glass door, holding an earnest conversation on his cell phone, eyes darting about as he talked. When his roving eyes spotted us, recognition clicked, and a frown followed by a toothy grin spread across his grizzled face.

"Bernie," I mouthed after swallowing the cherry I'd been sucking on. "Don't look now, but we have a friend standing just outside the shop." I pointed with my chin.

Bernie took a peek over her shoulder. "Well, I'll be..."

She didn't say any more as Bobby had popped into the shop and was at our table in two long strides. "Hey, there, ladies," he greeted us with a smile that stretched from ear to ear but didn't seem to reach his eyes. "Enjoying some ice cream, I see. I'm picking up some for my girls, too. Good day for it, huh? Well, gotta run. See you." And without waiting for either of us to respond, he turned on his heel, pushed ahead of the line to the counter, made his selection in rapid time, paid for it, and was out the door before Bernie or I could blink, let alone swallow.

"Good grief." Bernie leaned back in her chair.

"Yeah," I stared out the picture window at nothing in particular. "Good grief is right. Is it my imagination or was he one up-tight young man?"

"God, it must be this humidity. The whole damned place is crawling with crazy whackos. Sheesh."

"You're telling me. Double that sheesh."

Bernie tossed her bouffant head of hair and resumed tackling her ice cream. "Forget the loonies. This is sooo good. Probably..." lick... "the best..." lick... "ice cream I've..." lick... "ever tasted..."

Spooning lumps of chocolate covered cherry vanilla into my mouth prevented me from responding so I rolled my eyes, nodded, and left her to do the interpreting.

When we finished—feeling a tad nauseated from too much sweet stuff in too much heat—we tossed our trash and ambled over to the wall displaying videos for rent. Bernie spied *Dreamgirls* and snatched it up as though someone might put up a fight for it. I followed her to the counter, where the congenial proprietor waited to check us out.

I gave him the necessary info about where we were staying, and Bernie showed him her driver's license and paid the rental fee.

"Enjoy," he said, grinning, "and come back. I could see how much you enjoyed your ice cream."

Bernie made a face. "One of my many vices."

"Good one." His grin widened then faded. "And remember to lock your doors. We had a break-in last night."

"*You* did?" I exclaimed in total shock.

He shook his head. "No, not us. By 'we' I meant here at the beach. One of the beach houses was broken into—the folks weren't there—and some stuff was taken." He shook his head again. "Not big stuff—just some cameras and a ring and stuff."

"How'd you hear about it?" I asked.

Color flooded his cheeks. "Oh…I, uh, am friends with the, uh, local authorities around here and…well, I guess I shouldn't have told you. Keep it under your hats, okay?"

We both nodded, thanked him, and left, rendered speechless for several seconds. Once out the door, however, I spoke in a rush. "Okay. They're here. They're here. I can't believe it."

Bernie put her weight on one leg, thrust out her hip, and scowled at me. "*Who's* here?"

"Bonnie and Clyde, of course. Who else would rob a house down here? Wake up, Bernie."

The look she gave me was the patented one she'd given Bart Heilbronner some twenty-nine years ago when he'd chosen to use the words *but* and *butt* as examples of homonyms in eighth grade grammar class. The very same glare that had sent the six-foot tall, 150 pound eighth grader to the boys' lavatory in tears, while the mob of hormonal teenagers in the class howled with laughter.

Sixteen

As soon as we got back to the condo with our video and our still-nauseous stomachs, we headed for our respective bathrooms for showers, to be followed by naps. I blamed it on the heat. Bernie blamed it on me. She said being around me was exhausting. I didn't deign to address *that*.

By evening, we were ready to watch our movie. Dinner was *in*—as opposed to going *out*—and comprised of hot, buttered popcorn, a tall glass of Diet Coke for me and a similar one of Diet Dr. Pepper for her. To give the impression that we were educated and well versed on the latest nutritional findings, we also prepared a plate of raw veggies and a small bowl of 'light' Ranch dressing. We were content.

The sun had melted into the horizon long ago. I turned on the lights so Bernie could see as she knelt before the video/DVD player, trying to figure out how it worked. I'd set the food on the coffee table and was about to take my seat when I remembered I was close to the end of my novel and needed another one.

Getting the keys from my gaping handbag, I said, "Bern...I'm going out to the car for a sec. I have extra books in the trunk."

Her reply was a mere nod and a low grunt.

I let myself out, leaving the door open but the glass outer door closed, and padded down the steps. It was dark now and the space between condo complexes even more dense due to the number of trees with mossy stoles. The scattered solar lights implanted close to the ground were hardly adequate so I took my time. Coordination and I weren't the best of friends, and I'd been known to trip or lose balance over a gum wrapper.

Rounding the corner of our unit, I leapt out of my skin and let out a loud shriek when a dark form suddenly took shape in front of me. "*Lionel.* Oh. You scared me spitless."

He'd stepped out of the deepest shadows so was visible, and I could tell he'd been as unnerved as I. "Oh. I'm sorry...I'm so sorry..." he stammered.

"What were you *doing*?"

"Doing? Oh. I, uh, I thought I saw something move under your unit...wanted to see what it was..."

"Well, what was it?"

"Nothing. That is, I couldn't see anything when I got here. Probably a raccoon..."

"Or a gator. You know they walk across the golf course at night to get to other ponds."

His entire body stiffened at that and it almost cost me a laugh. "Oh. Well. Wouldn't want to meet up with anything like that," he said, still breathing hard.

"No, neither would I...though it would be fun to see one... from a distance."

He nodded. "Yes, yes, it would. Well, Vicki is probably wondering where I am, so I'll get back to my place." He swatted the air and then smacked his left arm. "Damn mosquitoes. You better not stay out here too long. They're really biting."

"I'm just getting something from the car. See you, Lionel." And with that, I jogged to the car, retrieved my book, and sprinted back to our unit. By the time I stepped into the living room, I was panting like I'd run a marathon. Bernie looked up in surprise.

"What took you so long? I was about to go looking for you." Her eyes narrowed. "And why, for crying out loud, did you run?" Her mouth curved up in a sly grin. "Saw some boo-daddies, did you?"

I fell onto the couch and pushed the sweaty bangs off my forehead. "No...I...didn't see any...boo-daddies." I sucked in a shaky breath. "But...I did run into Lionel. And I do mean 'run into'."

"*Lionel?*"

"Yes, Lionel. And you'll never guess where he was standing...or hiding...or...whatever..."

"Where?"

"Right next to that panel thingy with all the meters and widgets for our complex."

"And?"

"C'mon, Bernie. Don't be dense just to annoy me. Why was our neighbor from the *next* building standing in the dark next to *our* electric meter thingy?"

Bernie's sigh was a tad over-dramatic. "I don't know, Mike, did you ask him?"

"Well, of course I asked him. I mean, I asked him what he was doing, and he said something silly about thinking he'd seen something under our building and wanted to see what that something was. Or, something like that." I winced.

"So, did he say *something* else about this *something* he saw?"

"Oooh." I writhed in my seat. "No. Nothing. Said he couldn't find anything...said it probably was a raccoon, if you can believe that malarkey, and I said it could've been an alligator—"

"—Would you drop this fixation on alligators, for crying out loud?"

I pressed my lips together and glared at her for one very pregnant moment. "Bernadette...for the last time...there *are* alligators here."

"Fine." She had the audacity to smile sweetly at me. "So, what did he say to *that?*" Her voice dripped superiority.

"Nothing much. He was stammering a lot, and even in the dark I could tell he was blushing. I think he's one very suspicious character."

"No, he's just one very dweebish individual who's been bossed around by women all his life. You see it all the time."

It was my turn to smile. "You are *such* an expert on human nature, Bernadette…"

After that the subject was closed and we turned on the movie.

Halfway through, Bernie struggled to her feet, pushed pause, and stretched. "Potty break time."

We each scuttled to our bathrooms and came out at almost the same instant. "Okay, I feel better. Let's get on with it." I said, snapping my fingers. "Jennifer Hudson is remarkable. She certainly earned her Oscar, in my book."

"I agree."

I sank into the sofa cushions, raised my feet to the coffee table then grunted. "That's how we lost it."

"I beg your pardon?"

"The electricity. Remember how odd we thought it was to be the only complex without electricity?"

"Well, y—"

"Lionel. Lionel cut our power. That's why he was standing by our meter thingy."

Bernie looked at me like I'd returned from a trip to The Pig with a pierced nose and snake tattoo. "*What?*" She snorted. "*Why,* for heaven's sake? Why would he cut our electricity? What's the point? And, furthermore, how *could* he? I mean, not everybody can hotwire a car or snip red and blue wires in seconds without giving themselves a shock to remember. Sheesh, Michaela."

"Well-l-l…"

"I repeat…*why* would he even remotely *consider* doing such a thing?"

"Because…" I wracked my brains for a plausible answer. "Because…"

"Because he's really Lord Voldemort and is determined to make us go insane."

I gave her my most withering look. "Oh, *please*. I'm trying to be serious here."

"Okay, okay, then tell me why he'd want to cut our power? I

mean…poor Melba would be unable to watch her shows…and what about the youngish couple with the innocent little child upstairs?"

I closed my eyes in frustration then snapped them open when a brilliant idea struck. "Of course. Why didn't I think of it right away?" I slapped my head. "I'm a numbskull."

"We finally agree on something," Bernie beamed.

I ignored her. "No, listen. What were we doing when the power went out?"

She looked puzzled for a second then shrugged. "Nothing much…just watching the news…"

"You got it. Don't you see? He didn't want us to see the newscast about Bonnie and Clyde. Oh, this just proves I'm right. Vicki and Lionel are Bonnie and Clyde. Oh, this is so exciting. To actually help solve a real, honest-to-goodness mystery. Oh, Bern—"

"Hush."

That stopped me mid-sentence. "Huh?"

"Just calm down for a minute, will you?"

"But this is exciting."

"No…it's probably the stupidest thing you've come up with yet."

"Oh, you're just jealous that I have an intuitive, er, analytical, brain. You're ticked off that you didn't figure it out first."

This time Bernie looked pained. She sighed, then sighed again. "Michaela, Michaela, Michaela…what am I going to do with you? You were like this back in your twenties and you haven't changed. You work yourself up into such a frenzy that it's no wonder you get sick and have to go on antibiotics all the time—"

"—Not since I retired. It was the stress of teaching that made me sick." I said, a trifle defensively I admit.

Her smile patronized. "Dear, *dear* little wacko…just listen to you. All worked up over nothing. For once and for all, Vicki and Lionel are not—and I repeat—are *not* Bonnie and Clyde."

"You don't know that for sure," I muttered under my breath. I wasn't pouting, just annoyed at her condescending manner.

"Okay. Let's drop the subject for now and finish our movie."

"Fine."

We watched the remainder of the video, shoveled in the popcorn and veggies, and mentioned nothing else about Vicki and Lionel. I stored it at the back of my mind, however. I still wasn't convinced that I'd imagined things. Bernie would never, ever, hear the end of this if it turned out that I was right and she was so *completely* wrong. When Vicki and Lionel were hauled off to the slammer, I'd crow. Yes sir. I couldn't wait. The last laugh would be mine.

Seventeen

After attending Sunday Mass the following morning in a small modular building posing as a church that was actually very pretty on the inside, we returned the movie, then headed to The Pig to stock up on the necessities of life: crackers, onion dip, diet soda, and cantaloupe. Even on a Sunday, the local grocery store was over-flowing with throngs of people doing the same thing we were. Amazing.

On the way home I regaled Bernie with the bittersweet story of my fateful tumble from my bicycle two months ago when my hubby and I were staying with my sister and brother-in-law at the condo and using the bike path that ran through the heart of the island. Every time I brought up the subject I got riled up all over again. This time was no exception. And Bernie appeared to be listening.

"I'd pedaled miles and miles—"

"Yeah, right."

"—Around the length and breadth of the *entire* island only to be mercilessly *thrown* to the ground and *thoroughly* bruised from head to toe by a careless cyclist—"

"Your husband."

"Stop interrupting. Yes, my husband. Darn idiot failed to notice that I'd slowed to admire a butterfly and plowed right into me."

Instead of inquiring how injured I'd gotten, Bernie laughed long and hard at the mental image of my short, plump little body toppling head over heels, landing in the gravel, stunned, disheveled. Not unlike her altercation with the ocean waves, now that I think about it. It was such an entertaining tale—at my own expense—that she was still laughing when we turned into the resort. I refused to let my feelings be hurt. After all, I'd laughed at her.

There must be something inherently wrong with two long-time friends such as ourselves getting that much enjoyment from one another's mishaps and mayhem. Anyway, I ignored her, preferring to put all my attention into my driving. That started Bernie cackling once again, much to my disgruntlement.

"I don't see why you find everything about me so funny," I fumed.

Brushing a hand across her face, Bernie shook her fluffy head, smothered two more snorts, and said, "I-I don't…really…sorry. I-I'm glad you didn't break anything…important…"

"Uh *huh*."

Still chuckling, she donned her best pseudo-sympathetic smile. "What did Joe do when he discovered you'd really been shaken up?"

"Joe? Humpf. My dear husband was dutifully remorseful and solicitous of my well being for a good two days following the accident. All it took was for me to show my sister and brother-in-law my sore ribs, scraped knees and elbows, and the magnificent purple-green bruise running the entire length of one thigh." I sighed. "Oh, man, did I ache all over. Couldn't sit, couldn't roll over in bed. Had a heck of a time getting in and out of the tub, too. I mean, sheesh, I could've broken a bone. Even my neck. And I've told Joe, I don't know how many times, not to follow so closely when we ride the bikes as you know how wobbly I am. Sheesh. But does he listen? Noooo. He never listens to a word I say." I looked at my companion, waiting for a comment or two… or three. Bernie's eyes looked out the window into the great beyond. "Bernadette," I reprimanded, "are you listening to me at *all?*"

Bernie blinked, focused on me, and cleared her throat. "Oh,

yes, yes, of course. I heard you. I did. Glad Joe finally came around. Yes. Men are so clueless sometimes, aren't they? But, you know? I've been thinking about the mystery that seems to be unfolding right here in our little vacation community. On the surface, everything is as it should be. The sky is blue, birds are flying hither and yon. Golfers are slicing and divot-ing to their hearts' content. Families are biking up and down the quiet streets. Yes, a perfectly normal summer resort, resorting in perfectly normal summer activities." She pointed with her chin. "And then there's Melba."

I swiveled around to see sweet Melba shuffle across the complex's parking area—ancient flowered dressing gown proclaiming her total lack of style, taste, and decorum. She was searching the pine needle-strewn asphalt as if she'd lost something.

As soon as we climbed out of the car, I chirped, "Hello, Melba. What's going on? Lose something? Can we help?"

Melba glanced up, saw us, yet seemed unaware of who we were or why we were speaking to her. With a shrug, she resumed her study of the blacktop, pushing aside lawn debris with her terry-clad toe. Bernie and I blinked at each other in surprise. Both hesitant to intrude on her mission, yet curious about what had inspired this meticulous screening of the parking lot, we stood and watched her for several minutes.

A thousand and one heartbeats later, Melba looked up and registered our presence. "Oh, my," she whimpered. "He was here just a few seconds ago. I don't know what's become of him." A long sigh illustrated her keen disappointment.

"Who are you looking for, dear?" I kept my tone light. "Maybe we could, uh, help…"

"Well, I certainly hope you can help me. But you better move your car first. You have parked your car in Trudy and Anita's parking spot, and they will be back soon, and will be ever so annoyed that you have taken over their parking place. By the way, my name is Melba, like the toast, and I live in 214, and you are…"

Deciding that it was pointless to continue the conversation, I completed the sentence with, "…exhausted. We are utterly exhausted. We'll talk to you later, Melba. Okay?" Then my Christian upbringing came to the fore and I added, "Unless, that is, we can help you in any way."

Melba's brow puckered. "Have we met?" The woman's voice was tremulous. "Who told you that I was here? Is he looking for me? Have *you* seen him? Is it time for *Jeopardy*? I love *Jeopardy*. Don't you? And *Wheel of Fortune*. Dear Vanna comes from Charleston, you know," Melba bobbed then executed a graceful pirouette. She shuffled toward the wooden steps that led to her unit, shaking her white head from side to side. Talking to herself, she muttered something about people taking liberties with other people's parking spots. Then, in a louder voice, said something about Hostess Cupcakes, followed by a comment about Jay Leno's chin. We trailed behind her as she hauled herself upward, step by step, to arrive in one piece at her own front door. In a flash of floral confusion, she disappeared into the dark recesses of her apartment, with only the faintest essence of Honeysuckle talcum lingering on the porch as a reminder of her presence.

"Whew." I exhaled.

"Amen."

I opened my purse and began rummaging.

"I've really had about enough." Bernie huffed.

"Look, you could demonstrate a little patience here." Just a shade on the defensive.

"No, no, I'm not talking about the keys…although it *is* ridiculous the amount of time you waste looking for them. I mean, normal people can find their keys within seconds but not you. But, no, that's not what I was talking about," Bernie retorted.

As soon as we stepped inside, my eyes bored into hers. "It's Melba, isn't it? You are confused and/or concerned about our dear little Melba. Face it, Bern…*Melba* is confused and/or concerned about Melba."

At that precise moment, a solid rap on the storm door startled both of us. We whirled around in synchronized surprise to see our condo door thrown open as a sprightly Vicki invited herself in, at ease and not a bit concerned with invading our personal space. Uninvited.

We stared with mouths open. Once again Vicki had outdone herself in the wardrobe department. She was the poster child of glamour gone haywire. A mental image of a scene in the delightful movie, *The Devil Wears Prada* came to mind, and I nearly choked. When Bernie hissed under her breath, "I swear the woman doesn't own a mirror," I let out a strangled gurgling belch.

Vicki was indeed a vision…or, perhaps, nightmare is a better word. She had on something that I guess was *supposed* to pass as a blouse or shirt or—it doesn't matter. Suffice it to say she was wearing an article of clothing not up to snuff in the covering of her generous endowment department. I mean, June was busting out all over…and then some, if you get my drift.

"Hey, y'all." she sang, oblivious to our malcontent over her barging in like that. "Y'all having a good time here in Fun City?" One well-manicured hand brushed at her frizzy bangs. "Lionel and I have just *marveled* at your get up and go. You two are *always* on the move, aren't ya? High-tailin' it everywhere like you do."

"Uh huh," Bernie said dryly. "We only have ten days in which to spread our wings. So…we're, uh, spreading."

Vicki beamed. "Oh, I think what you two're doin' is simply *wonderful*. Wish *I* had a gal friend I could up and leave with. Go on a cruise, maybe, or—"

"Can we help you with something, Vicki? We're planning another sightseeing trip and need to get a move on."

"Ohh. Sorry." She rolled her eyes. "Silly me. Lionel is forever sayin' that I can go on and on and on and on—"

"Vicki?"

"Oh. I'll get to the point then. We—me and Lionel, that is—would like to invite you two over for a real Texas barbecue. This evenin'. Can you come? Or isn't it enough notice? I know it's rather short notice, but you two are pretty darned hard to catch up with." She giggled.

Bernie looked at me, her eyebrows almost to her hairline. I

took that to mean she'd like to so nodded. "Sure, Vicki. We can come. Thank you for thinking of us. Would you like us to bring over something?"

"Heck, no. You'll be our guests. Hope you like pork steaks on the *bar*becue."

Coming from Missouri, Bernie certainly did. "Yes…that would be great. What time?"

"Oh…come along over 'round six-ish. That isn't too early, is it?"

"No, that'll be fine. We'll see you then." Bernie started walking forward, which forced Vicki to back into the doorway. She giggled, waved, and let herself out. Bernie closed the door behind her, turned and faced me. "Well?"

I did a jig. "This is great. This is really great."

"You like pork steaks that much?"

"No. But I do like the chance of getting a peek inside their condo. Don't you?"

"Ohhh. You mean a chance to see where they've hidden all that pilfered loot. Right?"

I smacked my lips. "You got it."

"Humpf. Texas barbecue, my ass-pirations. Everybody knows Texans barbecue beef, not pork. Pork is a Mid-western thing…or, maybe, a Southern thing. Texas barbecue. Who does she think she's kidding?"

Eighteen

After Vicki pranced out of our unit, I ran both hands through my short hair, causing it to stick up in several places. Of course Bernie had to point that out to me by placing both hands on my shoulders and turning me around to face the decorative wall mirror. And, of course, she was laughing. I didn't care. We were knee-deep in some serious business.

"Bernadette," I said between clenched teeth. "We've got to do something."

"About your hair? I'm afraid th—"

"Bernie."

"All right. So, what's your plan? What can we do about it—whatever *it* is?"

"Well…I guess…first off…we have to somehow get inside Melba's apartment…"

"*Melba's?* I thought you were hell-bent on checking out Vicki and Lionel?"

I gave her my most withering look. "Oh, Bernie…for crying out loud. Wake up. Just a few minutes ago you, yourself, were fretting over Melba's…well, lack of sentinence—"

"*What?*"

"Sentinence…you know—intelligence…awareness—"

Bernie was laughing so hard now, she had to sit down. "The word is 'sentience'…" Another snort. "Sen-ti-ence…not 'nence'…" A choking gurgle. "And you're an English major…" More snorts, guffaws, and gurgles.

I glared at her. "Okay, okay. Let's get back on track here, please. You've had your laugh therapy for the day. Help me think."

"You're beyond hel—"

"*Bernie.*"

"Okay." She sobered and donned her principal-parent-teacher-conference mask. "So, how do you want to go about it—getting inside Melba's unit, that is?"

My eyes darted about our small kitchen. "Bring her something? But what? I need an excuse to go over there in the first place. I can't just knock on her door and walk in."

"I don't know why not. Vicki did."

"Yeah, well, I'm not Vicki."

"Thank God for small favors."

"I know. I'll take her a few of the peaches we bought at George and Pink's produce stand." I dashed to the drawer that had plastic grocery bags, whipped one out, and began selecting the best-looking peaches from the basket we had sitting on the counter. "You think three's enough?"

Bernie grimaced. "Yes. It means three less that we get to enjoy. And I *was* enjoying those peaches. Best I've ever eaten."

Ignoring her, I picked up my sack, glanced in the mirror to be sure my hair wasn't still sticking up in half a dozen places, and marched to the door, paused, reached into the bag and retrieved one of the peaches. Taking two steps backward, I set the fruit on the counter and made a face at my cohort. "There. Two're enough. Okay. I'll only be gone a minute. Don't go anywhere."

"Where would I go, for heaven's sake?"

I shrugged. "I don't know. Just don't go."

A dozen steps brought me to Melba's door. I could hear the faint voices of talk TV. She was watching her shows, of course. The only thing she seemed to do, poor thing. Taking in a deep breath—I was nervous and didn't know why—I knocked on her metal door. It took forever before I heard shuffling footsteps approaching.

"Who is it?" Her flute-like voice called out.

"It's Mike, Melba…from next door…Bernie and I have a couple of fresh peaches if you'd like them…"

There was a clicking as locks were turned, and then the door swung open to reveal a darkened room and a flickering television set. Melba was still wearing the flowered dressing gown and the terry cloth slippers. She looked at me like I was an auditor from the IRS.

"Hi, Melba. We thought you might like some fresh peaches… from that wonderful fruit and vegetable stand…with the colorful sign…past Botany Bay Road…you know…" I winced at the sound of my own inane rambling.

Melba's round face brightened, and she stepped back and motioned for me to come inside. Since that is exactly what I'd hoped she would do, I crossed the threshold. It took a while for my eyes to adjust to the dimness, however, so I stood there helpless for a full minute before setting the sack on her already crowded counter. Then my eager eyes swept the room.

Her place was a nightmare. Not only was the small kitchen counter hidden beneath stacks of dishes and boxes of various foodstuffs, there were magazines piled high on the floor. Stacks and stacks of back issues of several ladies' magazines…*Family Circle…Women's Weekly…Cosmo—Cosmo*? Anyway, there were newspapers and magazines and paperbacks everywhere. Downright claustrophobic.

"Would you like a tour?" Melba asked, her voice trembly with excitement.

A tour was the last thing I wanted but knew I had to do if I was to get any information, so I said, "Oh, that would be nice." and followed her down a dark hallway to the bedrooms and bathrooms that were a mirror image of our own.

"This is *my* bedroom," Melba twittered as we stepped into the smaller of the two rooms, done in several shades of pink and rose.

"Oh…you don't use the master bedroom—the bigger of the two?" I was surprised.

She tittered as though that idea was extremely funny. "Ohh,

no…no…that room is used for storage…my nephew…his apartment is so small…and he and his lovely wife collect things…Jessica is such a talented little gal…makes lovely ornaments for Christmas…and she can knit…I do love a person who can knit, don't you?"

Nonplussed, I said, "Uh, huh."

"And this is my *bath*room…" She pushed open the door and switched on the light. "I chose lavender for the color…my nephew painted it for me…wasn't that sweet of him?"

"Uh…" I was rendered dumb after seeing a reflection in the mirror of a ghastly specter from my childhood. Hanging on the closet door was one of those old-fashioned, archaic, torture devices that my own Aunty Bea had used whenever my cousin Penny had had a stomach ache, a head ache, a pimple, an F on a test, an eyelash in her eye—whatever. A large, red rubber water bottle with a long white hose attached—its prime responsibility: the giving of an enema—hung in mute testimony to our not-too-distant uncivilized, barbaric and primitive Past. Something I dreaded more than the Plague when I was a child, visiting my aunt and cousin. Something, thank God, my own mother had never ascribed to. And here it was, hanging in all its glory, silent yet mocking, reminding me of terrible deeds done for terrible reasons. I shuddered.

"You cold, dear?" Melba asked sweetly.

"Huh? Oh. No, no, I'm not cold, 'though you do keep your AC a tad cooler than we do. You, uh, you're right about the color," I prattled, "Lavender is a pretty color for a bathroom…really pretty…"

"Can I get you something to drink, dear?"

"Uh, no, thank you, Melba. I can only stay a minute."

"Why didn't Sylvia come over with you?"

"Syl—oh. Bernie, you mean. Well, uh, Bernie was in the bathroom…getting ready…we're, uh, going out…" I brightened. "But she sent her love along with the peaches. Hope you enjoy them. Gotta run. We'll visit longer another time." And with that rather lame exit line, I hurried to the door and let myself out. In seconds, I was behind our closed door and breathing hard.

Bernie, still sitting on the over-stuffed chair with her feet on the ottoman, looked at me, one eyebrow raised. "Well? How was it? You were gone longer than I expected. And why so out of breath? Did poor Melba scare you?"

"Don't be silly," I snorted as I flopped down on the couch and put my feet on the coffee table. "Oh, Lord…it was awful in there…really awful. Stacks of newspapers, and magazines, and about a million paperback novels, strewn everywhere…junk and more junk…and I could hardly breathe…and—oh my God. Bernie. In the bathroom…in the bathroom, she had one of those archaic rubber hot water bottle thingies they used for enemas hanging on the door. Oh, it was ghastly, I tell you. Ghastly. Dear God, my Aunty Bea used to have one hanging on her d—"

"Please, spare me the details," Bernie barked. "Just tell me what you found out."

I stuck my tongue out at her and slumped back further into the cushions. "Well…I didn't really find out much of anything, except…"

"Except?"

"Well…she uses the small bedroom as *her* room…and keeps the master bedroom for *storage*…don't you think that's a bit strange?"

Bernie pondered that for a moment then nodded. "Yes, as a matter of fact, I do."

I sat up as a surge of excitement geysered. "You know. Now that I think of it, all that malarkey about her nephew needing storage 'cause his apartment is so small is…well, it's suspicious…suspicious, I tell you…*mighty* suspicious…a conundrum…"

Bernie snorted. "You think every*one* and every*thing* is suspicious. For crying out loud, Mike. To hear you go on, you'd think this sleepy little sea-island town was a hotbed for Al Qaeda."

It was my turn to snort, and I did. Loudly. "Oh, Bernadette. That's a *gross* exaggeration, and you know it." I pulled at my T-shirt and adjusted a bra strap. "Don't you think it's funny that her nephew has all this stuff that he just can't seem to find room for at home so has to store it in the small apartment of his dim-witted, elderly aunt who is so vague she doesn't know what day it is half the time?" I sucked in a ragged breath.

For once, I'd rendered Bernie speechless. She stared at me for a full minute then shook her head in disbelief. "Okay, okay…let's say, for the sake of argument, that Melba's nephew is using her… for what, I haven't the foggiest. But, for the sake of argument, I will agree with you that said nephew using her master bedroom to store stuff is, well, is pretty weird. But—"

"I knew it."

"But. That's as far as I'll go. I mean, it isn't a crime to use your dithering old auntie's place for free storage. And we may be doing the fellow a disservice. He may be paying the old gal some rent. She's getting money from *some*where, and it certainly could be from him. Maybe it's his way of saving her some pride…paying her to store stuff for him and his wife. Don't you agree?"

I closed my eyes and groaned. "Okay…yes…I agree you make sense. Still, it's more fun to see it my way. Be honest, Bernie…wouldn't you like to solve a real mystery like the heroines in books do?"

Bernie had the grace to grin. "Well-l-l…sure. I guess I would. Only if it's a real, honest-to-goodness mystery, though. I sure as hell wouldn't want to be the laughing stock of the county just because I had a few random suspicions…like some doddering old busy-body."

I sighed. "I'm right, you know. This complex seems to be *wallowing* in intrigue. Just think about it. There's Vicki and Lionel who are the absolute personification of criminality, due, most likely, to a lifestyle of accelerated spending." Bernie snorted. "And then," I glared back at her, "there's Melba with the not-so-up-and-up nephew. Oh. And how about Jorge?"

"*Jorge?*"

"Yes, Jorge."

"What's so suspicious about poor, hard-working Jorge, for crying out loud?"

"He's always around…in the background…watching…observing…pretending he's so humble and subservient…"

Bernie exploded into laughter over that. I let her get it all out of her system before continuing. "Fine. I won't *bore* you any more with my keen observations. Just you wait, however. Time will tell…time *will* tell…and I'll prove to you just how keen an intelligence I have. Keen, I tell you. Sharp as a tack."

Bernie laughed so hard at that I thought she'd need *Depends*. "Ohh, and don't forget Dixon Lee," she wheezed. "Remember the stories he told on the tour about the spirits and mysteries and swamp gas and strange goings-on. We have more clues than we can keep track of, and they're piling up into one huge mound of suspicion. Am I right, Miss Marple?" Bernie leaned over and nudged my foot.

"Well…okay…" I relented, "maybe you're right. Maybe I *am* letting my imagination run away just a bit. But…then again…what if there is a shred of truth somewhere in all this strangeness?" I grabbed a couch pillow and hugged it. "There's something about little Amanda's beauty mark that bothers me."

That innocent remark had Bernie doubled over and shaking from spasms of uncontrolled cackling.

Nineteen

We'd dropped the subject like a spoiled potato after Bernie needed almost the entire box of tissues to mop her tearing eyes from her obscene fit of hilarity. We'd been quiet, sitting for the past hour, reading our respective novels. There'd been no more conversation, no utterances of any kind…just the quiet complacency of understood friendship and a comfort zone that belied the years. Until, that is, I could contain my suppressed excitement no longer and blurted out, "So. What're you wearing?"

"*What?*"

"What're you wearing?"

Bernie glanced down, rolled her eyes, and whined, "I'm wearing a sleeveless cotton blouse with little red and blue squares—"

"*Ber*nie. I mean this evening. What're you going to wear over to Vicki and Lionel's barbecue? Sheesh."

She made a face. "What I have on…"

"You are? Not me. I'm changing into something cute and sassy."

"So you're going to strap on a brassiere for the occasion?"

"That's hilarious. I'm soooo glad you're soooo amused by my underwear challenges. Give me a break, will you? We have to look presentable."

"Why?"

"Wh—oh. For crying out loud, Bernadette. Snap out of it."

Bernie grinned at my frustration, enjoying her innate ability to aggravate me with little effort. It had ceased to become a challenge. "Okay...sorry...I'll change," she mumbled, the grin playing at her lips. "However...if we're going to socialize with these people simply because we want information, well...isn't it rather hypocritical to pretend anything else?"

I squirmed a little in my chair in anticipation of having to don the bra. Or, perhaps, it was plain downright, unadulterated annoyance. "No, it isn't," I grimaced. "Of *course* we're going for some information—that's a given. But we also have to put our best foot forward. We still have to be polite."

"Just in case we are absolutely and totally mistaken about them and would be mortified if they suspected that *we* suspected… Is that it?"

I rolled my eyes at that one. "Oooooh. Yes...that's it. Get into the spirit of this thing, will you, Bernadette? We'll go over, eat their barbecue—"

"—*Texas* barbecue—"

"—Texas barbecue...and smile and be polite and have a good time."

"And eat too much and laugh too loudly and be so damn clever they'll be astounded by our social prowess. Yet, all the while, we'll be snooping around with eagle eyes and bloodhound noses."

"You got it. Right on target, missy." I grinned then stuck my tongue out at her.

✱

Since the evening had already been planned and plotted, and Bernie didn't feel like wrestling with her swimsuit, we had the remainder of the afternoon to check out all the tourist traps. Visa and Mastercard in hand, we strode to the trusty Neon for yet another ramble into the tiny town. Demonstrating how familiar every thing and every place was to me, I drove up and down lane after lane toward the busy shop, just across the bridge that connected the beach—a barrier island in itself—with the main island. Popular with the tourists, it featured a wealth of desirable oddities.

The building was long and housed three separate departments:

a clothing shop, a general store, and a gift shop filled with lamps and scented oils and framed pictures of the area's hot spots. Pulling into a parking space, I cut the engine and grinned at Bernie. "You're going to love this shop. If I had money to burn, I'd buy a ton of stuff from here."

Bernie squinted at the display window and grunted. "Looks to me like typical souvenir shtick. You know…unique items that *demand* purchase, beckoning the easily *impressed* with *extraordinary* beauty and originality, and then morph into something *totally* awkward when you put them on your mantle in Missouri. They should have named the souvenir shop, *What WAS I Thinking?*" She made a face and released a long sigh of resignation.

"Oh, pooh," I wrinkled my nose. "You're full of hot air."

"Well…wallowing in it, at least." Before I could respond to that quip, she added, "I want to get Molly a T-shirt."

"Great." I nodded, glad that she was showing some positive spirit for a change. Leaving the car, we pushed through the door to the clothing shop and right away I spied something I liked. I pounced on a gaudy T-shirt featuring two over-the-hill, dumpy, matronly-looking ladies in swim attire. The slogan said, 'Girls' Day at the Beach'. "Oh, Bern, this is wonderful. Look. Isn't this just the cutest thing?"

Bernie raised her eyebrows and looked at me like I had my blouse on backwards. "No, sweetie…I think it's sadly lacking in the whimsically droll department. Can't you find something a tad more subdued?"

"Oh, Bernie. You're no fun. Let's buy one apiece to wear around, proclaiming our scandalous independence."

She gave me a withering look. "No way, darlin'. And anyway, they don't have my size."

That challenge inspired me to rummage through the stacks to make sure. They didn't. The sizes ranged from small to medium. No larges; no extra-larges. The frazzled saleslady followed us from stack to stack, straightening, re-folding, and giving us the evil eye.

We drifted into the general store, then into the gift shop, where Bernie saw several items that might be worthy of closer inspection. I mean, who wouldn't want a half-naked mermaid perched precariously on a dried starfish?

A dozen curiosities appealed to me. "My sister would love this," I gushed, holding up a sturdy little pelican with a limp fish in its beak, which had me anticipating one less Christmas present to purchase in six months.

Next, I was slathering on half a dozen potent body lotions, sniffing myself over and over, and trying to decide which I liked best. In a matter of minutes, I smelled like a citronella candle gone rancid, and neither the mosquitoes nor Bernie could stand to be next to me. Bernie had the grace to tell me so.

"Lord, Michaela, you smell like a brothel on Mardi Gras."

I sniffed my arm. "Oh, jeez…I *do* stink like a bordello. What will people think? Do you think people will wonder what I do at night?" I tried to keep my voice this side of a wail.

"Don't fret, sweetie, it's not that awful. Really. You know how I like to tease you. You smell just fine…well…not too bad, anyway."

Of course I didn't buy that consolation, and feeling like a disappointed child, replaced the smelly stuff on the shelf where it belonged. "Damn. I know better than to do that. Happens every time I go to *Bath and Body*."

"It's okay. Honest. And anyway, the cheap stuff always wears off quickly and before you know it, you'll be welcome back in public."

We spent fifteen more minutes just wandering through the shops, then I announced we had one more store to visit. Bernie complied, having selected two shirts for Molly but nothing for herself. She paid for her purchases and followed me out of the cool store into mind-numbing heat. Of course my little car was a veritable inferno.

Bernie began fanning her face. "God, it's hot in here. Believe it or not, I am almost tempted to suggest we go to the beach."

My heart leapt with joy. "You are? Th—"

"I said *almost* tempted. Heat stroke does evoke peculiar reactions in women of a certain age, you know."

My heart plummeted to my ankles.

The second shop was okay, though not Bernie's or even my taste. Over-flowing with outlandish creations created by local artisans, it reminded Bernie of the annual Art Fair at the high school, where treasures appeared on display, only a mother could appreciate. The stuff was funky and eccentric and far-out, but not for her.

I *did* like the homemade jewelry, however, and spent a good ten minutes 'oohing' and 'ahhing' over chunky necklaces and bracelets and dangling earrings that would've bounced off my 'girls'. Bernie's snide remarks about aboriginal art and ostentatious efforts by talent-impaired artisans were lost on me as I picked up one bracelet after another. Sensing my arty nature coming to the fore, she urged me to hurry, saying that we needed time to bathe and nap before our big night out. I capitulated, bought a pair of earrings made out of 'sea' glass that Bernie insisted had never seen the ocean, and left the store.

Annoyed and aggravated with the oppressive heat, Bernie couldn't wait to get home. After staggering up the stairs to our condo, it was all she could do to control her sarcasm as I fumbled once again for the key. I was relieved when a door shutting upstairs accompanied by the sound of footsteps drew her attention away from my frantic search.

Bobby clattered down the steps, wearing a wide grin. He raised a hand when he saw us. Bernie nodded and returned his smile. "Hi, Bobby."

"Hey, there. Looks like you gals went shopping."

Bernie held up her plastic sack. "Yes. Two T-shirts for my daughter back home…a little something to remind her of how much I enjoyed my vacation." I snickered and she grimaced, but Bobby wasn't listening anyway. "And Mike got some earrings," she added as an afterthought.

He chuckled. "Cool."

"You guys headed for the beach?" My pal's question sounded innocent, but I knew better.

His face clouded a little. "No...no, uh, we don't go to the beach." Bernie's eyebrows rose half an inch and he rushed on. "A-Amanda is terrified of the ocean—can you believe that? Totally freaked her out when we took her the other day." He laughed and stuffed his hands in his pockets in obvious discomfort.

"Oh, that's too bad. Sheesh. And here you are at the beach, no less. How 'bout the pool? Just across the street and pretty neat looking, if you ask me. Sure are a lot of kids enjoying it," I offered.

He rolled his eyes. "Yeah, I know, but...believe it or not, the pool freaks Amanda just as much. Poor Brenda is pulling her hair out keeping the kid entertained." He laughed again then shrugged. "Well, gotta go. I'm off to the grocery store. Can I get you guys anything?"

"No, thanks. We'll be seeing you." Bernie smiled and pushed me through the now-open door ahead of her. "Hurry," she hissed. I picked up my pace and she slammed the door shut behind us. "Whew. *That* was the be all to end all."

"What? What's gotten into you?" I huffed, tossing my purse in a corner.

Bernie dropped her purse and sack on a dinette chair, yanked open the fridge, selected a Fuzzy Navel wine cooler, then fell into her favorite chair. "Seriously. Of all the far-fetched stories I've ever heard, that one takes the cake. Who does he think he's fooling? I could read him like a book."

I reached under my shirt, fumbled and twisted, then succeeded in removing my bra, which I tossed on the couch. With a sigh of relief, I strolled to the refrigerator, retrieved a cold bottle of Busch Light, and collapsed onto the couch. "Ahhh...I'm beat." I took a long swallow, sighed again, and then had the grace to look at her. "So...what were you ranting and raving about?"

It was Bernie's turn to sigh. "Didn't you hear what Bobby said out there?"

"Yeah...something about Amanda hating the beach...so?"

She shook her head in absolute disbelief at my obtuse remark, and I felt a sliver of compassion for poor Bart Heilbronner pass through me. "Michaela," she enunciated like the ex-schoolmarm she was. "Have you *ever* heard of parents spending the kind of *money* it takes to come here, with a child who is *mortally* afraid of the ocean—or water of *any* kind—and then remaining holed-up in their *quarters* for lack of anything to *do?*" She sat forward. "Well, *have* you?"

That got me. "Gosh…when you put it that way…no." I sat up. "So, why? Why did they come here, then? Why? It doesn't make any sense."

"That's what *I* say. Why, indeed? I mean, for heaven's sake, there's bike riding and miniature golf, not to mention the kiddie playground by the pool…or just plain walking around the resort. Plenty to do, yet they hang inside, watching TV, coming and going at odd intervals and seemingly only to the ice cream shop… Strange…mighty strange…"

We each pondered that dilemma for the next few hours as we showered then went to our rooms for a lie-down. I was too tired to think about the barbecue looming on our horizon. Right now, it seemed too difficult to even think about breathing, let alone smiling and coming up with clever and witty repartee.

Surprising, therefore, that we both awoke from our naps feeling refreshed. Bernie blamed my remarkable energy upon waking on the delicious anticipation I felt for our upcoming snoop-fest. To tell the truth, I couldn't keep from babbling on and on about nothing and singing snatches from Broadway plays. It was enough to cause one to drink. And I'm not referring to diet Dr. Peppers, either.

At three minutes to six, dressed in stylish capris, we left our unit and made our way over to the next complex. Vicki and Lionel had their front door wide open, and cute little napkins and a platter of nibbles already waited on their deck. Believe it or not, the appetizers looked pretty good.

Vicki saw us coming and met us as we stepped onto their

veranda. "Well, hey. Lionel, honey. They're here. C'mon and have a seat. I dusted off the chairs just a minute ago. What can I get you t'drink? We have beer, wine coolers, and iced tea."

"A wine cooler sounds great," Bernie said with her best smile.

I bobbed my head. "Yes, that sounds good for me, too." I'd been perched on the edge of a chair but bounced up. "May I help you, Vicki? Please." I saw Bernie wince at the blatant eagerness in my voice. I had to cool it a few degrees or I'd give myself away.

Vicki didn't appear to notice, however, and just smiled. "Why, y'sure can. C'mon." With a wave of her brightly painted fingernails, she ushered me into their apartment. I glanced at Bernie over my shoulder and had the audacity to wink. Bernie just made a face.

Lionel pushed through the storm door at that moment, bearing a plate of raw pork steaks. He leered at us and stomped down the steps to his Weber grill, where he proceeded, with much fanfare and a loud, slightly off-key rendition of 'Home On the Range', to initiate his Texas barbecue. Tempted, I almost asked if he planned any more excursions to our electric panel thingy, but kept my mouth shut instead. No point casting aspersions.

I returned to the deck with two frosty bottles in my hands and a glass under each armpit. "Here," I said under my breath. "Take this." I rolled my eyes and bit my lower lip. "Ohmigod, Bernie…" I hissed, "it's exactly—"

"Well, isn't this *nice*." Vicki's shrill voice interrupted my piece of scandalous revelation. "I think this is just *so* nice," Vicki's voice percolated. "I'm so *glad* you could come. I just *adore* parties, don't you? *Any* excuse for a party, I always say. I could party *all* day and *all* night."

Bernie looked up from pouring her wine cooler into the glass I'd provided from my left armpit. "I enjoy a party or two myself. Your appetizers look delicious, Vicki. Did you make them?"

Vicki jiggled up and down, causing her opulence to bounce along with her. "Ohh, I did, I did, indeedy. I got me one of them books on entertainin' and copied out some of their neat little tidbits. I hope you like 'em. Those over there are made with pimento cheese and those..." she pointed one long red fingernail, "are made with cream cheese and green olives."

I reached for one of the latter, popped it into my mouth, and rolled my eyes. "Ummm, goo'," I said around a mouthful.

Bernie chose one of the pimento rolls and bit into it. Her eyes widened. "Mmm, nice, Vicki...really nice."

Our neighbor beamed. Her happiness was short-lived, however, when we all noticed an increasing number of mosquitoes crashing our little party. With a loud moan, Vicki picked up the tray. "Darn little buggers. Let's take this here party inside where we won't be bothered by them nasty critters."

Bernie and I left our chairs, each carrying a glass and bottle, and followed our hostess into her apartment. Vicki shut the storm door but left the main door wide open for Lionel. "Poor baby," she clucked, "I hope he isn't bein' tor*men*ted by them horrible bugs and chewed alive. He's so brave, standing out there by that hot grill, just a grillin' away. He does love to make the meat."

I know my eyes widened at that, and Bernie shot me a pointed look. Bernie had enough trouble keeping her own mouth closed without having me say something sarcastic to light her fuse. I mean, we were guests, for crying out loud. And our hostess meant well. I was now a firm believer that the size of one's bust was not an indicator of one's cerebral capacity... But... *But*, still and all, dear Vicki was putting on a good show. One glance at Bernie's face and I had no doubt she was beginning to see our Vicki in a whole new light, too.

Twenty

My feelings toward mosquitoes took an upward swing that evening. I blessed them for being the cause of our admittance into Vicki and Lionel's inner sanctum. My brief sojourn inside earlier had allowed only a glimpse of the kitchen and living room—enough to whet my appetite.

Crammed in a ten by ten space was a sofa, two recliners—all leather—three tables with decorative lamps and knickknacks, a display cabinet exhibiting all manner of exquisite ornaments, and a vase big enough to bathe little Amanda in. And every bit of it expensive. Now that we were inside, I knew I'd have a chance to use their bathroom, thereby getting a peek inside at least one of the bedrooms.

Sitting on the sofa beside Bernie, I did my best to chat about our excursion into Charleston, the tour, and various other outings. Bernie, of course, was at her glib best, describing our adventures as only she could. She had us in stitches with her piquant descriptions of personalities and locales. And she was a social studies major, no less. Do wonders never cease? But it was Vicki who stole the show. I nearly choked on my cream cheese and olive appetizer when our hostess bounced up and down in her jeweled flip-flops then pranced across the room to retrieve a large photo album. "Would y'all like to see pictures of our first house?"

"Sure," Bernie murmured. "In Columbia?"

Vicki rolled her eyes and giggled. "Ohh, no. Lionel and I met in Vegas. I was workin' as a cocktail waitress at Sam's Town."

She must have read Bernie's and my confusion because she giggled again. "That's a casino. It's not on The Strip but it sure is a magnificent place. Always filled with oodles of people from *all* over—even *Canada*." She opened the large binder to the first page and pointed to a much younger, much sexier version of herself. I swallowed a nervous giggle and refrained from looking at Bernie, who was doing her best to appear interested in the collection of snapshots of a wilder time and place.

"Here's my sweet teddy bear-of-a-man. Isn't he just the cutest thing? He had hair in those days. I sure did love running my little ol' fingers through that head o' hair of his." Another giggle. "And here's me with Wayne Newton. Y'all know Wayne Newton?" We nodded. "He was *such* a dream back then. I sure did *love* to hear him sing. I've driven by his ranch more'n a hundred times." She sighed like that was a little bit of heaven, right here on earth.

It was somewhat of a relief when Lionel brought up the sizzling pork steaks, and we gravitated to the table in the little dinette. Vicki had made very attractive place settings that even Bernie couldn't criticize. She'd laid out dark blue place mats, with red, white, and blue paper plates, cups, and cutlery, and bright red napkins. The centerpiece was a cute little paper boat with white sails. I made a mental note to ask where she'd gotten them.

The pork steaks were, well, pork steaks. I guess they were good by the way Bernie, Lionel and Vicki were consuming them, shoveling in one bite after another. I wasn't that fond of pork steaks, finding them too fatty and greasy for my taste, but I cleaned my plate all the same. Vicki had made a wonderful potato salad with dill pickles and radishes and some seasoning I couldn't make out. It was different from the potato salad I made but I thought it delicious. I made another mental note to ask for the recipe.

Vicki also had soft yeast rolls, a congealed salad full of vegetables, and a plate piled with slices of cantaloupe. Believe it or not, I was enjoying the company, the conversation, and the food. But I couldn't wait to go to the bathroom.

Finally, after we'd pushed away from the table, groaning

that our stomachs couldn't take any more, I asked to use the little girls' room. Vicki grinned at me and waved her hand. "Well, sure, honey. You oughta know where it is." I smiled, nodded, and sprinted down the hall, pausing to sneak a quick peek inside the first bedroom.

It was an office cum guestroom and filled to capacity with desk, futon, shelves, computer, printer, telephone, television, and radio. Heaven knew what was jammed inside the closed closet.

I was disappointed to see that the master bedroom door was closed, and of course I wouldn't dream of opening it so had to be content with using her prettily appointed guest bathroom. It was decorated in blues and greens with an inordinate amount of mermaid paraphernalia scattered about. It was very apparent that Vicki loved mermaids. The wallpaper depicted mermaids frolicking in a foamy sea; the soap dish and candle were in shapes of curvaceous mermaids; the guest towels had embroidered mermaids on them; the shower curtain had a vivid nautical scene starring nude mermaids; even the light fixture was one buxom mer-gal. It was hideous and at the same time, entertaining. Yet, it almost made you want to rush, having so many voluptuous sea-women staring at you from every corner of the small room. It was giving me the willies. I wished I could show Bernie but knew that would be too obvious. I'd have to pray that Bernie'd need to use the bathroom before we left.

She didn't—much to my dismay. After another hour and a half of teasing banter and congenial conversation, Bernie and I thanked our host and hostess for a wonderful meal and a great get-together and bid our adieux. Vicki and Lionel walked as far as the yard between our two complexes, chattering all the while about how delightful we were, and how much they hoped we'd be renting #215 again soon. I reminded Vicki that since my sister and brother-in-law owned the condo, I'd most likely be down sometime in the near future. Bernie, however, told them that she'd not have another chance in a long time to repeat this little getaway—much to her dismay. A consummate actress, my Bernie.

This time I had my key ready and opened the door to our unit in record time. Bernie gave me a look of approval and I smirked, "Hah. See? I can find the key when it's all I have to handle."

We each grabbed something to drink then sat down to unwind before heading to bed. Bernie sighed, screwed up her face, and then sighed again. "Well. Whew. So. What did you think about all that?"

I proceeded to describe all that I had seen in the office and guest bathroom. Bernie listened then offered one raised shoulder in a half-hearted shrug when I finished. I gaped at her. "*So?*"

"So..."

"Don't you think their stuff was a bit out-of-this-world in the price department?"

Bernie wrinkled her nose. "Not especially. I mean, their stuff was nice, but not so nice that I was suspicious or anything. Just looked like the kind of stuff people with their means would have."

"A Fab-something egg? Filigreed in gold? *Here?*"

"Faberge..."

"What?"

"Those eggs...they're called Faberge—from Russia—and, yes, they are very expensive."

"See? Who'd leave something as exquisite as that in a glass case in a beach house? I mean, sheesh. Who'd *have* one in their *town* house even?"

"Well, *I* wouldn't and maybe *you* wouldn't, but Vicki obviously would and *does*...hence the glass case filled with fine pieces."

"But here?" I was incredulous. "And *Vicki?* The gal who reads, and I quote, 'them trashy romances'? You talk about inconsistencies with the couple upstairs but what about Vicki and Lionel acting like Li'l Abner and Daisy Mae and collecting fine art?"

"To each his own, Mike. So they have an eye for beautiful art..."

"You should've seen her bathroom..."

"Her bathroom?"

"Oh, yeah. It was decorated in modern mermaid. Everything—

and I mean *everything*—had a mermaid on it or was in the shape and form of a mermaid. It was so gaudy and...and...*cheap*. I mean, I bet it was all really expensive and everything, but cheap *looking*, sort of like Vicki, herself. Too much, too loud, too bright, too glitzy."

Bernie laughed. "Oh, come on."

I made a face and sank lower in my seat. "Okay...but...it just wasn't the kind of stuff I'd expect in someone's vacation home. You know?"

Bernie picked at a hangnail. "Fine, but that's still not enough to incriminate them. You heard Lionel talking about his computer job. He's apparently good at what he does and has made a few bucks along the way. Enough, anyway, to own a home in Columbia and the condo here."

"Yeah," I muttered, "but just the same...they had too much expensive junk crowded in that tiny condo for just a vacation getaway. And they said they don't rent it out. Just makes me feel funny about the whole thing."

Twenty-One

Morning dawned on the eighth day. It was incredible to think that our little escapade was winding down. We'd had so much fun laughing, crying, sniping—sending pointed quips to one another like die-hard politicians—that it depressed me to think it would all come to an end sooner than we wanted. I woke up feeling great but the joy was raveling along the edges. As they say, 'this, too, will pass'. Oh, fudge.

When I straggled into the living room, Bernie, for once, was already sitting in her favorite chair with her slippered feet propped up on the ottoman. She had her omni-present glass of diet Dr. Pepper and was writing in a spiral notebook.

"Good morning. You're up before me. Sleep okay?"

Her head snapped up and a grin spread across her face. "Uh huh," she smirked.

"So, what are you writing?"

"Oh…nothing much…just a few notes about our vacation so far…but, damn. It's hilarious, if I do say so myself."

"Oh, that's just dandy," I muttered as I set about getting my coffee ready. "I can only imagine what you've said about me." That produced a loud snort. "Oh, come on, Bernie. Be nice. You better not be saying things you shouldn't. Remember what they say. Never put in writing what you don't want to see printed on the front page of *The New York Times*."

Another snort followed by a cackle. "Don't worry…I'm just highlighting the events so far…all truth and no fabrication…"

More cackles, snorts, and wheezes.

Time to change the subject. "Gorgeous outside…and there's a breeze. I'm taking my coffee out on the deck—"

"—Veranda."

"Veranda. Join me?"

Bernie let loose one more titter and tossed the notebook aside. She replenished her drink while I poured my coffee, then we ambled out onto the veranda.

"Gotta enjoy it while it lasts." I sighed. "In another hour or so it'll be hotter than Hades."

Bernie grunted. "Just how hot *is* Hades?"

"I'm sure you'll be able to answer that yourself some day."

We sat and sipped in silence for several minutes. Then a clicking upstairs made us both look up at the same time. "Upstairs," Bernie mouthed, pointing with her chin.

I nodded and we sat still, expecting one or the other of the adults to show. Neither appeared. Instead, a diminutive figure dressed in green shorts and a striped green and white top came very carefully on tiptoe—one step at a time—down the stairs. Little Amanda was grinning from ear to ear.

"Well, good morning," Bernie greeted the child. Amanda lowered her eyes shyly but came over to us. In one chubby fist was a Pop Tart with god-awful purple frosting. "Is that your breakfast?" Bernie prodded. The pixie nodded and took a huge bite, oblivious of crumbs cascading down her front.

"Well, it sure looks yummy in the tummy," I said as I leaned forward to smile at the little girl and brush off some of the crumbs clinging to her chin and shirt.

Amanda's eyes widened. "That's what my mommy always said."

"Yummy in the tummy?"

"Uh huh. She always said that…ev'ry time we had veg'ables."

I laughed and Bernie chuckled. Little Amanda giggled and took another bite from her pastry. I was just about to ask whether she was having a good time here at the beach when a sudden bang upstairs startled all three of us.

"Amanda. *Amanda*."

Bernie's head jerked up. "She's down here, Brenda," she called. "Don't worry. We have her."

A clomp-clomp-clomp and Brenda appeared over the railing at the top of their stairs. Again her long, stringy hair reminded me of the Spanish moss hanging on the trees. She was breathing hard. "Amanda. You get back up here. You know what I told you about wandering outside."

Amanda's round face seemed to crumple, and a lone tear snaked its way down a flushed cheek, past the tiny mole on the right side of her little chin. "No, Bwenda. I wanna stay here. I don't wanna go back inside. I wanna stay with my gwammas."

Brenda disappeared for a second then reappeared on the staircase. Her chest was heaving and two spots of color stained her cheeks. "Amanda. Don't you *dare* sass me. Now get back up here before I tell dada what you've done. You're a very bad little girl. You'll have to go to your room for some time out, young lady. I said hurry."

Amanda threw down the fragment of Pop Tart remaining, stuck out her very purple tongue at us, and dashed back up the steps. A great slam of the door and silence descended upon us like a shroud. I looked at Bernie, who had her mouth open in complete and unadulterated shock.

"Well," I exhaled. "What do you make of that pleasant little scene?"

"That was nothing short of criminal. Imagine saying that to a baby who'd just come down a few steps to chat with the neighbors."

"Yeah...they keep a pretty tight rein on that little one. I mean...I sure don't go for today's cavalier way of raising kids... you hear about so many of them getting snatched while the mother's back is turned for just a second...but...I don't know..." I slumped in my chair and let out another long, drawn-out sigh. "I sure didn't like Brenda's manner. Wasn't nurturing...or loving... My nieces are so good with their little ones...always kisses and hugs and fun little activities planned for them. And my Abby is always reading aloud to her kids and teaching them new games and things…jeez…poor little Amanda…"

Bernie grunted. "Yes…poor little Amanda. I do *not* like that young woman."

"Me, neither…but Bobby's nice…don't you think so? I feel sorry for him, married to the likes of *her* and raising a child, too."

"She's a witch…although we spell it a tad differently where I come from."

"Yeah, but you know…we may not have the whole story here. Remember the Amber Alert. Maybe Brenda is just a young, inexperienced mother who's afraid of losing her child. They're not at home, surrounded by familiar things…perhaps she's just overly protective. Let's give her the benefit of the doubt."

"Well, perhaps…but I still think it's criminal."

"It wasn't pretty. But she's probably just over-heated and tired. Remember what Bobby said about Amanda being too freaked to go to the beach or pool? Brenda's probably doing just what he said, 'pulling her hair out', trying to entertain the kid."

"They could play miniature golf," Bernie muttered.

"Oh, Bernie, stop it. They're just a young couple who still needs some parenting skills. Too bad they don't require you take a course before having a child."

"Okay, okay. I was just surprised at her tone of voice. I've seen so many abused kids in so many classes over the years, and…well, don't get me started. I just didn't like the way she spoke to her little girl, but, on the other hand, I've been known to raise my voice at my kids, too, so…well, maybe she's got a headache with this heat, like you said. She's over-weight and—and…well, over-weight is over-weight. Most of the world's problems are caused by situations pertaining to someone being overweight. I have a theory…"

I chuckled. "Isn't everyone in America over-weight? I'm over-weight and feeling this heat, too, but I'm not snarling at everybody." Bernie's look took the wind from my sails so I leapt from the couch and clapped my hands once. "Okay. Enough said on that subject. What do you want to do today? We're running out of days and should fill them to the nth degree."

"The 'nth' degree?"

"That's what I said. Let's go to the beach."

Bernie's face clouded over like Kansas during a thunderstorm. "Oh, Mike...isn't there someplace *else* we can go? You mentioned something about an interpretive center or some such thing—"

"Yeah, there's the Interpretive Center..." I gave her the eye. "*Or*...we could go to the Serpentarium..."

"Serpen-*what?*"

"Serpentarium...which just means a reptile house with snakes and turtles and alligators—"

"Oh, Lord. Here we go with the alligator thing again." Bernie ran a hand over her face and groaned.

I crossed my arms over my chest. "It's either the beach or the Serpentarium. I'm giving you a choice. Which will it be? Come on...you're an educator. You surely can't be adverse to broadening your perspective. It'll be good for you."

"Fine. We'll go to your Serpentarium. But so help me God, Mike...I'd better not come any closer to a real live snake *or* alligator than a dozen yards."

Twenty-two minutes later we were pulling into the parking lot of the island's famed Serpentarium. I hopped out of the car in high spirits while Bernie dragged herself out like a child on his way to the dentist's. "C'mon, Bernie...this'll be fun. Maybe I can get a picture of you petting a snake."

"Over my dead body," she murmured

We purchased our tickets, and I was happy to know we were in time to see the live snake demonstration. I'd witnessed it several times before with various grand-nephews and nieces and was excited about seeing Bernie's reaction to a four-foot rattler being dangled in front of her face. Well, within her twelve-yard radius, anyway. It should be worth a few laughs. Lord knew I deserved them, seeing I'd been the butt of her needling and teasing for most of the vacation. Far too much talk about butts during this trip anyway. And boobs, too, for that matter.

Passing through the gift shop, we lingered in the main hall where a large pit in the center of the room offered the casual visitor a good view of over fifty thick-bodied brown water moccasins. I peered over the chest-high wall and couldn't help an involuntary gasp as several of the venomous snakes writhed and wriggled in and over one another.

Bernie took one look and shuddered. "Oh, my God," she groaned. "What have I let you talk me into, *this* time?"

Since the show was about to start, we made our way outside to a small, covered amphitheater where about a dozen people already had seats on the curved benches. The only seats left were right in front. I was tickled to death to have Bernie that close to the demonstration. I just hoped she wouldn't make a scene or faint on me. My little amusement would backfire if she did.

Bernie disappointed me. As the handler—a tall young woman in her thirties, dressed in natty khaki safari-like garb—lifted one snake after another and recited her spiel regarding habitat and diet and strength of toxicity, Bernie remained passively disinterested. True, her eyes never left the center-stage, but she didn't moan or squeal or do anything remotely indicative of her squeamishness—much to my chagrin. My little sport hadn't exactly backfired, but it hadn't sparked any hilarity, either.

After the show, we headed down the cement path to where open-air pits displayed more snakes and turtles. Beyond that, a fenced-in area housed alligators of all sizes, weights, and girths.

An older gal, somewhere in her sixties or seventies, crouched on a high platform, overlooking the alligator pen and tossed raw chicken down to the hungry lizards. The sudden opening of giant jaws, revealing sharp, yellow teeth, was an awesome spectacle. I poked Bernie and grinned.

"See? Alligators. Nice big, fat alligators…with mouths wide enough to swallow a horse."

"Humphf." Was all she said.

On our way back to the main building, we passed a pit that stopped us in our tracks. Half a dozen small trees grew from the center; trees whose branches seemed to be rippling and moving until we got a closer look. Snakes. Hundreds and hundreds and hundreds of black, brown, yellow and green snakes, all writhing and undulating and squirming. It was enough to make us sick. I began to itch all over.

Bernie stared at the awesome sight—her eyes unblinking round orbs of awe and wonder and just plain, everyday, common variety horror. "Oh...my...*God*..." she breathed.

I couldn't think of anything suitable to say so just stood beside her, mesmerized by the gruesome display. Then I spotted something even more appalling. A turtle with a snake latched to its behind, trying to swallow its tail. "Oh, Bernie, look. The poor baby. I don't think I can take another turtle being violated." I looked around in desperation and spotted the gal in safari attire. "Ma'am." I called, waving for her to come over. "A turtle needs some help here."

She came right over, sized-up the situation, gave a low grunt, then hefted her bare leg over the side, and jumped down into the pit of hell—as far as Bernie and I were concerned, that is. I know I let out a surprised little squeak as Bernie clutched her shoulder bag tightly against her chest, mouth wide open.

The ranger—or whatever she was—stooped down, picked up the turtle in one hand and the snake in the other and proceeded to free the turtle from the jaws of death. Overhead, writhing serpents rolled and crawled and twined and undulated. Underfoot, more snakes curled and stretched and wriggled and slithered. It was a nightmare. I couldn't believe a human being would actually be insane enough to let themselves get that chummy with a zillion snakes, even if they weren't venomous. Like I said, it was a nightmare. If one—just one—of the loathsome creatures should slip off a branch and fall on her bare head or—worse—down her neck, I knew I would lose it and start screaming my head off.

Nothing like that happened, however, and in less time than it took for me to tell it, the young woman-with-the-nerves-of-steel had separated the two reptiles and had rejoined us on the right side of the wall. "Thanks," she said brightly and sauntered off.

"We have to go," Bernie hissed in my ear. "We have to go, now. *Right* now. And I *mean*, now."

I didn't argue. I'd seen enough, myself, and knew I'd probably dream about this for nights to come.

Twenty-Two

I felt a little green around the gills as I turned on the ignition, backed out of the parking space, and pulled onto the two-lane road. Bernie chuckled. I glanced at her. "What's so funny?"

"You."

"Me? Why? Now what'd I do?"

"I knew all along you had your little heart set on giving me a hard time back there at that hideous snake house."

"Did not."

"Did, too. But I'll be truthful. I did have a hard time—can still feel slimy things crawling up and down my back—but. You be truthful, too. You got more than you bargained for with the turtle and snake incident. Right? You are as grossed out as I am. Right?"

I winced. "Right."

I looked out the window at the passing scenery so unique to this part of the world and tried to clear my head of lingering visions of writhing reptiles when all of a sudden a thought hit me, and I let out a bark of laughter.

Startled, Bernie turned and watched me shaking with mirth, my square hands tightly gripping the wheel. After a long moment she asked, "Now what's so funny?"

"Oh, n-nothing," I hiccuped.

"Oh, it's something, all right. Let me in on the scathingly droll joke. I'm *dying* to know."

I glanced her way and chuckled again. "I was just remembering what Amanda said this morning when her mom yelled at her to come back up."

Bernie smelled something rotten in Denmark and wrinkled her nose. "Ohh-kay…and that was?"

I grinned. "She said, and I quote, 'I don't wanna go back inside…I wanna stay with my gwammas'." I wiggled my eyebrows. "'Gwammas', Bernie…grandmas in *your* language." I tittered again, relishing the whole idea.

Bernie sniffed, and pretended to be offended. "Cute, Mike, really truly adorably cute. You realize the word was plural, don't you?" I just kept on grinning. "Good. As long as we both are on the same page, I can enjoy the little witticism. Just don't bring up the 'mommy' incident and we'll be fine."

I nodded then lifted my chin and peered into the rearview mirror. "Darn. I'm too *old* for a pimple."

"A what?"

"A pimple…or, what refined seventh graders refer to as a zit. I've got one sprouting on my chin." I thrust said chin at her. "See? Right on the right…same place Amanda has her mole…wish mine were a mole…or, maybe I don't…seeing that moles sometimes turn nasty…"

This was going where Bernie didn't want to go. "Enough, already. So you have a blemish on your chin. So what? Put some astringent on it and it'll go away. And, for your information, Amanda's mole is on the left side of her chin…not the right."

"It is not. Amanda's mole is on the *right* side of her chin. I remember thinking it was like Elizabeth Taylor's beauty mark the first time I saw her that evening they were going out for ice cream. It's on the right…right here…" I pointed to my own chin.

Bernie forced a patience she obviously didn't feel, probably recalling a recalcitrant student from bygone days, and smiled patronizingly. "No, sweetie…Amanda's little mole, which is no bigger than a minute, is on the *left* side of her cute little pointed chin. There is even a slight cleft in said chin. And two dimples, one in each round cheek, make for a calendar-perfect face. She has dark brown hair cut in a pixie. She is no more than a yardstick in height. She is—"

"Bernie. Quit it. I don't want to argue with you over some silly mole…but…it *is* on the right side of her chin." My head swam as another senior moment washed over me. "Or…at least…I *think* it is." I exhaled a loud whoosh of air in frustration, gripped the wheel tighter, and grimaced. "Ohhh, that's what's been tickling the back of my subconscious for the past few days. That blasted mole. I swear one minute it's on the right side of her chin, and then…" I took a curve a tad too fast and had to concentrate to stay in my lane. "And then, the next time I see the child, the blasted mole is on the *other* side." I stole a quick look at Bernie, who'd refrained from commenting or interrupting and was just staring out the window as though in a trance. "Bernadette." I squeaked. "Say something. Please."

Bernie cleared her throat and drummed the fingers of both hands on the dash that was almost in her lap. "All right. I'm stymied at the moment so will not belabor the point. We won't settle this by verbal fisticuffs. Let's remember to look carefully the next time we see her and settle the matter then. Okay?"

"Okay…if we ever *do* get to see her…the way Brenda keeps her under lock and key…"

"We will…never fear…"

"Yeah, Bernie is here."

"You got that one right."

"But…and I know this sounds loony, but…even if we see her again and determine, once and for all, which side the mole is on…well…it won't explain these creepy senior moments I've been having…*seeing* the mole jump from one side to the other." I sucked in a deep breath. "I'm almost be ready to believe there are *two* Amandas. Crazy, huh?"

"You got that one right."

✴

The days were flying by, and the paradox of mixed emotions ran high. Bernie and I had welcomed each morning, anticipating some new and wonderful adventure or other and had enjoyed our week in this sleepy beach town. But lurking in the recesses of our minds was the titillating though somewhat unsettling thought that an honest-to-goodness mystery was unfolding right under our noses and somehow we were just too daft to catch on.

Because our time was running thin, Bernie agreed to my strident plea to go to the beach one more time. So, this afternoon we were returning to the sea, challenging all that was good and right and proper by squeezing into bathing suits specially designed and constructed to 'go with the flow'.

Still sensitive about her disastrous encounter with the crashing waves earlier in the week, Bernie suffered occasional flashbacks about mooning the beach-goers on that fateful day she was swept off her feet, kicking and clucking. I agonized over the prospect of her hating the ocean, since she knew *I* knew she was opinionated and had a tendency to establish and maintain immovable notions and obstinate ideas. And stuck to them. Tenaciously. Yet, my bosom—oops, that word again—friend agreed to approach the mighty ocean with the Queen of Sea and Pluff Mud one more time since the fateful departure day was all too rapidly approaching.

Right on cue, I popped from my bedroom, flip-flopping across the living room's laminated floor, beach bag clutched close to my chest. I was again a fashionable vision in black and netting, beach hat smooshed down on my head, sunglasses perched on the end of my sunburned nose. The faint aroma of Coppertone wafted across the room as I began the litany of 'thou shalt take it to the beach or do without and suffer the consequences'.

With well-honed disregard, Bernie hauled herself out of her favorite chair and, sighing, shuffled with blatant resignation toward the front door. You can only do so much with a swimming suit at our age, and there are reasonable limits to modest coverage. Bernie's cover-up started at her chin and cascaded to her knees. Add an over-sized beach towel, cavernous beach bag filled with dire essentials, a hat, sunglasses, and sandals, it was almost more trouble than it was worth. At least to *that* Missouri gal.

From around the corner of our condo, Jorge appeared in a

cloud of noise and dust, his ever-present blower and extension cord in tow. He nodded to us, eyes averted, trying not to stare—probably trying not to laugh. Dutifully, Jorge went about his business, neat brown uniform reflecting the intense heat and humidity. Bernie and I waved at him, but he seemed engrossed in the task at hand as he climbed the stairs toward the upstairs units.

"Ready?" I chirped.

Bernie grunted an affirmative, and we, the troublesome duo, dragged all our paraphernalia toward the tiny Neon.

Somehow sensing my buddy's preoccupation with humidity, blistering beach sand, and rogue waves, I refrained from chattering and we rode in silence for a couple minutes. Until I couldn't stand the silence a second longer.

"Bernie?" I dared to venture into her reverie. "Are you having fun?"

"Hmmm?" she responded noncommittally.

"I'm just wondering where you are. You're obviously not here with me. What's up? You're not fretting about going in the water are you?"

"Hmm, no…no, it's not that. Nothing, really…just watching Jorge…and thinking…" Bernie shifted in the miniscule front seat, attempting in vain to cross and uncross her legs.

"Good. This time you're going to love the ocean. I promise."

After the now-familiar ritual of choosing a parking spot, usually the easiest place to park regardless of proximity to the target, Bernie and I rolled out of our seats, blinked at the Sahara-like sun, and scanned the sandy shore for a likely spot to pitch the beach umbrella. Wherever we went, we seemed to cause a scene. Why was that? Beach-goers already engaged in their own sunny activities stopped to stare at us, and nudged each other. I tried to fool myself into believing it was due to their unquenchable interest in a couple of mature, well-preserved women. I preferred to think of us as women who embraced Mother Nature; reminiscent of intrepid gals like Jane Goodall or Amelia Earhart. I refused to believe their interest was indicative of a devilish delight in seeing a veritable comedy routine entering from stage left.

As soon as we waded into the gently rolling ripples of the sound, I was relieved to see Bernie begin to relax. It appeared she would not be wrestling with Dame Neptune today, or be subjected to never-ending humiliation. And I…I was in my element as I melted into my noodle, one with the sea, bobbing and floating, unencumbered by gravity, head tilted back, blissfully happy. Naturally, this would be the moment Bernie, of all people, chose to discuss our self-imposed mystery challenge.

"I'm still wondering why Bobby and Brenda are here," she mused.

"Ummm…me, too."

"Utterly ridiculous, if you ask me."

"Umm hmmmm…"

"They could have spent the money somewhere else."

"Ummm…"

Bernie sighed, splashed a little, hoping to elicit a more articulate response from me, but I continued to ignore her. Another sigh, louder this time, and still I gave no reaction to the less than subtle cues.

Eyes closed, floating languidly, I'd hung out my official 'do not disturb' sign. No use trying to get through to me now. She'd have to try later when I regained consciousness and returned to the real world of mystery and intrigue and a vacation running amuck.

Twenty-Three

Why is it always much harder going home from doing something fun than the process of getting there? Does that make any sense? By the time Bernie and I dragged our sodden carcasses out of the car, we both looked like we'd taken an active part in the digging of the Panama Canal. Stringy, salt-encrusted hair, sandy feet, sunburned ears and noses, squinty 'aviator eyes', and insatiable thirsts made up our deplorable countenances. In short: we were a mess.

And we were exhausted. We were rattled, therefore, when we noted the other car in our small parking lot parked in what I'd considered my spot for the last eight days. I was a little vexed at having to park in another spot, farther away from the path leading around to the stairs. "The nerve of that person." was uttered through pursed, sun-chapped lips.

"I wonder who it is? Somebody visiting Bobby and Brenda? Or, of course, sweet Melba could be having company…" Bernie mused.

"Maybe it's her beloved nephew, bringing more stuff for her to store."

"Or it could be the upstairs unit next to Bobby's…it's been empty this whole week. That's who it is…just another vacationer…"

We trudged up the wooden steps, praying that we wouldn't bump into anybody, desperate for showers and some clothes first. Luck was with us. We made it to our door without seeing anyone, and I had the key in my hand, much to Bernie's warped titillation.

Showering in record time, we reunited on the veranda, frosty glasses in hand, and settled in the plastic deck chairs to relax, enjoy the arrival of early evening, and to make snide remarks about various unwitting golfers who appeared on the sixteenth hole from time to time.

"You know...this really is the life," Bernie sighed.

I was in the middle of swallowing a mouthful of hard lemonade so could only grunt.

"It'll take a bit of concentration to—" Bernie stopped as the sound of a door opening next door alerted us to Melba's presence. We both lowered our legs from the railing and sat up straighter, ready to par with Her Royal Vagueness. We were surprised when a man appeared, followed by a simpering Melba. He stopped in his tracks when he saw us—looking, for all the world, like a four-year-old caught with his hand in the cookie jar.

"Hi," Bernie said with one of her most ingratiating smiles.

The man—somewhere in his thirties, I'd guess—was rendered mute for several seconds. It was Melba who cracked the silence. "Ohh, Billy...here are Donna and Kristen...my dear friends from next door...we've had such good times together...wonderful neighbors...hello, dears..." She beamed at us like a Sunday school teacher pleased with a correctly recited verse.

"Hi, Melba," I added to the burgeoning conversation.

"I'm Bernie and this is Mike," Bernie offered.

The man had recovered somewhat, donned a mask of civility and took a step forward. "Hello. I'm Bill Thomas...Melba's nephew. Enjoying your stay here on the island?"

We nodded and Bernie replied, "Oh, it's been a blast. Packed a lot into one week already and hope to fill the remaining days just as well. Do you live here on the island?"

He scrunched his face—a facial tic he'd been demonstrating for the past few minutes—and shook his head. "No. I live in Mount Pleasant."

"Near the Yorktown," I interjected, for the inane reason that I felt the urge to show off my enormous base of knowledge.

He smiled, the tic doing its thing, and Melba twittered, "Billy sells antiques and has his very own shop…don't you, dear? And he's very good at what he does, aren't you, dear? Tell Marcia and Susie what you do on your days off." She took hold of his arm and hugged it. "Tell them about your hobby, dear."

Bill, or Billy, made a face, gently disengaged his arm from his aunt's grasp and sighed. "Oh, auntie…they don't want to hear about all that. Now you be a good girl and walk me to my car. Jessica and I will be back next weekend, and we'll all go out to dinner…maybe to the restaurant at the clubhouse. Would you like that?"

Melba's head bobbed up and down. "Ohh, yes. That would be lovely, dear." She glanced at us. "Maybe Cathie and Theresa would like to join us?"

Poor Bill recovered from that one in record time. I was trying to swallow the convulsive giggles levitating up my throat and was relieved when Bernie took reins in hand. "Oh, thank you, Melba…that sounds lovely. Unfortunately, we won't be here next weekend. We're sorry to say that our vacation is coming to an end. We leave Thursday. But thanks, all the same."

Before Melba could utter another word—her face had clouded over like the prelude to a summer storm—Bill had firmly taken her arm and pulled her along with him as he descended the stairs. With only a quick nod in our direction and a terse goodbye, they disappeared beneath the deck and were around the building and out of earshot.

"Hmmm, interesting…" Bernie muttered.

I skewed my chair around to face her. "What? What did you think?"

Bernie made a face, took a sip from her drink, lifted her legs onto the railing, and sighed. "He was strange…"

I sat forward. "How strange? What do you mean, strange? I mean, *I* thought he was strange, really strange—did you notice that facial tic he had? Sheesh. If that doesn't spell out nervousness I don—"

"Michaela. Stifle it for a minute."

That put a cork in my bottle of enthusiasm, and I bit my lower lip, sat back, and waited for Her Royal Glibness to resume.

Bernie grinned. "I just don't want you to get so worked up. Yes, I thought his behavior decidedly strange and a tad on the down side of nervousness." She chuckled. "Reminds me of Mr. Manheim... You, of course, haven't forgotten him...took your side in everything..." Now her grin was malicious. "I was under the impression that he had a serious crush on you—"

"Ted Manheim? The seventh grade math teacher? You've got to be kidding. Teddy was bald and portly and wore checkered shirts with plaid pants. You think he had a crush on *me*? You are *way* out of your mind, Mrs. North. Way out. I never *once* gave you or anyone else the impression that Ted Manheim and I were interested in one another. Not *once*."

"Well, all I can say is that it's a good thing your Joe came along or you could've been married to Ted."

"Ohh, Bernie. You ma—"

"Yooohooo, Christine? Virginia? Are you still up there?" Melba.

We both sat up, waiting for our plump, floral-robed neighbor to climb the steps to the deck. We remained silent as one faltering step after another made its way up the stairs. After an eon of waiting, she emerged, face flushed from the exertion, curly hair reminiscent of orphan Annie, jewels of perspiration crowning forehead and enhancing upper lip. She beamed when she saw us still in our deck chairs.

"Oh, hello...so glad you're still here...thought you said you were leaving...your vacation is almost over...so sad to have to say good-bye..."

"Your nephew on his way?" Bernie asked.

Her eyes glistened and her head bobbled up, down, from side to side. "Ohh, yes...Billy is gone...I do miss him...love it when he visits...but next week...next week, Jessica and he will come and we will go out...we will go to that lovely restaurant by the clubhouse…where they have those darling little golf carts…I do love seeing the men driving those darling little golf carts…women drive them, too. They are so cute, don't you think? Compact yet plenty of leg room…and airy…quite well ventilated. I've always thought I would like one…to drive to the grocer's and back, don't you know…but Billy says—"

Bernie cut in, exasperated with Melba's ramblings. "That's great. I'm glad to hear your nephew is coming back next week. I'm sure you'll enjoy your time with them, and next week's not so far away. Anticipation is half the fun."

Melba nodded, did the hula wave, and headed for her unit. Three steps then she stopped and turned to face us again, smile bright as a light bulb. "Do you know what Billy brought me *this* time? It's an amazing thing. I have never seen anything so amazing. He bought it and then couldn't find anywhere to put it… so silly…just like his father…Martin was forever buying things they didn't have room for…used to make my sister so angry… though Eunice never got *really* angry…she was so tenderhearted, my Eunice…but Bil—"

"Melba." Bernie interrupted. "What is it—this amazing thing your Billy brought over?" Bernie twisted in her chair, transmitting a very suggestive look my way so I made every effort to appear keenly interested, too. Melba glowed with the kind of pride a mother has for a beloved child. It was clear as glass that she doted on dear Billy, and dear Billy could do no wrong, was the apple of her eye, a shining star, a man-among-men, and every other cliché in the book. I held my breath and waited to hear what the amazing *it* was. The glassy-eyed look on Bernie's face almost made me erupt into giggles.

Melba rolled her eyes and sighed. "That precious boy brought one of those computer machines with a darling little mouse and a printer that will print anything you want in color and…" she inhaled, exhaled, and rolled her eyes again. "…And he told me I could use it anytime I wanted. Isn't that nice?"

Bernie smiled and nodded. "Yes, Melba, that sounds like a

lot of fun. Will you use it?"

The older lady giggled, tossed her fluffy head from side to side. "Oohh, no…no, I don't imagine so. It's far too complicated for me. The dear boy tried to show me how, but I'm afraid I didn't quite get past how to turn the amazing thing on. I'm just too old, I think."

"Oh, Melba," I spoke up. "It's really very easy. Bernie or I could walk you through it again, if you'd like. I think you'd have a lot of fun using it."

"Ohh, I don't know…"

"Are you hooked up to the Internet?"

"The what, dear?"

"The Internet."

"I have a hair net in my bathroom, dear, but no inter-net… not that I know of…"

"Uh huh," I said, not wanting to belabor the issue. I glanced at Bernie whose bemused expression hadn't altered. "Well, you think about it. If you change your mind, you let us know, and we'll be more than happy to help you."

Melba cocked her tousled head, shrugged, then turned in a rustle and flurry of caftanned glory. "Ohh, no, dear…I don't like those things and don't plan to use it. My goodness…whatever would I do?" She was halfway to her unit when she twirled around on the tips of her slippered toes. "But I do thank you. You're both such dears. Bye-bye." She opened her door then turned again. "It is an amazing thing, though, don't you think?"

"It certainly sounds like it. But if you're not going to use it, why did he haul it over and go to the trouble of setting it up?" Bernie asked even though I was fairly sure poor Melba hadn't a clue, and Bernie knew this but was just baiting her.

The old gal's pale forehead puckered then cleared. "Oh, I don't know, dear…he's such a thoughtful boy…always looking out for his dear, old auntie…thinks I'm lonely…but between you and me, I think my sweet boy just needed the room…his apartment is so tiny, don't you know, so he brings the things he can't keep to me…and I put them in my spare room. I don't mind…I'd do anything to help him, and he and Jessica have so much to do just minding their little shop, and they both have so many other little interests to keep them busy…Jessica does crafts, you know…she makes such wonderful Christmas ornaments and can knit beautifully. Have you seen her crocheted pillows? She has sold them in the Market in Charleston. Have you ever been to the Market in Charleston, dears? I must take you there sometime…you would love to see all the sweet things for sale…I know…I have been to Charleston ever so many times…"

"That's great, Melba…we'll do that sometime. Well, thanks for telling us about the latest surprise from, uh, *Billy*. We'll talk to you later." We both beamed at her and waited as she smiled, patted her downy head, and finally disappeared into her apartment. Once she was safely behind her closed door, we let out collective whistles.

"*Well*…that was interesting." Bernie said on an exhalation of air.

"I'll say. Sheesh. That old gal can sure go on and on and on and—"

"Michaela."

Twenty-Four

Planning to eat later at the clubhouse, we fetched snacks, replenished our drinks then retreated to the couch and chair to begin untangling this mess we seemed to have gotten ourselves into.

"Jeez." Bernie exhaled as she reached for a handful of peanuts. "My head is swimming with questions and thoughts and random accusations. I mean, okay, even the least perceptive landlubber would realize that darling Melba is being manipulated and maneuvered by her slick 'nephew'. I mean, really."

"Yeah."

"Gosh, these peanuts are good."

"Yeah, nice and salty."

"Remember to get more next time we go to the Pig."

"Sure."

A minute of silent ruminating and masticating went by before a sudden dizzying thought whacked me on the side of the head.

"He's never anywhere but here." I announced, almost spilling my drink. I shook my head and gasped. "Ohmigosh, Bernadette. That's *it*. I've got it. It's him—uh, I mean, *he*." I glanced at Bernie, saw her look of utter stupefaction, glared at her, then added rather petulantly, "Stop staring at me as though I'd suddenly announced my intention of joining a convent, for crying out loud."

Bernie blinked, tossed her humidity-fluffed hair with one hand and returned my pointed stare. For maybe the second time in her life, she was rendered speechless. My seemingly irrelevant announcement stunned her. After an epoch of watching me twitch and wriggle and blink as the wheels turned in my fertile brain, she demanded, "*What* are you *talking* about?" She maneuvered Doritos and cheese dip and cashews without missing a syllable or crumb—years of practice paying off.

"Jorge." I couldn't hold it in a second longer.

Bernie nearly lost a dollop of dip from her cracker but recovered. She looked over at me, eyebrows in a knot, yet not distracted from her feeding spree. I suppose she thought *I'd* had one too many *lemonades*.

"I thought we were *utterly* fascinated by Melba and her darling nephew. Or was it the dynamic duo of Vicki and Lionel? Anyway, what does poor *Jorge* have to do with anything?" She'd managed to lose a glob of oily dip on her new capris after all.

"*Exactly.*" I stated and crossed my arms.

"Too much sun," Bernie muttered, poking through the dwindling pile of snacks for more cashews.

"Bernie…we've driven through this complex…what…twelve, fourteen, *twenty* times, right? Even walked around a bit, checking out the neighbors and their condos, *right?*"

"Uh hmmm," she hummed.

"Okay. And Jorge is *always* around, cleaning up, doing his job, *right* on schedule, blowing and cleaning and tidying up," I added.

Bernie leaned forward in her chair. "Right," she agreed. "And…?"

"*And*…have we *ever* seen Jorge anywhere else in this humongous complex besides right here at our own place? Have we seen him down the road, or across the lane, or down by the gate, or policing the other units? Well, have we?" I questioned, tugging at my T-shirt and pulling on one side of my shorts.

"Well…no…I guess I never noticed him anywhere but here… except that time at the beach…" Bernie replied, not sure where this conversation was headed.

"And Melba's place is being used as a storehouse for a creepy nephew who says he's a nephew, but who really knows for sure, and now there's a brand-new computer, and the leaf blower thing is always running right on schedule but nowhere else, just around *us* and—" I sucked in a deep breath.

"For God's sake." Bernie interjected. "Take a breath. Settle down, Michaela. You are hyper-ventilating."

"But don't you get it?" I cried.

"Michaela, you are bordering on hysteria. The last time I saw you *this* excited was when you encountered the tiny mouse that'd taken up residency in the glove compartment of your Volkswagen Rabbit, and had invited friends and family to join him in the plush, luxury accommodations. Missouri winters can be beastly, I know." She popped another chip into her mouth.

"Forget that nonsense. Somehow this is all connected. It *has* to be." I leapt to my feet. "It's just all too strange and odd and— And our vacation's almost over, and we're not going to discover the end of the story, and—for crying out loud, Bernie. Will you *please* stop eating long enough to listen to me? We have a real, live adventure here, and time is running out."

Flopping onto the couch, exhausted from my tirade, I fidgeted and squirmed, popped my neck, and glared at my annoying comrade.

"Mike," Bernie warned, "you're going to break something. Stop the Pilates for a sec and chew on *this*. One, this complex is so big, I'm sure they have a dozen men going around with blowers and such. Two, I'm sure that each man is assigned a territory or section or whatever, and keeps to that location, which, of course, ensures that the job gets done and nothing is overlooked. Right?"

I nodded and frowned.

"Third, just because *we* think we haven't seen anybody else do the job doesn't mean they haven't. Truthfully, have you *really* cared one iota whether someone was blowing debris two units down?"

I grimaced then shook my head. "No…I guess I haven't…"

"On the other hand…I think it *is* mighty strange that we've only been aware of *Jorge* being around and nobody else. I mean, why zero in on Jorge? He's not particularly large or excessively handsome…and yet, we seem to be fixated on him and him alone. Why? What is it about him that has enslaved our senses?"

I stared at her, sparks shooting from my narrowed eyes. "Wait just a darned minute, Bernadette North. First you go on and on, telling me how silly *I* am, and then you go 180 degrees on me. Do you just *enjoy* tormenting me?"

Bernie grinned, cracked open a pistachio and stuck the nut into her mouth, keeping one eye on the slide show of emotions displayed on my perspiring face. "Okay…you're right. I am only baiting you, but. Even though I think we have just missed seeing other gardeners around, I do agree that Jorge does seem to be always *here*, which does make him a *tad* suspicious…of what, I haven't a clue."

"He probably works for the CIA or FBI or NSA or—"

"Mike." Bernie was shaking with convulsive laughter and could hardly get the words out. "Mike…you're…incorrigible." Another spasm. "As I said earlier, you need an outlet…a job…*something* to occupy that fertile imagination… FBI? *NSA?* You've *got* to be kidding. Next, you'll suggest he's affiliated with NCIS."

"I happen to like that program," I muttered darkly.

"You have a crush on Mark Harmon, Charlton Heston—may he rest in peace—Lorne Greene—gosh, he's dead, too—George Clooney—"

"Stop it." I glowered at her. "You admitted he looked suspicious…"

"Yes…but more in the ballpark of illegal alien or something… certainly not," A loud snort. "FBI or NSA. Ohhhh, Lord, that's priceless."

"But that's why he's so good at what he does," I whined. "He's *perfect* for his surveillance job for the very reason that he doesn't look like he's perfect for his surveillance job."

"Run that by me again?"

I picked up one of the couch pillows and flung it at her. With force. It landed square in the open container of onion dip.

"Ohh. Now look what you made me do. And that's my sister's pillow. Now I'll have to wash it somehow, and dip is oily and will probably leave a stain and she—"

"*Mike.*" Bernie's voice was so loud it did the trick. I deflated and slumped against the remaining sofa pillow. "There…now just calm down. We'll clean the damned pillow. Right now, we have better, more constructive things to do."

"Like what? I mean, if I knew there was actually something we could do, I'd jump at the ch—"

At that precise moment, the whirring howl of Jorge's leaf blower punctuated my dramatic gyrations. I sat bolt upright, transfixed by the noise and whirlwind of dust and pine needles that announced the groundskeeper's arrival.

"3:30." My voice was hoarse. "Now, what do you make of *that?*"

"You know, sweetie," Bernie replied cryptically, "that twenty-four hour walk-in medical clinic we saw on highway 17 could probably see you right now, no questions asked."

"3:30, Bernadette." I repeated, desperate to make a point that seemed lost on her, since she'd left her chair and was once again foraging in the refrigerator. I knew Bernie could *hear* my impatience without having to see it. My bare foot tapped on the laminate floor, attempting to command some semblance of attention from her, but she was otherwise occupied and therefore unimpressed. However, sensing my eyes boring into the back of her… well, her posterior…she rose to full stature, closed the refrigerator in resignation, glared at me and flopped back into her chair.

Seizing the opportunity to make my point or lose the moment forever, I declared, "Jorge *never* comes around at 3:30. It may be 9:00 in the morning or 11:20, and once almost noon, but never-*never* has he swept the deck at 3:30. Something's up."

Looking like she hoped there was more to this sudden, though remarkable deduction, Bernie motioned for me to go on. So I did.

"Don't you see? Everything we thought was regular and ordinary and usual and common is…well, *ir*regular and *un*ordinary and *un*usual and *un*common."

"Sweetie, truthfully, I suspect that maybe it's *you* who is irregular. May I suggest something soothing and natural to *rectify* the situation?"

"Bernie. Stop being so difficult and listen to me. It's a *conspiracy*. What can we do? We've got to do *something*."

"Okay. Then we will."

"Huh?"

"I said, we will."

"We will? Like what?"

Bernie slipped on her sandals and struggled up from the chair. "I think we need a little exercise and fresh air. Don't you? I think a nice stroll around the complex would be just the ticket."

Now *I* was dumfounded.

Twenty-Five

It took me a minute to run to the bathroom, comb my hair, struggle into a bra, stuff my pockets full of Kleenex and house key and join Bernie on the veranda. We sprayed our ankles and behind our knees with bug repellant then made our way down the wooden steps to the parking lot. We couldn't see Jorge but we could hear him. He was on the far side of our building, blowing to beat the band.

"Okay," I hissed, "now what?"

"We walk. We look devil-may-care. We breathe in the fresh air. We watch his every move...without being conspicuous ourselves. Got that?"

"Oh, right...uh huh...sure. Like *that's* going to solve anything...or *prove* anything..."

"Look...you're the one who wants to solve a mystery..."

"You do, too..."

"Yes...therefore, we embark on an afternoon stroll about the grounds..."

"Oohh, you're just patronizing me again."

We rounded the corner, came up behind the gardener and skidded to a stop. Bernie raised her eyebrows but didn't say a word. I kept my eyes glued on the man, watching his every move. He seemed complacent enough, doing his job with the same meticulous attention, blowing debris hither and yon, but every once in a while his head turned upward, and he stared at our complex.

I nudged Bernie and hissed, "Why's he doing that?"

"Haven't the foggiest."

"Whose unit is he interested in? Can you tell?"

"No."

"Is it Melba's or Bobby's or ours?"

"Don't know."

"This is killing me. He's definitely consumed with curiosity about *one* of them."

"Doesn't appear to be concerned about Vicki and Lionel's…"

"Yeah…at least, not right now…"

Just then Jorge snapped off his blower and the silence was deafening. We didn't want to look conspicuous, standing there like idiots, spying on him, so stumbled into one another in an attempt to turn around and retreat. We made it to the parking lot, overcome by a spasm of strangled giggles. Bernie snorted and choked, while I bent over with uncontrolled laughter.

"I..I…" I gasped, "haven't laughed…like that in…years. Oh, Lord…it hurts…it hurts…"

"We're acting like…a couple of silly junior high…ninnies. So glad…no one I know…was here…to witness that…" Bernie panted, fanning her face with a Kleenex. "God, now I need to use the bathroom…"

That brought on another series of convulsed giggles, and I had to lean against my car for support. "S-stop it…*please*…you're killing…me…"

We were so caught up in our childish regression into an unbridled, total lack of self-control that we didn't hear our neighbors until they were upon us. To our complete and mortified surprise, Bobby, Brenda, and little Amanda approached, looking inordinately interested in what we two old gals were doing. Bernie recovered first.

"Oh, hi, there," she said with just a hint of embarrassment.

Bobby grinned. "Someone tell a good joke?"

"Oh, we were just reminiscing about old times…get a little slap-happy when we get going… You off to the ice cream shop? Again?"

"Yeah, we are. Mandy wants a cone. Don't you Mandykins?" The little girl craned her neck and stared solemnly up at her dad. He tweaked her nose but she didn't flinch. Somewhat flustered, Bobby looked at us and shrugged. "Woke up from her nap on the wrong side of the bed, I guess." His grin returned. "Well. Nice to see two old friends having such a great time. We'd better get going. We'll be seeing you."

"Have fun," I said, lifting a trembling hand in an awkward wave.

Bobby laughed. Brenda, on the other hand, scowled. We watched as they got Amanda secured, climbed in, then left the parking lot with a squeal of tires.

I looked at Bernie, swallowed, choked then gasped, "H-her mole...was on the l-left side of her chin."

"That's what I've been trying to tell you," she made a face. "But it wasn't the mole that I zeroed in on," she muttered.

"Yeah. Little Amanda didn't seem too overjoyed at the prospect of yet another ice cream cone, did she?"

"No, she di—" Bernie stopped in mid-sentence and her eyes narrowed. "Well, well... don't look now, but we've got company."

Turning my head slightly, trying to be nonchalant, I looked behind me. At the corner of the building, partially screened behind a thick live oak, stood Jorge. In the shadows, his face half-hidden beneath the brim of his cap, we couldn't tell what had snagged his attention. He was too far away for us to even call out a greeting without sounding like we were nosy, in-your-face neighbors.

"He's watching us," I whispered, feeling the need for a bathroom, myself.

"Hmmm, maybe," Bernie mused. "Or maybe he was interested in our upstairs neighbors...could be...could be..."

"Bobby and Brenda? Yeah...but why? And, what do *we* do now?"

A strange look crossed Bernie's face. One that I'd seen on a number of occasions in the past, boding no good for the recipients. I thought of burly Bart Heilbronner crumpling beneath her stern gaze, and the obnoxious Pine sisters who'd been brought to their knees after a 'talk' with Mrs. North. What did she have up her sleeve now? I wondered, feeling rather uncomfortable.

"Bernie…what are you going to do? I know that look. *Tell* me. What're you cooking up?"

Bernie smacked her lips, crossed her arms against her chest, and marched straight over to where Jorge was in the process of winding up his long extension cord. I trotted alongside her, now nervous as heck. "Bernie…Bernie…what are you *doing?*" I hissed.

"You just watch," she mumbled.

Twenty-Six

"G'morning, Jorge." Bernie called out in his general direction, smiling and striding with purpose toward the groundskeeper.

Jorge seemed to shrink in stature as she advanced, so reminiscent of all those mischievous little junior high kids who visibly melted when they realized they'd been *discovered* in some major misdeed or other.

"Do you have just a moment?" I knew from her tone that the inquiry was only a gesture, and that Jorge *would* have a moment whether he had one or not. The Spanish Inquisition was about to take on a whole new perspective.

Jorge removed his weathered cap, clutched it to his chest, and averted his peat-brown eyes. He was bobbing and nodding and mumbling something in a mix of languages that implied he couldn't or wouldn't or shouldn't understand the impending dialogue.

Undaunted, Bernie let loose with a string of questions, hardly allowing Jorge time to answer or even indicate whether or not he understood her at all.

"Have you had this job for long? Where are you from—originally I mean? Do you have family here? For whom do you work? Do you have a schedule? I mean…we seem to see you *here* every other day, but seldom see you anywhere else in the complex. Do you understand? Jorge? Do you understand what I'm asking you?" She fired rapidly as only a veteran principal could.

Jorge had the deer-in-the-headlights look that so many former students utilized, while enduring one of her barrages, to no avail. Fear was not a factor. It was answer or else. Still, Jorge just looked bewildered and unsure of what, if anything, he'd done to warrant this verbal salvo. Somehow he'd crossed this menacing lady with the fluffy hair who spoke so quickly and with such authority that it upped his anxiety.

"Bernie," I whispered, elbowing her. "He doesn't seem to understand you at all. Leave the poor man alone. We can look into this some other way. You're frightening him. Actually, you're even frightening *me*," I insisted, all the while smiling and nodding at Jorge.

Bernie ignored me. "Jorge…who *are* you, really? You're not a gardener, are you? Who are you watching, and why?" Bernie demanded.

Distracted by my pointy elbow nudging and jabbing, she unlocked her eyes from Jorge for a fraction of a moment to glare at me. The diversionary tactic worked, for as soon as she turned away, Jorge beat a hasty retreat to the back of the condo, disappearing into the underbrush.

"Way to go, Mike," Bernie sighed. "Now you've let him get away, and he will avoid us like the plague now that he knows he could be attacked at any moment."

I had the grace to look repentant. "I'm sorry…I just felt sorry for him…he looked so scared. You were coming on pretty strong, there, Mrs. North."

"Yes, well, he may have a very good reason for looking scared, and now we'll never know just what that reason is."

Somewhat dejected, we walked toward the deck steps, shaking our heads at each other's ridiculous actions.

Twenty-Seven

"I can't believe you did that," I said for the third time, somewhat out of breath, as we climbed the stairs to our unit. "I mean, I admire your penchant for taking charge of every single situation, probably because you think that I'm not capable…"

"Oh, you're capable enough. Capable of a vivid and random imagination, capable of making a mountain out of a molehill, capable of thinking you have this tremendous insight into everything and everybody…"

"You know what I mean, Bernadette. Stop belittling everything I do and say. Besides, you're changing the subject. I can't believe you did that. Don't you have *any* fear in you at all? I mean, I almost died when you said that to him. I thought I was going to wet my pants. I was ready to burst out into nervous giggles at any moment. I was—"

"*Mike.*"

"Sorry…I'm still reacting…"

"Well, stop reacting. Your inane prattling is getting on my nerves."

"Well. Ex*cuse* me."

I unlocked the door and walked in ahead of Bernie, still a little miffed by her tone, and went straight to the refrigerator for something cold to drink. I wanted something alcoholic, but decided against it since we'd soon be headed for the clubhouse restaurant and maybe getting a cocktail there. Finding a can of diet soda, I stomped over to the couch and sat down.

Bernie, meanwhile, fetched her soda, kicked off her shoes, and sat in her favorite chair, feet up on the ottoman. She gave me one of her most ingratiating smiles. I tried to hang onto my peeve but found my resolve slipping. When she smiled like that I had to give in.

"Something's not right," I muttered, as a way of reopening the conversation.

"They've got pills for that, nowadays."

I refused to bite. "Bernie...Bobby and Brenda just don't mesh."

"Don't mesh? Now that's insight for you."

This time I glared at her. "Bernie. I'm serious. There's something wrong with Bobby and Brenda. I can't put my finger on it, but something's not right. Not to mention that damned mole."

"Sheesh. This is like a Ping-Pong match...or tennis. You bounce from one culprit to another. Can't you make up your mind?"

"You were suspicious of Jorge, too. *And* Bobby and Brenda..."

Bernie nodded. "You're right. I was. I am."

"So, back to what I was saying. Something's not right upstairs with our young couple and their darling little girl with the dancing birth mark."

"Well, it's what I've been saying all along."

"I know, I know...and now I think it, too."

Bernie chuckled. "So Vicki and Lionel are off the hook, are they?"

"Please, Bernie...don't patronize me. Yes, Vicki and Lionel are now on the back burner of my suspicions." Bernie snorted, coughed, choked, then snorted again. I gave her my best 'look', left over from *my* teaching days. "Are you all right, dear?" She nodded, one hand hiding her mouth. "Good. Now, let's discuss this in a calm and rational manner, shall we?" More snorts, guffaws, and gurgles.

I set my soda on the coffee table, stood up and stretched. "I'm going to the bathroom. Maybe by the time I return you will have gotten a hold of yourself and have managed to regain some semblance of self-discipline. We still have a mystery to solve." I left the room, conscious of her smothered laughter trailing behind me.

Four minutes later I was back on the couch, still chewing on our bone of contention. Bernie had picked up her spiral notebook, and was furiously writing. I wasn't about to give her the satisfaction of asking what about. I knew already. Her muffled snorts and choked giggles were like a neon sign. Refusing to give her any satisfaction, I picked up the closest magazine. It was a traveler's guide to Charleston, which I'd seen a zillion times, but I wanted to appear blasé and not in the least emotional. Bernie fed on that and used it against me again and again. Then, like a gut-punch, it hit me.

"That's *it*. I know the *answer*. *I do*." I couldn't be more pleased with myself.

"Of course...Professor Plum in the dining room with the candlestick," Bernie said, with just a smidgen of sarcasm.

"You're being insufferable. Don't you want to see justice done?"

Bernie grinned. "Of course."

"Then put down that pen and focus."

"I will."

"Good. Okay. Now, listen to what I've come up with."

"I hope it's not contagious."

"Ber*nie*..."

"Okay, I'll be good. Just can't wait to see what amazing theory you've come up with *now*."

"Okay. Let's start with the Teals."

Bernie glanced at me, then looked down at the magazine in my lap, then back to my, oh, so earnest face. She sighed, put her notebook and pen on the floor beside her chair and picked up a bag of potato chips. "I now realize that all the innuendoes and flip remarks and sleuth-type observations have piled up, and you are bound and determined to land us knee-deep in some sort of conspiracy or other whether I like it or not." I was about to protest but she put up a hand and I bit my lip. "I confess, there are a few undeniable, immovable, carved-in-stone Mike-isms, such as love your family, even if they make you nuts, laugh until it hurts, if it tastes good, eat a lot of it, and never, ever, under any circumstances, walk away from a challenge. I accept all this. This, in fact, is what endears you to me."

I allowed ten seconds to pass before I huffed, "Are you *through*, Mrs. North?"

Bernie had the grace to lower her eyes, nod her fluffy head, and smile. "Yes. Thank you. I think I've gotten it out of my system."

Now that I had Bernie's undivided attention, and even her interest, I settled myself into the pillows on the couch, wrestled with the girls until they rested comfortably, and summoned my very best authoritative look-what-I've-figured-out voice.

"Okay. Now listen. What if…what if Bobby and Brenda are 'Bonnie and Clyde'? What would you say to that? Hmmm?"

Certainly not the reaction I'd desired. My keen observation produced a sudden bark of laughter. I glowered at my incorrigible friend. "Oh, for crying out loud. Bernie, you make me so *mad* sometimes. Can't you *ever* be serious? Oh, you're serious enough when it pertains to *your* insights and all, but, when it comes to anything *I* think is important, well, you jus—"

A crash overhead startled both of us. Bernie squeezed the potato chip bag she was holding, thus causing a volcanic eruption of greasy chips to rain all over her. I, on the other hand, sat up so suddenly that I kicked my soda off the table, spilling its contents in a wide arc of stickiness on the laminate floor.

"Lord, what was that?" I exclaimed, jumping up to get some paper towels.

"I don't know," Bernie muttered picking chips off her chest, lap, chair and surrounding floor. "But it came from directly above us."

On my hands and knees, I craned my neck to look up at her. "I thought so, too, but, Bernie…nobody's home upstairs. They went out for ice cream, remember?"

Bernie paused, stared out the picture window, and sucked in a deep breath. "Yes…they…did…didn't they…"

I mopped up the spill then ran to my room to get my shoes.

"C'mon, Bernie," I panted, "we've got to go upstairs and check it out."

"Now wait a minute, Mike. What is it you think we can do? If no one's home then the door is locked, and I certainly don't want to be seen standing by their sliding glass door with my nose pressed to the window, looking in like some low-life felon."

"But we have to see what made that loud noise."

"Maybe they have a cat."

"Oh, no, they better not. I know the couple who owns that unit, and they don't allow pets. The real-estate agency that handles the renting of that apartment would've made that clear to the Teals. Besides, have we seen or heard a cat around?"

"One doesn't hear a cat walking around, sweetie."

"Oh, fine. Whatever. I know it's not a cat. Let's go."

I led the way. My heart was tripping like it used to do when I was ten and playing hide-and-go-seek with the neighborhood kids. It was a delicious feeling, being so keyed-up that your hands sweat, little chills ran up and down your spine, and the hairs at the base of your neck tingled. I hadn't felt this way in decades. I glanced over my shoulder at a still-scowling Bernie and had to giggle. Her scowl deepened and she groaned.

"Oh, for goodness sake, Michaela. You're acting like a fourth grader."

"I feel like a fourth grader." I giggled again.

We climbed the second series of steps to the upstairs units, senses on high alert. We didn't want to be caught upstairs when Bobby and Brenda returned from the ice cream shop. My giggles erupted for the third time. "I know this is insane, but I really feel we need to do this," I whispered.

"For crying out loud, Mike, why are you whispering?"

"I just feel like it."

"Quit behaving like a moronic school girl."

"You quit harassing me."

"You quit—"

A sound sliced through that sentence like a guillotine. We

stopped, held our breaths, stared at one another for what seemed an eon, then Bernie stepped up to the Teals' closed door and put her ear against it. I scooted over to the large sliding glass door and peered through the partially open blinds. "I can't see a thing," I muttered.

"Interesting," Bernie grumbled, "but we're wasting our time. Let's go back to the condo before someone sees us being so ridiculous."

"That sound we just heard *definitely* came from inside this unit."

"I know that, Mike, but we can't see inside, can't break in, so standing here bemoaning the fact is rather silly, not to mention the insignificant little detail that Bobby and Brenda could be returning at any moment and then where would we be, hmmm?"

Disappointed, I turned around and hurried down the stairs. A fresh wave of nervousness washed over me as I anticipated our neighbors' return. Plus there was always the possibility that sweet, vacant Melba would appear, and that would be an annoyance in itself.

Once back inside our unit, we both let out whistling sighs through gritted teeth. I flopped down on the couch and moaned, while Bernie settled in her favorite chair. "Oh, Bernie, this is killing me...really killing me. I just know something isn't right here, but I can't decide exactly what the problem is. You know?"

"Yes, I know...and I also know that you're predisposed to letting your imagination run away with you—by-product of being an English major and drama teacher, I suppose—and when you get worked up, I, *too*, have a tendency to get worked up, and therein lies the problem."

"Huh?"

"By that I mean, I don't use common sense and discretion. I let you tease me into predicaments of one kind or another and, well, there you are. You'd think I'd have acquired some sort of immunity by now...but, no...I'm just as ditzy as I was back in the seventies, where you're concerned."

"Thanks a lot," I muttered, although I was secretly kind of pleased with this power she credited to me. "So." I sat up. "What I want to know is, do you or do you *not* agree that something here isn't legit?"

Bernie chewed on that for a moment then nodded. "Yes…I guess I'll have to admit that there is something not quite kosher in this quaint little beachside resort. *What*, I really don't know. Right now—and perhaps it's due to being hot and tired—I suspect just about everybody. Vicki and Lionel are a bit too much—almost caricatures of themselves—and sweet Melba and her less-than-scrupulous-seeming nephew are subject. Then, of course, there's my first choice, the Teals…don't know what to *think* about *them*…just know they both give me a strange feeling in the pit of my stomach…of course, that could be just the onion dip protesting, but…" she shrugged, "I just don't know."

"Don't forget Jorge."

"Ah, yes…dear, innocuous Jorge…"

I clenched and unclenched my hands then stood. "Okay. I say we go to the clubhouse now and volley our dilemma back and forth over a nice dinner…maybe have a drink to celebrate."

"Celebrate what?"

"Uh, well…we can celebrate the fact that we're having fun and are hell-bent and determined to solve a mystery before our vacation is up…how's that?"

Bernie smirked. "Sounds like as good a reason as any I can think of. Okay, then. Let me go to the bathroom, change into capris, and we can go."

I glanced down at my wrinkled shorts. "I guess I should change, too. You never know whom you'll meet, and I want to be prepared for anything."

"Planning on being discovered by a vacationing talent scout?"

I made a face. "You never know. Stranger things have happened, my dear."

"Oh, I agree. I'm just wondering which of your many *talents* could get you noticed without being arrested."

Twenty-Eight

Fifteen minutes later we were in the car and driving the short distance to the clubhouse and its newly upgraded restaurant. We could've walked it, but after a big meal and a cocktail, being able to ride home seemed the way to go. We weren't as young as we used to be. Actually, we weren't as young as we were fifteen minutes ago. And, besides, the mosquitoes were awful after sunset.

We were shown to a corner table by the window, sat down at a ninety degree angle in order to talk without being overheard, ordered our drinks—another margarita for Bernie and a Singapore Sling for me—and then stared at one another, waiting for the other to speak first. After an epoch of silent thought, I cracked the silence. "Okay, Bernadette...*now* what do you think about this entire situation?"

She rolled her eyes and gave me the 'look'. "For crying out loud, Michaela...give me a break. I've hardly had time to delve any further into our 'situation', as you call it, since the last time we discussed it, which was all of fifteen minutes ago. Therefore, I haven't the foggiest what to say next. I only agreed that we *had* a mystery, never once indicated that I *knew* what that mystery is. How about you? You're the one with the conspiracy theory. You tell *me* what the mystery is."

"Darn you, Bernie," I hissed. "Don't throw all this in my lap. You think the Teals are suspicious—have since day one. Right? *Right?*"

Bernie closed her eyes and sighed. "Y-ee-sss, you're right.

But that's all I have. Suspicions and feelings. Nothing tangible."

I took a sip of my drink, smacked my lips, then folded my hands on the table and leaned forward. "Okay. Then listen to this. What if Bobby and Brenda aren't who they say they are?"

Bernie sniffed. "We've already gone over that. For the last time, they are *not* 'Bonnie and Clyde'."

I wrinkled my nose. "Oh, Bernadette, *really*. I'm not talking about 'Bonnie and Clyde'. Now don't interrupt me again."

"*Again?* You asked *me* a question."

"Fine." I waved my hand in dismissal. "Now, listen. What if Bobby and Brenda aren't really mommy and daddy—er, 'dada'—after all? What if—and I hesitate to bring this up because you will swear I'm hallucinating or getting emotional or *something*, but. What if there are really *two* little girls upstairs, even though we *think* we've only seen one?"

Sensing only the tiniest smidgen of resistance in the form of a smirk from Bernie, I lunged ahead. "And…what if…what if Jorge-the-diminutive-groundskeeper isn't *really* Jorge-the-diminutive-groundskeeper but is *really* Jorge-the-private-detective who is keeping an eye on the family because they are suspicious as hell and odd and out-of-place and are possibly holding two little girls in that apartment, maybe for an enormous ransom? What do you think of that?" I sucked in a shaky breath and tightened my already-clenched hands.

Bernie didn't speak, only stared at me like I'd just said that there was a huge undergarment sale at Macy's and I was determined to stock up on support brassieres. Empowered and encouraged by the fact that she had yet to fall off her chair in spasms of ridiculing and demeaning mirth, I continued.

"And…what if those two little girls look so amazingly alike, that hardly anyone can ever tell one from the other except for the mole? The mole that appears to hop from one side of her face to the other."

"The…mole…?" Bernie repeated, as if trying to fathom the

type of mind that was capable of conjuring up lurid stories, yet marveling at my amazing yet misguided imagination. Oh, I knew her so well. Her look spoke volumes—epics, in fact. She picked up her glass, took a long swallow, set it down, and gave her head a slight shake. "Mike…are you…telling…me…that you're basing this amazing deduction on…on a…*mole?*"

I could tell that Bernie was grappling with the real possibility that one too many lemonades—or, my Singapore Sling—had effected terminal damage on poor, addle-pated Mikey. My blood pressure jumped a notch.

"No, please, Bernie. Think about it. Where is little Amanda's mole?" I challenged. "Which side of her chin? Left or right?"

"Left," guessed Bernie.

"Right."

"So, it's on the right?" Bernie ventured, playing with the salt shaker.

"No. You're being an ass. I said it's right that it's on her left, except for the last time when we saw her, and it was most definitely on her right," I said, hoping that finally cleared everything up. "*Now* what do you think?"

"I think that's our waitress heading this way. I think it's time to order. I think, Michaela, you are getting to be a true eccentric…harmless…but certifiably nuts."

The congenial argument cut short by the appearance of our pert little waitress, I held my tongue, bided my time, and placed my order without the least bit of scatter-brained nervousness, of which—according to Bernie—I'm famous. I chatted with Nancy, our waitress, and chuckled over the pros and cons of shrimp versus scallops. I finally decided on salmon stuffed with crab and waited while Bernie chose crab cakes with asparagus and rice pilaf.

Then, as soon as Nancy was out of earshot, I attacked with both guns. "Okay. Now, listen to me without any cute comebacks or pithy remarks. Are you ready?"

"I've enjoyed most of my drink so I guess I'm as ready as I'll ever be. Go ahead," Bernie sighed with resignation.

"Okay. Do you remember the Amber Alert that kept replaying all last week?"

"Yes…"

"So—and don't jump down my throat—I think Amanda and whoever else is hidden upstairs are those missing twins." I know my face conveyed a smug expression, even though Bernie's was just plain annoyed.

Bernie smacked her lips, ran a tongue over them, and cleared her throat. "Okay…but I also remember seeing their picture flashed on the TV screen, and they didn't look *anything* like Amanda. Those little girls had long, blond hair and neither one had a mole on her chin, if I recall."

I wasn't about to be thwarted. "Okay…well…yeah, I remember seeing their pictures, too, but…well, jeez, Bernie…hair can be cut and dyed a darker shade—you know that. And, as for the mole, well…maybe…maybe the photographer digitally removed them when he spruced up the picture. I mean, you could tell it was a formal shot and not one just taken at home in the back yard."

Bernie mulled that over, still playing idly with the salt shaker, rolling it between her thumb and forefinger. "Okay…I'll buy that…although I believe it's less common nowadays to alter photos like you said, preferring to depict people as they really are. Besides, a mole like that is still considered a 'beauty mark', isn't it? Her little mole certainly isn't unattractive, and I'm sure nobody would cover it up. So?"

"So…so, what do you think about my theory?"

"I think…oh. Here comes our food. I think we should put your 'theory' on the back burner and enjoy our dinner. Okay with you?"

It wasn't but I acquiesced anyway. I may be impatient, and a little too creative and intense, but I was a good sport.

✯

By the time we returned to the condo, both of us were too full, too warm, and too tired to reflect over something as silly

as a mole. Or, at least, that's what we told ourselves, having exhausted the subject over dessert.
"I'm going to—"
"—Remove your brassiere—"
"—Take off my bra—"
"—And get comfortable," we finished simultaneously. I made a face at Bernie and hurried to my bathroom, while she shuffled down the hall toward her own. It really irked me sometimes how much she enjoyed toying with me and my emotions. She took fiendish delight in magnifying my petty eccentricities. It annoyed me, yes, but it also made me laugh, so I had to give her credit for that. Laughing really is the world's best medicine. Whenever we got to laughing over something, the troubles and grievances just evaporated.

I couldn't forget the time our parish priest—head of the small, parochial school where we'd taught—had taken the faculty out to dinner to celebrate the culmination of an especially long month, due to the ever-changing accreditation process schools must endure in order to maintain some semblance of equilibrium. A stuffed shirt with little or no humor running through his veins, he was a constant source of amusement for us. Bernie and I took special delight in playing practical jokes on the poor creature.

The afternoon of the dinner at an up-scale but trendy restaurant, I phoned in a request for a birthday cake to be presented to the Reverend Pastor at the end of the meal. Knowing that this schmaltzy yet chic establishment made a huge fuss over patrons celebrating any kind of anniversary, I couldn't wait until the cake, ablaze with candles, was placed before him. Of course Bernie was in on the brazen caper, and it was all we could do to keep our poise throughout the long, drawn-out meal, chatting with our peers as though we two innocents hadn't a thing suspect up our sleeves.

When the waiter, accompanied by three others, appeared with a cake, sizzling sparklers shooting off a thousand seeds of dazzling colorful light stuck on top, our dear boss nearly had a seizure right there on the spot. The poor man turned a delicious shade of purple, but maintained his dignity and hoity-toity-ness to near perfection as the four employees sang 'Happy Birthday' to him. Since it wasn't even close to his birthday, I'd say the man earned a Congressional Medal of Honor for keeping cool under fire. He knew right away who'd been responsible. Our reputation was such that there was no question as to who the culprits were. Of course, our flushed and triumphant faces hadn't helped either. Lucky for us the pompous old blowhard had been a good sport. It'd taken months for us to live down that prank, but we'd all had a great laugh at his expense, and that had been our goal. We'd been supremely satisfied.

Still laughing to myself over my trip down memory lane, I joined Bernie in the living room. She made a face at me and said, "You know, dear, if you continue to wear that silly, vacant, half-baked expression, your face will freeze like that, and we'll have no recourse but to send you packing to one of those mountain retreats. You know, where they are experienced in helping those who cannot help themselves."

I sent Bernie one of my most scathing looks but she just laughed. That irked me. "You are insufferable."

"I am, aren't I?" she admitted. "And very good at it, too, I might add."

Twenty-Nine

I was up the next morning before the sun. I was so excited I just couldn't sleep. And of course this was the morning that Bernie decided to sleep in later than usual. It was all I could do to keep a lid on my percolating emotions. Three times I went as far as her door, hand raised to knock, then thought better of it and went back to the living room to sip my coffee and pretend to read my novel.

Seventeen minutes past eight—an indecent time for an ex-teacher to arise—Bernie made an appearance. I bit my tongue as she shuffled into the kitchen, found a can of Diet Dr. Pepper, popped the lid, poured it into a glass, grabbed the bagel bag and container of whipped cream cheese and settled in her chair. One glance my way and a crease puckered her forehead.

"My God…you look as though you're about to break out in hives. What's the matter *now*? Finally decided to burn the brassieres and be done with them forever?"

I bounced a little in my seat. "Bernie, I thought a lot about our mystery last night and am convinced that there are two Amandas upstairs. I would swear on a bible that the kidnapped twins are living upstairs."

Bernie took a bite from her bagel, chewed, nodded, swallowed, then muttered, "Oookay…"

I brushed aside her lack of enthusiasm. "Is that all you're going to say?"

Bernie licked a glob of cream cheese off a finger and just stared at me.

My excitement deflated like a popped balloon. "Gee, Bernie... I really expected more get-up-and-go from you."

Bernie smacked her lips, drank from her glass of soda, put everything down on the floor beside her chair, and stood. "That just about clinches it, doesn't it?"

"Are you thinking what I'm thinking?"

"Probably not."

"Well, what are you thinking?"

"I'm thinking that you had a cocktail at dinner, read another chapter in your mystery novel, went to bed all keyed-up and dreamt an elaborate and bizarre sequence to boost your already too lofty imagination."

"*What?*"

She grimaced. "Now don't get all bent out of shape, Mike. I'm not saying that your conclusion or deduction or whatever is all hot air. We know for a fact that two little girls were kidnapped from a town not too far from our little resort haven. I'll give you that. But. We've been here over a week and have actually only ever seen *one* little girl. One, Mike. One very adorable, pixie-haired darling."

My balloon of excitement shriveled into nothing. "I know, I know, but what about the mole that changes places? That can't be just our imaginations and you know it. That blasted little mole has been seen on her left side *and* on her right side. How do we begin to explain that phenomenon? Huh?" When I only received an unblinking stare, I gave up. "Okay...okay...maybe I'm just being overly dramatic." I closed my eyes, drew in a cleansing breath then looked up at my friend. "But...what if there *are* two little girls upstairs, and we ignore the possibility and the kidnappers escape? We'd be like *accessories* to the crime, wouldn't we?"

"I'm not throwing out your suspicions, Mike. I just don't want to go off half-cocked. Today, we'll listen and watch and see if we can come up with something more substantial than perceived misplaced beauty marks."

"Okay…but we're running out of time…"

"Running out of time and sanity. By the time I get back to Missouri, who knows what senses I'll have left? Jack will probably have me committed."

Thirty

After allowing a brief time for digesting breakfast, I dragged Bernie outside with the announcement that we should take a walk while the temperature was bearable. I knew walking was the very last thing she wanted to do, but I was so hyper she agreed to walk as far as the kiddie playground and back. Good enough.

We'd no sooner reached the parking lot, however, than Bobby, Brenda, and little Amanda appeared around the corner. "Bernie," I hissed, jabbing her for the hundredth time with my pointy elbow.

"I see them. Hush," Bernie replied from the side of her mouth. She slapped on her most ingratiating smile as the Teals approached. "Good morning."

Bobby grinned. "Yes, it is, isn't it? You guys out for a walk?"

"Just a short one. This ol' body can't take too much exercise in this humidity."

"Don't you know it. The report is for occasional thunderstorms today, and it sure feels like a storm is brewing. Steamy as heck out here."

As I geared up for a whopper of a meltdown, having glued my eyes to little Amanda's chin and noting the tiny mole on the *right* side of her chin, Bernie shoved me forward. I got her message. We said good-bye to the Teals and started walking.

We trudged up the tree-lined street to the playground, pausing long enough to allow the Teals time to get into their car and drive off, then headed back to our complex. When the rattletrap disappeared around a corner, I let my shoulders relax. "Well.

That's it. I made a point to look at Amanda's mole, and it was on the *right* side of her chin. *This* time, that is."

Bernie grunted. "Yes. I made a note, also. So, next time we see her, we will know whether you need meds or I need meds or the whole damn world needs meds."

"Yeah. So, what did you think about Bobby and Brenda? Brenda sure didn't look like she was having a good time. Hasn't from day one. Bobby, now, he's different. He acts like he hasn't a care in the world. I kept my eyes on him to see if he'd reveal any nervousness, but he handled himself like a pro. And that is suspicious in of itself."

"Yes, well I've always said they make an odd couple."

Seven minutes later we were back on our deck, dying for some AC. Bernie headed straight for the fridge, grabbed a Pepper, then collapsed onto a dinette chair with a weary sigh. I, of course, headed straight for my room to remove my undergarment. So adept at springing my girls, I was back in the kitchen, had fetched a lemonade, and was sitting across from my pal at the table in less than four blinks of an eye. She raised an eyebrow.

"Don't start, Bernadette. This thing has hardly any alcohol and you know it."

That received a dry chuckle, which, of course, made me squirm with annoyance.

I knew she was enjoying the slide show of emotions playing across my face when a sound overhead—faint but discernible—snatched the chuckle right out of her throat. Bernie clamped her mouth shut and held her breath, while my eyebrows shot up and I whistled. "Did you hear that?" She nodded. "Well, shouldn't we go up and check that out?"

Before Bernie could utter a word, I scrambled to my feet, dashed to the back bedroom and peered out at the parking lot. "My green Neon is the only car in sight," I called back. "That battered old brown van of the Teals' is gone." I sprinted back to the living room. "Bobby and Brenda are still out. Let's hurry."

With a grunt, Bernie capitulated.

This time, Bernie led the way up the wooden staircase, and I trailed behind, my breaths coming out in little pants. I was allowing my imagination full rein, while Bernie, *of course*, was only seeking some answers.

"We're going to learn something. I know it," I said in a stage whisper.

"Hmmm…all I know is your inflated suspicions have tainted my own usually common sense to the degree that now even *I* am seeing bogeymen—or should I say, boo-daddies—under every bush and tree. You'd think I'd learn to take you with a grain of salt. But, oh, no…I don't seem to learn."

I marched straight over to the Teals' door and knocked. I sure as heck didn't want to discover that while we were in our unit, they'd returned and Brenda was inside with Bobby just out on another errand. I pounded on the metal door but no one came to answer it.

Bernie pressed her face to the sliding glass door and peered through the blinds, again to no avail. Since there were no other windows, we were stymied at further exploration. It was frustrating as hell.

"I can't stand this," I moaned. "This whole thing is just about killing me. They might've just gone to The Pig and could be coming back any minute, and we haven't learned a thing. And our vacation is almost over. And for a whole week, we've toyed with innuendoes and half-baked suspicions and now clues are running around all over the place. And *everyone* is as suspicious as heck, and I don't trust any *one* of them as far as I can throw them—even Jorge. And we'll leave never knowing the end to the story. Or worse, rescuing kidnapped babies."

"Sweetie, are you sure your degree was in English?"

"Hush, Bernadette. You know what I'm trying to say."

"And that's what unnerves me the most."

"Just hush."

"But you're right. We *did* hear something…"

"I know."

"So maybe, if we keep quiet, we'll hear the noise again."

I crossed my arms against my unshackled bosom and rocked on my bare heels. "Ohh, the suspense is killing me."

"Well, one thing's apparent."

"What?"

"You wouldn't make a good spy."

"Oh, I don't know…the very fact that I don't *look* like a spy is the reason I'd be perfect for the job. Just like *Mrs. Pollifax.*"

"Who?"

"The heroine in a delightful mystery series by Dorothy Gilman. Love 'em. Great stories. She's older than I and manages to work as a spy in very convincing situations, since she literally stumbled into her new vocation when she—"

"Michaela. Please. Focus."

"Oh, pooh to you, Bernadette. Get that rusty ol' imagination of yours out of storage and put it to good use. I'm having a heck of a good time with this-this *surveillance* of ours. Enjoy the moment."

"If you're finished with your 'Carpe Dium' moment, I will."

"About time."

Glancing left and right over our shoulders and peering through the deck slats, we determined that nobody was around—not even Jorge. We were safe to snoop about some more, stare through the blinds into the darkened interior, press ears against the front door, all the while pantomiming to each other wildly. We were a ridiculous composite sketch of Hercules Poirot and Magnum P. I and who? Lucy and Ethel? Very cool, from our perspective, but ridiculous to anyone else who may have observed our less-than-agile stumbling over cheap plastic patio furniture, and the inevitable head-bonking on the hummingbird feeder suspended mid-air by the front room window.

Confident that we were on the verge of a major discovery, we were stunned and mortified, therefore, when Vicki's lilting 'yoo-hoo' stopped us dead in our tracks.

"Hey, y'all, what's up?" Vicki demanded, hands on what

were once hips, tapping her glitzy sandal. "You lose something? Lookin' for that sweet, little family? They've gone to Charleston…saw them leave—"

"Charleston? We assumed they were going to the ice cream shop again," Bernie bellowed.

"Or The Pig," I added.

"Well, honey, not this time. I saw them leave when you two started on your little walk. Then as soon as you two gals rounded that corner, they came toodlin' back. Brenda went up to their apartment with little Amanda. She came back, draggin' that poor lil' darlin' after her, bawlin' her eyes out, got back in the car, and they were off. Course, I was out doin' my daily Tai Chi and so was right there. As they were gettin' into the car again, I hollered, 'Where y'all goin'?' And they told me, 'Charleston'. 'Bout time they did *somethin'* fun." Vicki wriggled her hips and frowned. "So, what are *you* two up to? Whatever did you think you'd find up *there?* Seems mighty strange to see you, all stooped over, *peerin'* into their window like that…what're y'all *lookin'* for?" Vicki fired her questions, non-stop, smiling but disgruntled.

And as if that wasn't enough, Lionel lumbered onto the scene, crashing through the hedgerow as though a man on a mission, beer in hand, cigar dangling from the side of his mouth. "What's going on there, sweet pea?" he inquired of Vicki, all the while riveting his gaze on the two of us—guilty as sin and looking the part. Rarely had we been on this end of a scheme. Bernie and I had spent half our lives breaking up fights, disassembling student plans for pranks and machinations, and were successful in catching culprits in the act. Our record spoke for itself. We were gold-medal achievers. Being on the receiving end of unwanted microscopic attention was disconcerting, to say the least.

Summoning my very best 'I am in control' posture, I returned Vicki's penetrating gaze, eye to eye, all the while keeping my arms crossed against my bra-less chest. Managing to control a tremulous voice, I smiled down at the two neighbors who'd botched our snoop session so effectively.

"Well...you see," I explained, a little out of breath, "I'm out of Diet Coke," It sounded ridiculous even to me. I saw Bernie flinch and knew she'd been as startled by the words as everybody else present. I tried to recoup. "You see...Bernie and I have just returned from-from a walk, and it's so steamy and, uh, *humid*, and..." I swallowed, grimaced, cracked my neck, then hugged myself tighter. "And we've had such a tedious morning, doing odd jobs, here and there, you know, tidying up the condo and what not, and so, well, I'm just too tired to go to The Pig and... and...a Diet Coke would be nice."

"Shut up," Bernie commanded under her breath, attempting to put a cork in my prattle since it was obvious I couldn't. Too late. Once unleashed, and nervous to beat the band, my tongue could wag at both ends for minutes on end. Always chagrined afterwards, of course, but during an episode, I lost all brain function. Bernie winced as I continued. "And then I thought... gee, maybe Bobby and Brenda have some Diet Coke and would be willing to let me have a couple cans..." The hole in the dike widened, no stopping the deluge. "But, darn...it looks like they aren't home—like you said—though we didn't know that at the time..." Then, oh, Lord. I giggled. "...We thought we heard them... when we were in our living room...so we dashed up here to see... and...and, well, nobody's home," I finished, hands out in the I-give-up gesture. Then I remembered my missing brassiere and wrapped my arms around myself for the umpteenth time, feeling heat flood my face.

Vicki and Lionel gazed at me as if I had horseshoe crabs crawling from my ears. They glanced at each other, back at me, then threw a curious look Bernie's way. Bernie just shrugged and shook her head.

"Bern—"

"Do *not* say another word," Bernie hissed out of the side of her mouth, smiling and waving at Lionel and Vicki. She placed her hands on my shoulders and guided me down the steps to our own level. Vicki and Lionel just stood there and watched, confused and more than a little suspicious, as Bernie and I descended. And then, as if that wasn't enough, right on cue, darling, doddering Melba arrived in a cloud of talcum and the disturbing aroma of honeysuckle and Ben-Gay.

"Oh, my," Melba groped for words, surveying almost half the neighborhood on or beneath her deck. "Oh, dear," she cooed, noticing that Bernie's hands were gripping my shoulders as she marched me toward the safety of our quiet little apartment. "Did I miss something?" Melba's voice was plaintive. "I'm always missing something, it seems. Too early for some things…too late for most things…too addled to know the difference, my dear nephew always says…" Melba's voice trailed off as she sighed and glanced upstairs at the darkened unit's deck we'd just vacated.

Was it my imagination or did Melba make eye contact with Vicki for just a split-second? Had they shared a tiny nod, a fleeting gesture? Or was it just my rabid imagination? Could be the countless murder mysteries I was forever reading; the many reruns of *Murder, She Wrote*. On the other hand, it could also be one too many hard lemonades. Whatever the case, my hysteria had me even suspicious of poor, sweet, senile Melba. However, I had more pressing issues at hand. Four sets of eyes focused on me.

Realizing I had a starring role in this ridiculous melodrama, I no longer needed Bernie's propulsion toward our door. My discomfiture at being bra-less in front of a gaggle of strangers took every ounce of what good sportsmanship I had left, and I didn't care that I was leaving Bernie to fend for herself with the neighbors and their confused expressions and silent accusations.

I mumbled a hasty good-bye and leapt for our door, wishing all the while that I could sprout wings and fly away. Then, as though to reinforce the notion that we were all taking part in a *Candid Camera* episode, Brenda appeared, stage right—obviously *not* in Charleston—with little Amanda in tow. Bobby was nowhere to be seen as the impatient and ever-perspiring Brenda hauled little Amanda up the stairs.

"Let's go, Amanda." she tugged on the little arm. "I told you we need to hurry back. Now, come on." Brenda urged. She pulled the little girl along with one hand, while clutching a small brown bag in the other. "If this ice cream's all melted, it's your fault for being so pokey." Brenda railed.

Such a small matter for so many reprimands. The tot was no bigger than a minute and Brenda was a domineering giant in comparison. Who wouldn't balk at going anywhere with the ogress?

Snatching a quick look at the little girl's face, I let Bernie shove me inside, close the door, and lock it. She collapsed in her easy chair and I on the sofa. We stared at one another in pregnant silence. After a full minute passed, Bernie exhaled, "Well. *Laurel and Hardy* meet the *Three Stooges* in *Oz,* no less. If that wasn't a comedy routine, I don't know what is. Lord, help me." She narrowed her eyes and looked me up and down. "And you. You never cease to amaze me, Michaela. You're a phenomenon, actually."

"Takes one to know one."

"And that young woman. My *God*, she is a piece of work."

"Well, I, for one, have had enough."

"I'm not going to touch that with a twelve-foot pole *or* Lithuanian."

I ignored that and puffed out my cheeks. "Forget witty repartee for once in your life and get serious. Did you or did you not see where the mole was on Amanda's chin?"

Bernie's face clouded. "Lord, no. I'm sorry, but I was so distracted, I didn't even think to look."

"Well, *I* did. And—you won't believe this, Bernadette—but the damned mole was on the left side this time. The *left*."

"Oh my God..."

"Yes."

"And I distinctly remember it being on the right the last time...just an hour ago."

"Yes."

"Oh my God..."

"Yes."

"I have to confess that I haven't a *clue* what to do next. I am thunderstruck. I am speechless. I cannot believe you actually were right about something so-so *ridiculous* and far-fetched and Disneyesque."

"Ooohhh. Once and for all, we are going to *settle* this matter." I leapt from the couch, stepped over to the window and peered through the blinds. "Bernie," I hissed. "Come here."

"*Now* what?" she whined.

"*Come* here."

Bernie leaned over and parted the blinds enough to see what had riled me even more. They were still out there—Melba, Vicki and Lionel—standing on the deck outside Melba's unit, engaged in what looked like a real conversation. Every once in a while Vicki and Lionel glanced in our direction, nodded their heads, but since they were keeping their voices low, it was impossible to make out what they were saying. But what piqued our curiosity even more was that Melba seemed to be a viable part of the discussion. *Melba?* True, her back was to us, and she was tottering on tiptoes, looking as though she'd topple over any minute, but from the way her curly head kept bobbing up and down, it looked as if she understood every word Vicki and Lionel were saying. She seemed to be listening while an animated Vicki waved her bare arms in wild gesticulations, and an uncomfortable Lionel kept looking around as though afraid of being overheard.

"This is like something from a nightmare, or a poorly done 1950s thriller. I half expect Vincent Price to appear," Bernie muttered, letting the blinds drop into closed folds. "Get away from that window, Mike. They're bound to see you spying on them, and then what will they think?"

"It's suspicious as all hell."

"You said it."

"Something's going on here, and you and I are out of the loop."

"No *kidding*."

"Two little girls are upstairs but the whole world is supposed to think only one lives there. Is it a kidnapping ring or whatever they call it? Are Lionel and Vicki in on it? And crazy Melba? Impossible."

"Uh, huh…something's fishy about the whole lot of 'em." Bernie sighed. "Ohh, *I* don't know." She pushed herself out of the chair and stumbled over to the refrigerator. "Time for some cheese dip and Fritos. Maybe a snack will clear my head. *Something* needs to."

Thirty-One

It was all just too much. All the speculations, all the innuendoes, all the keen observations that *could* mean something, but probably meant nothing at all. It was all just one big glob of confusion. Two days left of this 'vacation', if you could call it that, and we were so caught up in our fantasyland story that we were forgetting that time was hurtling past. Soon we'd be standing once again in the airport terminal, bewildered and befuddled as we said our good-byes, hugged and hugged again, and promised to phone and write and email more often. Then it would be too late to determine who did what to whom, and when and where and how and why and the never-ending stream of what-ifs.

Time for action. Today *had* to be the day. To reinforce that conviction, I blurted, "Today is the day we solve this mystery."

"Well, you're right. Today just about has to be the day if we're to salvage what is left of our feeble brains and fleeting vacation. But, sweetie, 'today' is clicking away so you'd better get going."

"Okay, so help me. Where do we go from here? Call the local police and say we suspect that the kidnapped twins are in the unit upstairs? Can we do something like that? Would they believe us?"

Bernie shrugged, popped a chip into her mouth and grunted. "Don't really know. Reality and suspicion have overlapped and intertwined so much that neither you nor I even know where to begin the untangling. I tried taking the direct approach with Jorge and you saw how far that got me."

"But we can't just give up. We have to *do* something."

Bernie offered me a languid look, tossed her fluffy head once, and returned to her dwindling pile of chips. "Don't know what we can do," she managed between crunches, carefully collecting each morsel with a practiced maneuver. "Don't think we can call the police but don't know what else to do."

I paced the small room. "We have to do *some*thing. We have all this…this…*evidence* right under our noses, have seen the mole jump from one side to the other, and if that's not proof, I don't know what is. But that isn't the half of it. We're drowning in crazy neighbors. Then there's poor, poor Melba, and the Mexican leaf blower guy who's probably not a Mexican leaf blower guy, after all, and-and the larger-than-life duo next door who've filled their condo with ridiculously expensive items that still may have been stolen—we don't know for sure—and," I sucked in a shaky breath. "I never knew this tiny hamlet was so…so darn whacko."

Much to my surprise, I got a reaction from Bernie. She sent me a knowing look, a fleeting smile, a shoulder shrug, and then exhaled. "You're right. I have to be honest. I apologize for toying with your psyche. You know me. But, I'll say it again. You are right. I do care about what has been going on around here. This place has woven a spell for me. I do want to help put aright anything wrong. I do."

Breathing more naturally, I nodded. "Okay. So. Bottom line. I don't believe that the group upstairs is what they pretend to be. And, for some reason, they are posing two little girls as one."

Bernie nodded, picked up the remote, and clicked on the TV. "I agree. And, not to say 'I told you so' just remember I was the one who suspected them first, while you, my dear sleuth, had your eyes on 'Bonnie and Clyde' next door."

A sharp tapping on the glass sliding door startled both of us. We looked up to see Melba place cupped hands on either side of her face, and press her weathered, powdered nose to the window. Melba peered inside, eyes wide in an obvious search for us. Somewhat agitated, Melba pulled away from the window—leaving a large nose smudge on what had been clean glass—and flounced back and forth across our deck, stopping again and again to peer in at us. She appeared to be on the brink of losing it.

"Oh, Lord, what *now?*" Bernie moaned, turning the volume up on the TV. Anything was more entertaining than watching Melba's tripping through the fields of dementia. She waved one hand at me. "Your turn—bra-less or not."

Thirty-Two

After my initial shock at this intrusion, and Bernie's less than chivalrous sending me into battle, I tiptoed to the door, opened it just a crack to peek at Melba, who now seemed disturbed about something.

My eyes followed Melba as she wandered to and fro across the deck, leaned over the railing, looked skyward as if something alien would soon descend from the heavens. "Are you all right, Melba?" I asked, stepping out onto the deck. Melba, startled by my voice, whirled around to face me. Her hand slipped into the pocket of her aqua terrycloth robe then pulled out what looked like a small caliber pistol. Extending a pale arm, the gun wobbled in her hand.

My heart leapt to my throat. "Whoa. Melba. Melba, what are you doing? Is that a gun?" I croaked, making a desperate attempt to get Bernie's attention. No help there. Bernie was engrossed in a *Golden Girls* rerun, and was oblivious to the impending near-death experience unfolding just outside the front door. Desperate for Bernie's attention, I twisted my arm behind my back, leaned back against the wall of the condo, and began tapping my knuckles against the siding. It worked. Bernie rose from her chair, eyes never leaving the TV, reached over and slammed the front door.

Nobody was more surprised than Melba. The stunned look on her face would've been comical had she not been holding a wicked looking weapon. She stared in disbelief at the gun in her hand, then at a terrified me, then back to the gun, all the while sporting a vacant expression of bewildered confusion. Like an uncontrollable reflex, Melba's fingers began to tighten on the trigger. She lifted the gun higher and pointed the barrel toward me, who was now certain that the last sounds I would ever hear would be Sophia's voice declaring she needed a bathroom. What irony.

Melba looked as if she was no longer in control of her actions; that her hand had somehow taken on a personality of its own over which she had no control. I was beside myself with fear and frustration. After years of facing obstinate, obnoxious students, traveling around the world and back again, and surviving my own moderately dysfunctional family, was I now to die on the deck of my sister's vacation condo—gorgeous view of the 16th green, not withstanding? Was I to miss saying good-bye to my best friend, Bernie, just inside the door, and be shot at close range by a weird little old lady named Melba, like the toast?

A pained expression crossed Melba's distraught face as she jerked her hand, applying a final squeeze of pressure to the trigger.

"*Don't.*" I screamed at the top of my lungs, just as a thin stream of lukewarm water squirted from the gun, hit me square in the chest, leaving a moist, dark spot on the plum-colored top that makes me look sultry and alluring. Stunned, I clutched my bosom, not entirely sure if the wet spot was water or blood.

Melba just stood there like a stone statue. Then she dissolved into body-shaking mirth. "Ohhh, my," she cackled, "th-that was hilarious...s-so funny...so very funny..."

Before I could assimilate what had occurred, before I could wrap my dizzy mind around what the old lady was saying, from overhead, came a shriek of childish laughter. Shrill, lilting giggles from a small child—no. Make that, *two* small children. Laughing and howling, just above my head. As I craned my neck to look upward, a chubby hand dangled through the slats of the upstairs deck rail, and a plaintive, tiny voice warbled.

"I dropped it...my squirt gun. I wan'it. Gif it back t'me." The words tumbled from her parted lips. "It falled right in her pocket." She pointed a chubby, dirty little finger at Melba. "Haaahahaha. Funny lady. It falled in her pocket, an' her tooked it out and squirted you. Hey…you all wet."

I confess I was so overcome with conflicting emotions, I couldn't tell up from down. All I could do was stare in complete disbelief at the round, sweet faces—yes, *faces*—of two identical little angels, one laughing merrily, the other somewhat frightened; both engrossed in the entertainment just below their deck. Managing to gather a few shards of my shattered wits, I turned away from a still-chuckling Melba and staggered backward. With both hands, I flung open our door and screamed at the top of my lungs.

"Bernie. Ber*nie*. Now. *Right* now. Get out here."

Through the sliding glass door I watched as Bernie leaped from her seat, stubbed her big toe on the ottoman, expletive deleted, and hobbled to the door. I was frantic, wet, and crawling out of my skin with excitement. I gesticulated and sputtered words and phrases like a woman possessed.

"Two of them. Look, Bernie, *two* of them." I jabbed my finger in the air. "Look. Look at them. Up there. Tell me what you see. *Tell* me."

Glancing upward, Bernie smiled and nodded, shrugged her shoulders, waved, then turned to glare at me as thought I'd gone stark, raving mad. "Michaela," she drawled, "have you lost your mind? What is the *matter* with you?" She sounded more than a little annoyed.

I looked up. Brenda was holding little Amanda by her chubby paw, staring down at us like a thundercloud ready to burst. The smudged-faced little angel beside her had her head lowered.

"The kid dropped her squirt gun," Brenda hollered down. "You seen it?"

Melba shuffled over to where the small plastic gun was leaking a trickle of water onto the parched deck. Smiling, she bent over to retrieve it. Waving it toward Brenda and Amanda, she chortled, "You have upset Carmen and Iris. I can't believe it dropped right into my pocket," she bobbed her head and flip-flopped over to the steps. Brenda met her partway down the stairs, snatched the plastic toy, mumbled her thanks, and disappeared up her steps, and into their unit, dragging little Amanda along with her.

I turned and stumbled into the condo as though in a trance. It was all clear as mud right now. My head was spinning. My poor heart was beating like *Riverdance*. My mouth was as dry as the Gobi Desert. If ever I'd needed a drink, this was the time. Yes, sir…right there in front of us, but we were in too much of a frenzy to assimilate any of it. I doubted that Bernie had even seen the two little faces. I doubted that *I* had even seen the two little faces. The key to the puzzle had been right before our eyes. The question: what was it?

We flopped down into our designated chairs in the living room. It was all too incredibly weird. We looked at one another in bewilderment. What had just happened? A gun? Two little faces at the rail? Confusion reigning supreme? I twitched and squirmed and tugged at my creeping underwear and shorts, while Bernie raised her eyebrows and sighed. Finally she broke the silence.

"I'm hungry."

"You can't be serious." I gasped, sitting bolt upright, forgetting about my demon underwear. "I thought Melba had a gun. A gun, Bernadette. And then, as if that wasn't enough shock for one day, I looked up and there were *two* Amandas." I winced, leaned back against the cushions. "Oh, Lord…and let's not forget Vicki and Lionel, who appear to know a different Melba than the one who haunts us, or, at least are able to *communicate* like normal human beings with her. And then there's Jorge, who probably *isn't* Jorge. And what about the ice cream shop?"

"Ice cre—"

"Bobby goes there everyday, Bernie. Every single day. For ice cream? You want me to believe it's for sticky-sweet *ice cream?* No way. We saw him on the phone. On the phone, Bernie. Probably because his phone is like yours and won't work here." I writhed and hugged a couch pillow. "Ooohhh. Tomorrow is our last day. And after everything that's gone on and everything I've said, you're *hungry?*" My voice rose an octave with each sentence.

"Now look, Michaela," Bernie rose to her feet, squared her shoulders, and towered over me. "I believe you. I do. I do believe there are two little girls upstairs. I even agree with you that there is something decidedly fishy in this quaint sea-island town. But. We have plans for dinner at the clubhouse again, and we better get going right this minute before the crowd descends, and we have to sit outside in those hard, uncomfortable, creaking rocking chairs for an hour before getting seated. We can decide what we're going to do after we eat."

"But—" I began but was squelched by a rambling, rumbling Bernie.

"No. Now you *listen* to me. There is a Spanish-Mexican-Cuban-Guatemalan gardener, who works himself ragged around here that I have terrorized to the point that he only comes around when we're not home. I cringe when I think about my verbal attack on the poor man."

"Well, he—" I tried to interject but the overbearing Bernie barged on.

"And," Bernie rumbled, "Vicki is a totally wacko *train*wreck, I admit, but she's as shallow as a puddle, and Lionel…he's just a big-bellied, hairy chested, balding *idiot*." Bernie put hands on hips and railed on. "And Melba…Melba needs help to turn the lights on when she enters a room. She is about as harmless and insignificant as they come." Bernie was on a roll. "And just because there are *two* Amandas, well, what does that *really* mean? Hmmm?"

"But…"

"Oh, I'm sorry I yelled, Mike. But…I'm tired and hungry and this is almost the last day of our wonderful interlude here on this wonderful sea island, and right now I don't care a hoot whether Vicki and Lionel are 'Bonnie and Clyde', or that Melba is certifiable, or that Bobby and Brenda are weird. Please. Let's just go and have a wonderful meal. Okay?"

"Okay. I just want to say one thing before we go. How do you explain away the two little Amandas? *Two* little girls…identical…

side by side…and then Brenda and Bobby pretending that there's just one Amanda. What are they hiding? Why? What's going on? I mean, it's a conundrum, Bernadette. A perfect conundrum. And it's not right. It's just not right. And you, of all people, know the law where minors are concerned. As teachers, we were told to report *anything* remotely suspicious when a child's welfare was at stake. Right? So, I'm asking you. What should we do?"

"I don't know. I haven't a clue. I'm as perplexed as you are." Bernie ran both hands through her hair, making it fluff up even more.

"Ooooooh, I hate this."

"It's only four-fifty-two. Let's sit for half an hour and cool down. You read your book, and I'll leaf through that magazine I picked up at the airport but never read. Once we're calm and collected, we'll go have a leisurely dinner. Then we'll discuss our problem in a calm manner and decide what to do. How's that sound?" Bernie flopped down in her chair and retrieved her magazine from under the stool.

For thirty-four minutes, we kept to our own thoughts and activities. Twice the phones rang—the landline once for Bernie and my cell once for me. My Joe had misplaced his wallet, *again*, but found it wedged behind one of the couch cushions after I walked him through his day's activities and discovered he'd spent most of the day on the couch watching the Military Channel. Then he spent another five minutes regaling me with a screw by bolt description of how a torpedo works and how amazing the ingenuity of our WWII Navy heroes was and how the kids today only have to push a few buttons on a computer.

By her one-sided conversation with Jack, it didn't take me long to catch on that Bernie was enduring an expansive narration from her spouse concerning the tractor tinkering he'd had to do on their son's farm. She looked only too glad to be disconnected after almost ten minutes of sympathizing and empathizing and murmuring how sorry she was that his back now ached and his finger nails had grease in them that he couldn't wash out.

Needless to say, those conversations exhausted us, riled us, and just plain annoyed us…if that makes any sense at all. We sat in companionable silence for the next eleven minutes.

When neither one of us could stand it one second longer, Bernie threw down her magazine, causing an ugly crease to appear on the lovely countenance of a pouty-faced but otherwise stunning Angelina Jolie, and sighed. "Okay. We're as cool and calm as we'll ever be. I'm famished. Isn't it time we got ready and headed over to the clubhouse for one last, glorious dining experience?"

I looked up from my book and grinned. "Yes, I believe it is."

"Good. Let's get ready and go, for crying out loud."

"I agree. Just give me a minute—"

"—To put on your bra."

I made a face. "Yes, Miss Smart-Ass."

"Watch your language, Missy. I'm older and smarter than you."

"Older, and smarter, and more opinionated, and resolute, and set in your ways, and impatient and sarcastic and…and…I hope you never, ever change."

"Of course I won't change," Bernie replied. "I am not one to mess with perfection."

"Just once, I would like to have the last word with you. I mean, you can't even take a compliment."

"Can too," Bernie muttered.

Thirty-Three

How does one explain the ability to maintain a friendship—even from long distance—for over thirty years? For over an hour, we shared memories over succulent shrimp and decadent pecan pie heaped with whipped cream. We smothered chuckles and snorts over the antics of near-by patrons. Bernie and I enjoyed our dinner, knowing it probably would be our last at this clubhouse restaurant overlooking a splendid green golf course dotted with palm trees near a luscious ocean beach. Time passes whether you want it to or not. You just can't freeze the moment, no matter how poignant or funny, laughable or bittersweet.

Our shared laughter lasted all the way home as I—just a bit tipsy—drove at a slow pace, talking non-stop about my beloved Gullah and alligators and all the fun we'd had. My reflections of the time we'd shared seemed to amaze Bernie.

"You know, sweetie," my dearest of dear chums said in a low voice, "I marvel at your tenacious desire to hold onto frivolous dreams and idiotic notions of how life should be."

I opened my mouth to protest but she went on. "I also admire you for your guileless childlike qualities."

Not sure what to say to that, I kept my mouth closed.

"Yes," Bernie grinned, "I have to say…this time has been a dream that I will remember for a very long time."

I sighed as I pressed my foot on the brake and rolled to a stop in our little parking space. I turned off the engine, pulled out the key, then looked at my friend. "Me, too." Then I added, "I love Tequila Sunrises."

Bernie barked with laughter. "Mike, oh, Mike. Sweetie, you really need a part-time job. You haven't enough to do; that's why your imagination is running amuck." She grinned at me as she hauled herself out of the cramped front seat.

I was so relaxed that I played along. "Oh, pooh. I told you I have loads to do. My gosh. Taking care of Joe is a full-time job, what with laundry and more laundry, and even more laundry. Then there's cooking, and cleaning, and keeping up with all his bizarre projects...I mean, jeez. He wears his best shorts to work in the garage and then wonders how he managed to make a hole in them, surrounded by a halo of grease. No, I don't need a part-time job, Bernie. What I need is a vacation." I slammed the door with a foot, punched in the remote lock, and careened up the walk to our stairway.

"*Vacation?*" Bernie exclaimed right behind me. "You just had one."

I paused on the fourth step and wrinkled my nose. "You're kidding. You call *this* a vacation? With all the stress and strain and work we've had to do in order to figure out what the mystery is? Whew. Bernie, Bernie, Bernie. You've got one very funny idea of what a vacation is like. My neck aches, my back hurts, and I'm tired of all this restrictive underwear. I have a sunburn, mosquito bites, and I've gained weight with all the great food."

Bernie cocked her head and gave me her famous 'look'. "Oh, please...now who's patronizing? This could have been and should have been a perfect holiday...and would have been had you refrained from letting your over-active imagination run helter-skelter."

"Listen to her talk." I put hands on hips and sashayed across the deck to the front door. "You're acting pretty poochie, Mrs. North."

Bernie groaned. "Oh, now don't start with that silly 'poochie' business. You are the personification of one of your famous 'conundrums' you're always talking about. You bounce from fifty-cent words that absolutely nobody uses or understands to these off the wall, made up words that only you can decipher. Come back to Planet Earth, Michaela."

I managed to unlock the door before Bernie started moaning that she needed time to think about her Christmas shopping list, and we entered, threw down our handbags, and collapsed onto our favorite seats. Bernie wasn't finished haranguing me yet, however. "Sweetie…I really have enjoyed my time spent here. I meant it when I said it was the dream of a lifetime, and something I will treasure forever. Really. But…"

"But?"

"But…you have to admit that this obsession with kidnapped twins and crime rings and larger than life whacko neighbors from Vegas, and dim-witted old ladies, *and* gardeners who aren't gardeners are, well…pretty damned far-fetched. Right? Am I right, Mike?"

I wrinkled my nose, twitched, pulled on my blouse, groaned, then bounced up to waddle down the hallway. One minute flat, I was back looking as though my load had lightened. Bernie grinned, which, of course, made me smile.

"Oh, Bernadette, wipe that malicious little grin off your smug face. My doctor said that any little stress can cause my body to react as though to an allergen."

That resulted in a loud, belching snort and a series of throaty chuckles that just wouldn't stop. Bernie's mirth was volcanic. I only glared at her. She raised a shaky hand and winced. "I-I'm s-sorry," she stammered through another eruption of snorting laughter. "I know that *you* know that I simply *adore* you. You'll never change, and that, in itself, is a miracle that must be preserved. You are a *gem*. A priceless *gem*."

I was rendered speechless for a nano-second, then, "Oh… yeah? Well…let me tell you a thing or two, Mrs. North. You… you are—"

In that moment, the lights flickered off, on, and off again. When we were plunged into darkness, Bernie gripped the arms of her chair and let loose a chain of expletives. We both had been startled out of our skins.

I grabbed a pillow and hugged it to my liberated chest. "Oh, Lord. *Now* what?"

As our eyes strained to get accustomed to the darkness, I tossed the pillow aside, got up and started to grope my way to the front window. Of course, I bumped into the coffee table—nearly catapulting over it—and sent a Cap'n Ron Sightseeing Boat brochure and a take-out menu for the *Sea Cow* restaurant skimming across the laminate floor.

"Mike. Be careful. You'll break your neck if you don't watch where you're going," Bernie croaked, struggling to stand as I pushed awkwardly against the ottoman at her feet in a vain attempt to maneuver around the coffee table.

"I'm…*trying*…to catch them in the act…" I muttered between clenched teeth.

"Who?"

"Them." I gritted. "Whoever. I sure as hell don't know. But somebody…did this. Somebody—probably Lionel—cut our wires or pulled out a fuse, or whatever it is they do to do this."

Bernie lumbered to her feet and helped me regain some balance, then we both unlocked the door and stepped out onto the deck. I rushed to the far railing and leaned over, desperate for a glimpse of The Culprit.

"Do you see anything or anybody?" Bernie asked, remaining beside the open front door.

"No, darn it. There's nothing out here but the stupid palmettos. Oh, and a couple of tree frogs. And a cat…yes, I see one of those damned feral cats, and…and…"

"Come on…let's get back inside where it's safe."

"Safe? Safe from what…or whom?" My voice was swelling with excited anticipation.

"Safe from the hordes of ravenous mosquitoes swarming around out here."

"Ohh...darn it all," my voice shriveled like a deflating, two-day old birthday balloon.

Bernie gave me a gentle nudge and I capitulated. "Let's play a game... How 'bout Yahtzee?" she asked, grinning as though nothing out of the ordinary had happened.

I just sighed. "Ohhhhh, all right...darn and double darn. I was hoping to finally catch someone in the act and solve this stupid conun—"

"Please, don't say that word again."

I sent my pal a look toxic enough to wipe out the dreaded Kudzu infestation in the entire state of Georgia.

※

I have to admit it *had* been fun playing our game with only two candles for illumination. Difficult to do the final addition in such dim light, but fun, nevertheless. We went to bed earlier than normal, slept through the night, and awoke on our last full day at the condo to a dismal, overcast sky. I was disappointed. I'd hoped for one last excursion to the beach. Without much enthusiasm, I got up, padded to the bathroom, washed and donned some clothes. It was a major bummer.

Bernie came shuffling in only minutes later, gave me a groggy smile, and went about her daily routine of fetching soda, bagel and cream cheese. She flopped down in her chair with the collected booty in her terry-robed lap and reached for the TV remote. "At least we have electricity again. This is the second time I've had to change that clock in my bedroom. Gets a little annoying..."

"This is our last day, Bernie," I moaned. "What's even more annoying is we can't go to the beach."

"Somehow I'll get over the disappointment."

"We have to make our last day here special. What should we do? Another trip into Charleston...or Beaufort, maybe?"

"God forbid..."

"Ohh, Bernie..." I couldn't think of anything else to say at the moment so put my concentration into spreading peanut butter on a piece of toast. After we ate our breakfast, we both headed for our prospective bathrooms to dress. I threw a few more ideas at her, and she fielded them like a pro, tossing out every one.

Bernie was sitting on the deck when I finished my morning rituals so I joined her. She had her long legs propped up on the railing and a look of content on her face that belied our last-day woes. One eyebrow shot up as I lowered myself into one of the plastic chairs. "Nice and cool out here for a change," she muttered.

"Yeah…I'll miss this…"

"So will I…I've thoroughly enjoyed it here…"

"Before we know it, it will be autumn…then Halloween…and Thanksgiving…Christmas…"

"Slow down…I'm not in a hurry to have another birthday…"

From across the rolling golf course, a small golf cart lurched into view. With two portly golfers, horizontal stripes and all, and two lurid-colored bags of clubs bouncing and clattering on the back, they made quite a spectacle on the normally peaceful and dignified landscape. After all the placid golfers who had come and gone just outside our place during the past two weeks, this duo caught our attention. In loud voices, they made bets on the odds of sinking their putts.

The two golfers surveyed the green, looked all around at the condos encircling the course, squinted at the sky, and then stopped dead in their tracks to stare at us. Taken aback, we glanced at each other, then back at the golfers, and then we, too, began looking all around. We couldn't imagine what had captured their rapt attention. Their blatant staring became more than annoying.

Both golfers stood straddle-legged, hands on bulging hips, and stared at our deck, transfixed by what? Our appearance? Eventually, one of the golfers belted out "What the hell is *that?*"

"Do you think it's obvious from that distance that I'm not wearing a bra?" I whispered.

"Don't be ridiculous," Bernie muttered. "I doubt they are staring at *you* or your *girls,* of all things."

Somewhat incensed, and deciding that maybe my thin T-shirt wasn't covering as well as I thought, I rose from my groaning plastic chair. Summoning as much dignity as possible, with arms folded across my chest, I marched inside the apartment, banging my elbow on the door handle as it swung shut behind me.

Refusing to wrestle with my bra, I opted instead for a thicker T-shirt and made a hasty change. When I returned to the deck, Bernie was sitting up straight in her chair, staring out on the green.

I stood beside Bernie's chair and followed her gaze. The two morons continued to gape back at us. Bernie muttered, "Okay, enough is enough." She struggled to her feet. "So, what *are* they staring at?"

We looked each other up and down but didn't see anything wrong or ridiculous, except maybe Bernie's plaid capris. I craned my neck from side to side, but saw nothing out of kilter that would cause such rapt concentration from the motley duo on the green. Then, from my peripheral vision, I detected just the slightest movement. Startled, I poked Bernie and pointed. To our utter astonishment, two men in camouflage outfits perched in the enormous trees just beyond the deck, looking like an absurd scene in a grade-B war movie.

What, for crying out loud, was taking place just outside our door? As we looked around in total bewilderment, uniformed men swarmed. Tucked in among the palmettos, under the deck, at the foot of the steps, up in the trees, peeking through the foliage. From either side of the condo, more uniforms appeared, weapons in hand. The two stupefied golfers turned on their heels and waddled toward their cart at break-neck speed, almost toppling the cart as they leapt into the seat.

Sensory overload ruled the moment. Bernie and I, turned to stone, gaped as men shouted directions, exchanged terse remarks via walkie-talkies, and raced up the steps to our deck, two at a time.

"Ladies." One of the men barked with undeniable authority. "Please go inside."

Terrified, yet still dazed, I grabbed Bernie's arm, and attempted to hide behind her imposing frame. Peering through her bent elbows, I tried to make sense of all the commotion. Finally regaining the power of speech, I whispered "Bernie…good Lord, did we do something illegal?"

Bernie looked at me with wide eyes. "Probably. We've been accusing everybody and everything for days. I'll bet we were reported for trespassing or frightening old ladies."

"That was not my fault," I muttered. "Melba's the one who pulled a gun on *me*. Whose side are you on, anyway? You've been—" My sentence was sliced in half by the thud-thud-thud of heavy boots below our deck. We stepped closer to the railing and peered over.

From around the corner of the next building, Jorge stepped into view, familiar blower firmly in hand. Several of the soldier-types ran toward him.

"I knew it all along," Bernie said. "He's an illegal alien."

I gasped. "Just like on *NCIS*."

Thirty-Four

What a circus. A veritable menagerie of performers, all shapes and sizes. Most in uniform, looking extraordinarily official, or, extraordinarily fictional. Whatever the case, an impressive amount of time, energy, and manpower had been directed to this quiet little alcove on the sixteenth green. As the drama unfolded, we soon began to realize that we were not the subjects of this enormous sting operation, or whatever it was. Yet, the powerful forces and important looking individuals continued to focus their attention on our condo. And even more amazing, Jorge was not under scrutiny after all. Rather, he seemed to be giving directions, talking with military types in uniform, and running the show.

Jabbing Bernie with my elbow, I exclaimed, "Look. Jorge's in charge. I *knew* he was somehow involved in all of this. I suspected all along that he was absolutely integral to the entire plot. And I know it's a plot. Now. How will they go about closing in on Bobby and Brenda without putting those two babies in harm's way?"

"Jeez Louise," Bernie puffed out her cheeks, released air like a teakettle, and crossed her arms. "I cannot *believe* this is happening."

"Look. *Look.*" I shouted in her ear "This is it. Here come the big guns."

Jorge, no longer encumbered with the leaf blower, was leading a small battalion of somber soldier-types up our stairs. He paused on our level and frowned. "You were told to go inside."

We opened our mouths to object but he snapped, "Stay put." We nodded like a pair of bobble-head dolls. Jorge's mouth twitched and he added in a softer tone, "This will all be over in a few minutes. We are sorry to be causing such a disruption in your day." Then he nodded again and, instead of proceeding on up the steps to rescue the little Amandas—*both* of them—from the clutches of a diabolical Bobby and Brenda, he and his men turned their attention towards Melba's place. Our bewildered and obsequious Clark Kent-of-a-Jorge had morphed before our very eyes into a veritable Superman.

Stunned by this incredible turn of events, Bernie stared in acute disbelief at me, while I, in turn, just stared back.

"Bernie…they're going for Melba…they're going for Melba," I murmured in bewilderment. "Melba's in on this, too. I knew she was into it up to her chins. I'll bet she works for the two of them—that nasty Bobby and Brenda. She probably even babysat for them, once in a while. And those stupid housecoats she wears. Anyone could see she was a bit off-center."

"Mike," Bernie's voice cracked. "Shhh, for a darned minute."

While we stood and watched in stupefaction, a sharp rap on her front door brought a dazed and confused Melba to the living room window. Her face fell and grew ashen as she determined that this big crowd swarming all over the grounds was here for her. *Her.*

"Mrs. Clinton," Jorge barked. "Please don't make this difficult. Open up."

As Bernie and I held our breaths, the door to the neighboring unit opened and Melba stepped onto the deck, her head high and her lips curled in an ugly sneer. With an exaggerated motion, she offered her pudgy wrists for shackling. She had the demeanor of a veteran criminal—one who'd been down this road before.

"Wow…who would've thought… Poor old thing," I sighed. "How did those two ever rope Melba into helping them? The very idea of manipulating that harmless old lady…"

"Doesn't look so old and harmless right now," Bernie said.

"Yeah…she's a different woman now, isn't she?"

"I'll say."

"This is crazy…" My voice trailed off as this already impossible scenario got even more complicated. Bobby and Brenda suddenly emerged from their apartment, transformed into normal-looking, fashionably dressed human beings. Two small, round-faced little girls, identical in almost every detail—except for the little moles on opposite sides of two little chins—were clinging to them like spider monkeys. I tugged at Bernie's sleeve.

"Would you look at that," my voice squeaked. "And *two* little girls just like I said. They look okay, none the worse for wear, but someone needs to grab them away from those awful characters. Poor little things…kidnapped from their home and family…"

Jorge waited while Bobby and Brenda descended the stairs then strode up to them, and extended a hand. He wasn't arresting them—he was greeting them. What in the world was going on? They seemed more like colleagues than enemies.

As we watched, dumbfounded, Melba was ushered down the stairs, an armed soldier-type at each elbow. She paused, two steps down to gaze at us—her usually dim and distracted eyes now sharp and focused.

"You two," Melba began sweetly, "were a real pain in the ass. A real pain. Just want you to know that, truthfully, I don't care much for either *one* of you, and I'd like to wring your necks," she finished. She took another step, glared at us one more time, and then submitted to being hauled off to an awaiting police car.

Bernie and I stared at each other in acute shock. We'd been nothing but friendly and sweet and charming to that woman. Well, maybe just a little nosy, but we'd been good neighbors, nevertheless. Whatever did the poor thing mean by that?

As soon as Melba and her entourage had left, a swarm of official types rushed into her place, cameras, and notebooks, and even a weapon or two ready. Bobby and Brenda strolled over to us two bewildered vacationers, who still stood there staring, and had the grace to roll their eyes and shrug their shoulders.

Bobby extended his hand and smiled. "Detective Robert Barstow, Miss Bernadette." He bowed slightly. "And Miss Michaela. Time we were formally introduced."

Bernie and I stared at the detective, loose-lipped grins on our faces, shaking our heads in confusion. The cherub on his hip, Amanda-Number-One, flung a half-eaten vanilla wafer toward us, and even though startled out of our loose skins, we both ducked the projectile. Years of lunchroom duty had sharpened our reflexes to the razor-sharp reaction time of a rabbit in flight. You needed to be quick to dodge grapes, cheetos, and French fries on lunch supervision duty, and we were pros.

Bobby shook the tot gently. "Stop that, kiddo. These ladies have had enough assaults for the time being."

Brenda stepped forward. "Hi. Sorry about all this." Her smile was ingratiating as she gripped Bernie's and my hands in turn with a firm handshake. "Detective Brenda Morganstern. Pleased to finally meet you two for real. I'm sure you thought we were incorrigible parents, right?" Brenda's chuckle was low and throaty. Amanda-Number-Two, clinging tightly to her neck, reacted to Bernie's and my weak and decidedly strained smiles by sticking her tongue out then burying her head in Brenda's shoulder.

Brenda smiled and gave the child a quick hug. "I know you two must be bursting with questions. Although I'm not at liberty to tell you much, just know that our Melba has been the subject of an investigation for quite some time." She pushed strands of hair away from Amanda's eyes and planted a kiss on the little one's forehead.

Bobby grunted. "Actually, Melba and her nephew have kept us busy for almost nine months. Young Bill has a quaint little antique shop in Charleston and takes great delight in dabbling in the import/export business." He chuckled. "And I use the term *business* very loosely here. Melba's place is jam-packed with valuable imports from all over the world—even a Monet and a couple Picasos that were *borrowed* from their owners without their consent."

Brenda made a face. "Oh, yeah. They've got quite a few illegal items stored in that tiny apartment, if you can believe it.

"And, believe it or not," Bobby continued, "that old gal is the mastermind behind an organization that excels in siphoning funds from various companies—from here and abroad—and has managed to wreck sweet havoc on their bookkeeping." He laughed. "Their accountants have been pulling their hair out. There are a lot of CEOs ready to call it quits."

"Yes," Brenda added, "and the dear old gal is quite adept at using her computer for other fun and games as well. I can't tell you how many identities she's 'borrowed' to feed what must be a voracious gambling addiction. Oh, we could go on and on. The story would curl your hair." Brenda rolled her eyes and chuckled.

"I'll say." Bobby exhaled. "You'd have to be sitting down with a stiff drink to hear this whale of a story. Unbelievable."

I smacked my lips. "I *knew* there was something wrong here but couldn't put my finger on it. Bernie and I have stewed over this conundrum practically our whole vacation. We were especially concerned with our Melba."

"Yes, and my oh-so-astute-friend here absolutely *knew for a fact* that you and Agent Bobby were kidnappers holding these babies for ransom," Bernie added. "And she *knew* that somehow Lionel and Vicki were—wait a minute. What *about* Lionel and Vicki?"

All eyes swerved to focus on Lionel and Vicki, who'd been standing in the next yard, hands on hips, waiting expectantly to be noticed for I don't know how long. Bobby grunted. "Who are they, again?"

"Vicki and Lionel," Bernie and I said in unison. Bobby only shrugged.

"That gal cracks me up," Brenda snickered. "Always tried to chat me up whenever our paths crossed. Nosy as all get out. Oomph, kiddo. Loosen the hold on aunty's neck, will ya?" Brenda made a vain attempt to smooth her crumpled blouse, then rearranged the position of the child clinging to her neck. "My sister has been using the unit next to ours—helping me with this little party—and is about ready to blow a gasket over having to keep such a low profile. It was imperative that she not be seen yet we needed help with the girls. Talk about juggling. Several times we were sure she'd been discovered and nearly went out of our minds with worry that we'd botched the whole sting. It hasn't been easy, let me tell you." Brenda laughed outright at this.

I happened to glance up and was surprised to see a pretty, dark-haired woman suddenly materialize. She leaned over the upstairs railing and smiled down at us. Brenda saw her, grinned, motioned for her to come down, then looked at us, her smile widening. "That's Joyce. Poor thing thinks it's about time she got some freedom to go to the beach and play with her kids out in the open. Don't you, Joyce?"

The young woman skipped down the steps, tossing her short hair and grimacing. "Well, gee, Brenda...almost two weeks of keeping quiet, watching TV, and reading and re-reading magazines is enough to make anyone go crazy. I felt like Anne Frank in hiding. This is the beach. I'm dying to see some sand. And I want *both* my babies with me instead of one at a time while you play detective." She laughed. "Tim's arriving today and he wants to play golf and swim and relax, so please don't get any more ideas about us helping you out with—how did you put it? Oh, 'just a little inconvenience' for a few days. No thanks. I'm through playing detective. And so are my babies."

Brenda laughed, squeezed the 'Amanda' in her arms, and gave her another loud kiss. "My little nieces sure have been wonderful, though. Just three and already seasoned agents. I'll bet they join the Agency in another twenty years or so. Don't you?" She threw her sister a saucy look.

Bobby laughed and lifted his 'Amanda' over his head, making her squeal in delight. "I think they'd make excellent agents. Right, Tammy? Is dada right?" The little mite bobbed her head up and down, still shrieking with laughter. He glanced at us and winked. "And for the record. Their names are Tammy and Tonia. Not Amanda and Amanda." He seemed to enjoy his own joke.

Meanwhile, poor Bernie and I just stood there, mouths gaping, feeling like utter fools, taking it all in as though we comprehended the whole, damn thing. After an eternity, Bernie gave her fluffy head a shake, licked her lips, and said in a very principalish tone, "This *conundrum*—if I may use Mike's favorite word—is making me *dizzy* beyond description, and I'm about ready to *explode*. Just what was the *purpose* of this charade, Bobby, er, *Robert*? I mean, I understand the bit about unscrupulous Melba, but what was the *point* of posing as a sweet little, dysfunctional family of *three*? And aren't there really some missing twins—little girls exactly Tammy and Tonia's age, making the news?" Bernie was on a roll.

Tammy and Tonia, A.K.A. Amanda One and Amanda Two, reached out chubby arms, each to the other, attempting to exchange partially devoured, soggy vanilla wafers.

"Well, the reason is," Brenda sighed, handing her twin over to the little girl's mother, "we were all set for our surveillance of Erma—Melba, to you—when our supervisor told us that the two of you had arrived on the scene." She paused as Bobby released his twin to her mother and jerked his thumb toward the parking lot as a signal he was leaving, tossed us a grin, then sprinted down the steps and out of sight. Joyce smiled our way then directed her daughters up the stairs to their unit, calling over her shoulder, "Nice meeting you. See you later."

Brenda tossed her head and grinned. "Thanks, hon. Bye-bye, girls. Aunty Brenda loves you to pieces." She turned back to us, exhaled loudly and blew out her cheeks. "So, where was I? Oh, yes, your arrival. Anyway, we'd hoped your unit would remain empty for the time being. We'd done our homework and knew the owners—a couple from Atlanta—had just been down for a week, so we weren't expecting them to return any time soon, and we knew they didn't rent the place out. Your arrival sort of threw us for a loop, but our boss told us you'd be no problem if we kept you diverted. You've probably seen our supervisor, from time to time, working as a gardener—"

"Ah-ha," I interrupted. "*Now* who is imagining things, Bernadette? Didn't I tell you all along that Jorge was a poser of some sort? Didn't I? Hmmmm? Go ahead. Just shout it out. I was right, wasn't I? I was right."

Bernie cast me a withering look, hunched her shoulders, and rolled her eyes at Brenda. "You were saying, before you were so rudely interrupted..."

Brenda had the audacity to wink at Bernie. "I was saying, your arrival really muddied the waters more than we'd expected. We didn't want your focus on dear Melba—whose real name is Erma Rae Clinton, by the way—thereby risking our little sting operation. We were finishing up our investigation and were ready to close in on her and her *darling* nephew. I confess I wasn't really aware of the Amber Alert for missing twins. Hadn't even considered you'd think we had two girls. Thought we were so damned clever about hiding our secret. No, we just hoped you'd focus on the strange couple upstairs, thinking they were nothing but a dysfunctional family of three. We were also hoping it'd distract Erma." She made a face. "At least, that's what we hoped, anyway. Sounds pretty lame now, I'm embarrassed to say, and pretending we only had one child was really getting old. Don't know why we thought we had to have only one kid. Doesn't matter now. Thank goodness it worked...fairly well, that is...I guess."

I bounced up and down at this point—then remembered the spectacle I might be providing, unencumbered by the loathsome brassiere and stood still. "See?" I chortled. "I had this whole thing figured out ages ago, except for maybe the part about you and detective Bobby, and maybe the part about the girls, and perhaps about the kidnapping...that was a little confusing. And I really had no idea your sister was hiding in the vacant unit upstairs this whole time. She's good, really good, at being quiet, I mean. Although a couple times we heard noises coming from up there when you weren't supposed to be there. But. Please tell us what the scoop is on Lionel and Vicki. I know they're guilty as sin but haven't figured out exactly how they fit in," I finished on a breathy note.

"Lionel and Vicki?" Brenda repeated.

"Yes. What's the deal with them?"

"To the best of my knowledge," Detective Brenda Morganstern muttered, "Vicki and Lionel have absolutely nothing at all to do with *any* of this."

"You're kidding." I made a face then stole a glance at Bernie, who looked like someone overdosing on Rocky Road ice cream.

⁂

A glorious evening. The setting sun stained the western sky a delicate shade of mauve as it melted on the horizon. The entire area was empty of detectives and babies and brassy neighbors and vacant, doddering old ladies—present company excluded—and we had the place to ourselves. The quiet was like a balm after our much-too-frazzled afternoon. We two old friends were finally able to slump into deck chairs, too drained by the day's drama to even venture out for food. Considering the excitement of the reunion itself, not to mention the emotional impact of a crime scene unfolding beneath our noses, plus the exhilaration of being involved in a drama that dripped with truth and consequences—well, it had been quite an ending to this whole bizarre, unbelievable and unexpected interlude in our lives.

Now, with our feet propped up on the railing, we gazed out across the quiet golf course, where no golfers or carts marred the landscape. It was like a piece of heaven on earth, this bit of muted landscape, cupped in the green hands of palmettos and live oaks, complete with a darkening blue backdrop. We sighed in tandem.

"This is nice," Bernie said.

"Oh, yeah."

"Look at that sunset."

"Yeah." I sighed again.

Then we both sat up and squinted at the horizon. We turned

to look at one another and then back again at the extraordinary vista before us.

At the farthest end of the course, practically obscured by the palmettos and Spanish moss, almost hidden in the deepening shadows, a long, fat, dark gray-green reptile crawled out of the lagoon and lumbered across the golf course.

Bernie groaned, shifted in her chair, glanced at me and lifted both hands in surrender. I leaned back in my chair, smacked my lips and beamed. "Soooo, dearest of dear chums, what do you have to say to *that?*" I put my feet back on the railing and folded my hands on my unshackled chest.

Bernie inhaled, exhaled, then drawled, "For crying out loud…"

Don't miss the next adventure...

DON'T ROCK THE BOAT
by Cathie Wayland and Theresa Jenner Garrido

The intrepid duo, retired teachers, Bernadette "Bernie" North and Michaela "Mike" Rosales are kicking up their heels again, this time on a cruise in the Bahamas. What could possibly go wrong on a self-contained ship out in the middle of the Caribbean? Plenty. The girls find themselves up to their necks in another mystery—one they are determined to solve.

About the Authors

Theresa Jenner Garrido is a graduate of the University of Washington, Theresa taught middle school language arts and drama for over twenty-five years before retiring to devote more time and energy to her passion of writing. She loves walking on deserted beaches, country roads, and eating chocolate. She thinks living in Alaska would be great but is content to stay in her small town in South Carolina.

Cathie Wayland is a lifelong Midwesterner, a wife, a mother, a grandmother, and a friend. After achieving a Bachelor's Degree in Education and a Master's Degree in Administration she has spent her entire adult life working with children in schools, first as a junior high level teacher, and then as an elementary school principal. Early on in her life, she developed a love for reading and writing, and enjoys interlacing her books, stories and articles with real-life incidents, accidents, anecdotes and memorable characters that have shaped her world. Her friend Theresa ranks among the very best of memorable characters! She has been blessed with a long and happy marriage, and an incredible family. Cathie would claim that defining moments of who you are and who you hope to be come when you least expect them.